THE TOURIST
TRAIL

THE TOURIST TRAIL

A NOVEL

JOHN YUNKER

Ashland Creek Press

The Tourist Trail: A Novel

By John Yunker

Published by Ashland Creek Press
www.ashlandcreekpress.com

Second Edition 2018

ISBN 978-0-9796475-2-9

Library of Congress Control Number: 2018907121

Cover design by Rolf Busch.

To Midge.

When the land has nothing left for men who ravage everything, they scour the sea.

— Tacitus

PART I

ANGELA

IN DARKNESS, Angela ascended the winding gravel road. She carried a flashlight, but she kept it off. She knew the path well.

The Clouds of Magellan illuminated the white bellies of penguins crossing up ahead. Most stood at the side of the road and watched her pass, their heads waving from side to side. When one brayed, the high-pitched hee-hawing of a donkey, the others responded in kind, forming a gantlet of noise. It was mating season at Punta Verde, and the males were rowdy.

At the crest of the hill, the road veered right and continued for half a mile to the vast empty parking lot where tourist buses and taxicabs disbursed their cargo during the day. Angela continued straight, onto soft dirt and dry patches of grass, sidestepping the prickly *quilembai* bushes and the cavelike penguin burrows. She stopped at the top of the hill and scanned the wide, arching horizon of the South Atlantic Ocean. A gust of wind nudged her from behind, and she leaned back into it, her eyes tracking slowly from left to right. The moon, about to rise, gave the sky an expectant glow. She looked for the telltale lights of passing ships but saw nothing but the stars.

He should be back by now.

The last she heard from him was a week ago. He was off the coast of Brazil and headed south, only eighty miles north of here. She had reviewed the weather charts, but there were no Atlantic surges, no last-second squalls that may have pushed him off course, delaying his return. Perhaps he wanted to stay close to the others. Perhaps he was simply taking his time. Each day, she invented another scenario for why he was not on her shore, carefully ignoring the more rational, more depressing scenarios.

She was only supposed to trek up here once a week, a routine she'd once welcomed, a break from the camp. But when she lost contact, she began visiting nightly. Not that she would see him. But perhaps she would see something to explain his absence.

A star crested the horizon. She watched patiently as the light strengthened and inched from right to left, south to north. It was probably a fishing trawler headed for Puerto Madryn, returning from the Southern Ocean, its cavities stuffed with writhing fish and krill and the inevitable, under-reported bycatch. She felt her stomach tighten.

The moon began to bleed out over the water, erasing the ship from view. Angela sat down in the cold dirt and waited. A penguin brushed past her sleeve on his way to an empty nest, where he stood sentry. He, too, was waiting, demonstrating his fealty for a female not yet returned, as well as guarding his home. Every year, the males were the first to arrive at Punta Verde to claim their old nests, under bushes or on the pockmarked hills, in burrows carved into earth. A hundred thousand of them, in a slow-motion land rush, scrambling over this nine-mile stretch of scrubland that hugged the ocean.

The females took their time at sea, gorging themselves on sardines and squid, gathering their strength for the six-month breeding season that awaited them, emerging from the water two weeks, give or take, after the males. Fashionably late. And if they were fortunate, if everything aligned, their mates were waiting at their burrows, their homes clean and dry, new twigs laid out to form a nest.

The males sang when their females returned, and the

females sang in response. They flapped their wings and dueled their beaks and circled one another, orbiting, an ancient bonding ritual, an anniversary.

But the penguin standing silently next to Angela would have no reason to sing this year. Of this she was certain. It was simply too late. The females that would arrive had long ago arrived. Chicks were already entering the world, some taking their first unsteady steps. In a few short months, it would be time for everyone to disappear back into the sea.

Perhaps this penguin was in denial, unwilling to accept his loss, or perhaps he was merely stubborn. Angela preferred to imagine the latter. He would stand by that empty nest until the end of the breeding season, and next year he would return and seek out a new mate. An empty nest rarely stayed empty for long. Angela often wondered if penguins mourn the missing, but universities don't award grants to answer those types of questions.

He should be back by now.

Angela waited another hour, until there were no more lights on the water. She looked one more time at the penguin at his nest, then stood and made her way, flashlight off, back down the hill.

ROBERT

AFTER THE DRINKS and the dinner service, after the lights were dimmed and the curtains pulled, Robert extracted the television screen from the armrest of his business-class seat. He was not interested in the movies. He switched the channel to the flight tracker—a cartoonish map of the Gulf of Mexico with a little white plane suspended above, pointed south, creeping toward the tip of Colombia. Every few seconds, the screen refreshed itself, updating Robert on the air speed, altitude, distance traveled, time remaining. The dispassionate data comforted him, reminding him that he was making progress, that he was not lost.

He leaned his head back and closed his eyes, hoping to join the symphony of snoring bodies in the darkness around him. But he rarely slept in public. On those rare trips when his body did relent, he would often jerk awake wildly disoriented, spilling drinks and alarming neighbors—a side effect of a life spent constantly on guard. And then there were those rarer occasions when a flight attendant would awaken him to stop his shouting—a side effect of something worse.

Robert opened his eyes, sat up, and took a deep breath. He would not sleep tonight. Instead, he'd spend the next seven hours and forty-three minutes watching a little white plane inch its way to Buenos Aires. He didn't mind; at least it would be a quiet night, bathed in the blue glow of the flight tracker, his guardian compass, his night-light.

The light did not bother the woman passed out in the window seat next to him. If only she could have stayed awake a few hours longer. Dina. A cute but unnaturally tan woman in pink sweats. She was a model from Dallas on her way to Argentina for breast implants.

"They're cheaper there," Dina told him after the drinks were served. "And the surgeons are world-class."

She flirted with him, drunk on pisco sours. He told her he was in sales, a safe cover. Up here, in business class, almost everyone was in sales. Up here, he could have been anyone, which was why he lived for these brief moments of recess, acting out the role of someone else high above the Earth, moments when he could imagine life as a civilian, unburdened by the nasty ways of the world, drinking pisco sours with Dina from Dallas.

She told him he should be a model, another cover he once used. She ran a hand through his dark hair. He ordered more drinks. He said her *before* breasts looked perfect as is. She gave him her business card and invited him to Dallas to test-drive the *after*.

For effect, Robert had opened his laptop, pretending to read sales reports. As if to taunt him, the computer too had fallen asleep. He checked to make sure Dina was still out, then poked the laptop awake. He studied up on the agent he was to meet in Buenos Aires, Lynda Madigan. She would be his partner for the duration of the assignment. Robert didn't want a partner, let alone an agent he didn't know, but he needed an interpreter, and she spoke fluent Spanish.

He imagined Lynda looking through a similar file, one on him, and he wondered what else Gordon, their boss, might have told her. Though they were all in the business of keeping secrets, Robert didn't want to share any of his. But even Gordon didn't know everything that had happened five years ago. Robert kept those other memories to himself, hoping that he could somehow suffocate them. Instead, he ended up preserving them, perhaps all too well.

Now, as he leaned his head back in his seat, he felt the memories returning. He could see the slowly undulating horizon of ice as he hovered low behind the controls of a helicopter, looking for a Zodiac, a break in the ice, a bright red parka.

As the clouds had descended, so had he, landing on a low, tabular iceberg. He left the engine running and stepped onto the ice. The fog surrounded him, leaving his eyes with little to do but dilate. He started off into the white emptiness, arms out in front, chasing every change in hue, hopeful that he was headed in the right direction, though in reality he was lost in any direction. When the engine noise faded, he called her name, hearing only wind in response.

The ice had begun to shift, growing pliable. He looked down to see the tops of his boots bathed in blue water. The iceberg was descending. He hopped onto a neighboring berg and called her name again, louder. This ice, too, became unsteady, so he hurried to the next iceberg, then the next. The icebergs, once joined together like a completed puzzle, had begun to separate, revealing expanding rivers of indigo, until Robert found himself stranded on a lone sheet of ice, his feet now immersed in the subzero water. He could no longer hear the helicopter. He screamed her name, his ankles now underwater, its icy grip working its way up his calves, then his thighs, and he whispered her name, prepared for the end, to be with her again, then his chest, then his arms—

Robert opened his eyes to see Dina, leaning over him, her hands gripping his shoulders.

"What?" he asked.

"You were shouting," she said.

Robert looked at the flight tracker—two hours and thirteen minutes remained until landing, the little white plane hovering over the southern half of Brazil. Dina took her seat again, and Robert reached for a water bottle. He wiped the perspiration from his face. He sat up and noticed the blinking eyes in the darkness around him. He picked up his laptop from the floor and turned to Dina. "I'm sorry."

"That's okay," she said. "Who's Noa?"

Robert didn't answer. He had already opened his laptop, pretending to read sales reports.

ANGELA

ANGELA WATCHED HER ASSISTANT extend the *gancho*, a long piece of rebar that was hooked at the end, into the burrow. Doug was on his knees, face to the ground, squinting into the tiny entrance, nudging the male so he could get a better view of the five-digit number on the stainless steel band wrapped around the penguin's left flipper.

"Three four six two seven," Doug shouted over the wind.

Doug was in his mid-twenties and, like most naturalists his age, looked more the part than old-timers like Angela, his senior by a decade. While she stomped around in worn tennis shoes and faded, thrift-shop khakis, he was a walking REI catalog: waterproof boots, camouflage pants with more pockets than objects to fill them, an Indiana Jones hat shoving his messy blond hair down over his ears, a blue bandanna around his neck. He was the type of assistant— *You say assistant, I say wingman,* Doug liked to say—that kept Angela's program running year after year, fresh from the classroom and eager for an unpaid adventure. Too young still to find the trip down here tedious—the ten-hour flight to Buenos Aires, the two-hour flight to Trelew, the four-hour bus ride on a gravel road to the research station. And it wasn't much of a research station at that: two cinder-block huts, one shower, and a public restroom they shared with the tourists who stopped to pay their admission fees and to shop for postcards and key chains.

Angela studied Magellanic penguins, named by Ferdinand Magellan in the sixteenth century when the Europeans were busy naming the planet after themselves. At last count, Punta Verde was populated by 200,000 breeding pairs—a count Angela was in the process of updating. The Magellanic species was the largest of the warm-weather penguins, its beak reaching the height of an adult human's knee, its dominant features the black upside-down horseshoe mark on its white belly and a circular white stripe that curved up either side of its neck to its eyes. Each penguin had a different pattern of black spots on its belly that tourists often mistook for dirt. This was not the penguin to inspire movies or stuffed animals—it was not as majestic as an emperor, nor as colorful as a macaroni. It lived in the dirt and the muck of wet spring days, snapped at hands that got too close, and often honked incessantly, emitting the sounds of a donkey, earning it the nickname *jackass penguin*. But even jackasses needed people to look after them.

"You get that?" Doug asked.

"Three four six two seven," Angela repeated back without looking up. She leafed through her notebook, her little *black-and-white book*, as she called it, looking for the five-digit number. She'd tagged thousands of birds over her fifteen years at Punta Verde; every penguin fitted with a tag was listed here, with a number, place, and date. Yet despite such a wealth of data, most numbers were entered once and never again revisited. Tagging a penguin was akin to putting a note in a bottle, tossing it out to sea, and waiting for it to return. At night. It wasn't enough for the penguins to come home; Angela also had to find each one, among thousands and thousands of nests.

"Did you hear that?" Doug asked.

"Hear what?"

"Sounded like an engine. A boat engine."

Angela looked up and tilted her head back and forth.

"Must be the wind," she said. She returned to her book.

"Red dot?" Doug asked, hopefully.

Angela didn't answer right away. While finding a tagged bird was not as statistically significant as winning the lottery, it certainly felt that way at times—and the greatest jackpot of all was when they discovered a red-dot bird.

A red-dot bird was a known-age bird, one that had been tagged the year it was born and hadn't been seen since. Young penguins typically spent four to seven years at sea before they reached breeding age and returned to their colonies. Yet not all penguins returned, and the reasons had been haunting researchers for years. Because red-dot birds had been tracked since birth, Angela and the other naturalists knew more about them than about any other tagged bird—and they still wished they knew more. But they took what they could get, recorded what they could measure. Whether five years or twenty had passed, finding a red-dot bird always felt like a family reunion.

But she was beginning to hope that this bird was not a red dot. She was reluctant to let Doug handle the bird, even though she knew he was due. It was the natural order of things, for researchers to pass on their knowledge and skills. Once they found a red dot, they had to weigh it, then measure its feet and the density of feathers around its eyes.

Doug hadn't yet weighed a penguin, and once he did, it would be one less thing he needed to learn from her. One less reason to join her on these trips. One day closer to not needing her at all. Not that he'd ever needed her to begin with. The life of a naturalist was a lonely one, spent more with animals than with people. This was what Angela had wanted, and at thirty-six, she did not harbor any illusions about having children—the birds were children enough—but she did have her illusions about Doug.

Over the past few weeks, Angela had adopted him as she

had the birds. Every morning, she was first out of the dining hall to select her assistant and set out for the day's assignment. Doug was always out there waiting for her, a smile on his tanned face, while the other assistants were still cocooned in their sleeping bags or brushing their teeth in the public restroom. She knew by now not to anthropomorphize the penguins, but she could not help projecting her attraction onto Doug. That he was simply an early riser did not dampen her belief that he had developed a crush on her, and that perhaps when he no longer needed her, he would still accompany her. A comforting thought, particularly since they had indeed discovered a red-dot bird.

She looked at Doug and nodded.

"Kick ass!" Doug leapt to his feet and emptied his brown backpack of a caliper, handheld scale, and nylon strap.

This one had been tagged five years ago. Finally ready to breed, this penguin was probably in his second season at Verde—returning to his natal colony to make a nest, find a mate, and begin a ritual that would last another two decades, if he was fortunate.

During Doug's first week at Verde, against her better judgment, Angela had let him extract a penguin from its burrow. He had only just figured out how to handle the *gancho* correctly, and she had been giving him free rein with the birds. He was so passionate that she could not have refused him the opportunity. The scrubby hills were like a playground to him, and she enjoyed looking at the world through his sharp blue eyes, eyes that would wink at her on occasion across the dining room, a wink that took a few years off her life. Sometimes she imagined herself his age again, not yet jaded by the drudgery of Ph.D. politics.

She'd always kept her hair short, but its deep red color invited attention. She never doubted her ability to attract men, only her ability to keep them around. Her life was a migratory one—six months here, six months in Boston, the cycle repeating over and over again. While most women her age were now cuddling their newborns, she was crouched over burrows in the relentless southern sun. Her face had begun showing signs of the mileage, wrinkles to the sides of her eyes, ridges that caught the dust like snowdrifts.

She remembered the first time she held a penguin in her hands, a fierce little lapdog, all muscle and motion; felt the tightly woven feathers; gripped that firm, fibrous neck as his beak thrashed dangerously about. She remembered the joy of holding this creature who spent most of his life in the water, that only for the sake of raising his young bothered to set food on land, that this gorgeous awkward creation was now between her two straining hands. She never forgot it. Her teacher was Shelly, who later recruited her for the job Angela had now: teaching Doug.

Shelly had waited four weeks before letting Angela handle a bird, but Angela was not as patient, not as thick-skinned, and when she first began working with Doug, she was quietly thrilled to have a handsome young man spending the day with her. She wanted to be the person that Doug would remember for the rest of his life. The woman who taught him everything. The woman who said yes.

Hold the bird, she'd told him that first time. *Firmly. Mind the beak. Grab the neck.*

Doug had been bitten so badly he had to be driven to Trelew for stitches. His natural instinct had been to pull away, but the penguin's serrated beak had hooked his flesh tightly and held fast as Doug tore what was left of his hand away. *It was like a Chinese finger prison*, he joked as the doctor sewed together the sinew of his left hand.

But Angela got what she wanted. He never forgot that day.

Now Doug used the *gancho* to pull the bird out of the hole by his feet, then clutched him swiftly by the back of his neck.

He clasped the neck with unflinching confidence, ensuring that the bird could not swing around and bite his arm. Angela slid the strap around the bird's waist, cinched it, and attached it to the scale. Then Doug let go.

The bird flapped his wings and snapped at the air as he twisted in circles. Angela read the weight aloud; Doug entered it into the notebook. Then Angela grabbed the bird and held him between her legs, to measure the feet.

The wind shifted. Angela heard an engine cough, coming up for air between the waves. She looked up, half expecting to see a boat cresting the hill, then heard a scream. Her own. The penguin had bitten the skin between her thumb and forefinger.

"Doug, take hold of the beak," she said, trying to remain calm.

Doug fumbled with the bird's wings, finally grabbing onto the head and prying the beak apart. Angela snatched her hand back. The bird squirted out beneath her knees and retreated to its nest.

Angela's fingerless ragg glove was shredded, and blood was beginning to bubble through the crevices and soak through the fabric.

She started up the hill, toward the sound. Doug followed.

"Where the hell are you going?" she said.

Doug froze.

"We're not done measuring," she told him. "Stay here. Don't let that bird go anywhere."

Angela stomped up the hill, angry with herself for making such an amateur mistake, for letting emotion get in the way of science.

The first thing she saw as she crested the hill were whitecaps blown backwards. She felt her body pushed forward by the stampeding wind, a breeze that had rolled off the Andes and gathered speed over hundreds of miles of nothing.

Then she saw him.

A man prostrate on a flat stretch of rocks that extended two hundred yards away from the beach. The remnants of an inflatable boat. It looked as if the boat had exploded, sending him and his belongings in all directions.

She hurried over sand and mussel-covered rocks, the sound of crunching shells in her ears as she neared him. He was facedown, a large man in a fluorescent yellow jacket and an early beard. The waves washed over his legs. She grabbed his arms and pulled him, as best she could, away from the water. And it was then that the body stirred and opened its eyes. He came to, as if from a deep sleep.

"What?" he asked.

"You were in the water."

"Goddamn piece of shit," he said, looking around. "The engine flooded. Wave tossed me."

Another wave crashed, dragging him across the mussels into Angela's shins, nearly taking her down. He spit out saltwater and looked up at her, confused. She helped him to his feet, and he leaned on her until they reached sand. She saw smears of blood on his jacket and arms and neck. She sat him down, pawing at his clothing, looking for the source.

"You're hurt," she said.

"I'm wet."

"You're bleeding. You need a doctor."

"No doctors."

"But you're bleeding."

"There are people looking for me. People who wish to hurt me. Do you understand?"

She drew away from him. He had the look of a merchant marine—a reddened face that rarely saw sunscreen and lines on his forehead and cheeks from a life spent squinting. He appeared to be in his early forties, and fit. His thick, dark hair could have used a haircut six weeks ago. He looked her up and down in a deliberate way, as if he only just noticed her.

"You're the one who's bleeding," he said.

She glanced down to discover the source of all that blood. Her ragg glove was saturated and dripping. She felt the sting of saltwater. She remembered Doug and glanced up the hill, relieved to see it empty.

"Let me look at it," he said. She offered up her hand, and he gently peeled back the moist fabric. "How'd this happen?"

"Penguin."

He looked up at her. "A penguin did this?"

She nodded. Though his face was sunburned and rough, his eyes were calm and steady, and for a moment Angela forgot the pain in her hand.

"And I thought I was having a bad day," he said.

Now was the time to return to camp and notify the authorities. Report what she'd seen; stitch her wound; document items recovered; note coordinates, date, and time. Normally that was what Angela would have done. She detested all nationalities of tourists and trespassers.

Yet this man was neither. He was wet and shivering and needed her help. And she had a soft spot for strays.

ROBERT

AT THE BUENOS AIRES AIRPORT, Robert held Lynda's picture, studying the faces of the people walking past, coming through the automatic glass doors that separated customs from the outside world. He himself had emerged from behind those doors only an hour before, weary from a sleepless night, wondering how he would make it through the long day ahead. With one more flight to go, and a partner yet to meet, he'd begun to entertain thoughts of turning around and heading home. He tried to remind himself why he'd agreed to this assignment in the first place.

He replayed the previous morning in his head, when Gordon had phoned him awake and told him that Aeneas had turned up again. *Like a bad penny*, Gordon said. He told Robert to pack his bags and get to the office.

But Robert had stayed in bed, staring at the bare walls of his "no personality" apartment, as an old girlfriend once called it. She'd been right. He used to blame the lack of decoration on living his life on the road. But the truth was, as an undercover agent, Robert had assumed so many personalities over the years that he had begun to question which personality was his.

Robert's one meager attempt at interior decorating was a laminated map of the world. He'd hung it in the kitchen, planning to use pushpins to mark every place he had visited— Amsterdam, Oslo, Osaka, Kuwait—but he abandoned the idea when he realized that most of those trips were classified.

And that morning, after he'd finally gotten out of bed and dressed, he wandered into the kitchen and stared at the northern reaches of the map, at the tiny islands of Svalbard, two hundred miles north of Norway, just below the polar ice cap. Places deserving of pushpins. Places Robert had nearly succeeded in erasing from memory, until Gordon had called and mentioned Aeneas.

When Robert had entered Gordon's perennially unlit office, Gordon was reclined in his chair, feet on the desk, keyboard on his lap. People often mistook the posture for laziness, but Robert knew it was intentional. Gordon once said the fastest way to get promoted at the Bureau was to pretend you didn't want to get promoted. Robert wondered whether Gordon's emerging paunch was part of the disguise, but he hesitated to ask. Gordon was only a few years older than Robert but looked twice that, heavyset, with a balding head framed by wisps of thin blond hair and wire-rimmed glasses.

Robert walked to the window and pulled open the vertical blinds to let in some light, revealing the top half of a naked tree. The night's ice storm had left a sheen on its branches, and they hung low under the weight. A dense layer of clouds threatened more of the same. Robert normally would have welcomed the change in scenery brought about by a new assignment, but not this time. He could feel Gordon watching him but resisted the urge to turn around.

Don't you want to know what he did? Gordon asked.

Not particularly.

I'd have thought you would relish a second shot at him.

And I'd have thought I would've graduated to pursuing real terrorists by now.

Oh, he's real, Gordon said. *Aeneas, too, has graduated. To negligent manslaughter.*

Robert turned to see if Gordon was joking. He wasn't. *Aeneas may be good at protecting animals,* Gordon said, *but he's not so good at protecting people. He let one of his crew members, a woman, die up in the North Atlantic. Details are sketchy because nobody's talking. She was estranged from her parents, and they want it kept quiet as well. But they've got connections in the Bureau, which is all we need to know. And, frankly, it was just a matter of time before he gave us another reason to come after him.*

Robert had looked back out the window, at the tree, at one sadly sagging branch. He felt the urge to exit the building, climb the tree, shake the ice off. Give the branch a break from the weight. A little temporary insanity might give Robert a break as well, a week off from work, an excuse. He knew he didn't need an excuse; he could just say no. Gordon certainly owed him. Back when Gordon had been working undercover, with Robert just out of the Academy, an arms dealer in Long Beach discovered a microphone in Gordon's briefcase—and Robert put a bullet in the man's head just as he was about to put one in Gordon's.

But Robert couldn't say no. He'd been the one to open this case, and he knew he needed to be the one to close it.

Still, he wished he hadn't been assigned a partner, that he wasn't still waiting for her at the increasingly crowded airport terminal. He noticed a woman approaching rapidly, pulling a wheeled carry-on bag, and he stepped aside to get out of her way. But she stopped, right in front of him.

"You Robert?" she asked. She wore a Red Sox cap that covered her short blond hair.

Robert looked again at the picture, expecting a brunette. The woman smiled. "That photo's from when I was working out of Boston. I'm in the Miami office now. Gotta blend in with the locals. I'm Lynda." She gave his hand a quick shake then started off. She was shorter than Robert expected, but she carried herself with a swagger that made up for it. "We've got to motor," she called back to him. "Next flight leaves in ten minutes."

Robert followed a step behind. She was still talking, but

he couldn't hear her over the public address system, and he got the sense that she didn't care if he heard her anyway.

On the plane, Robert took the window seat and, as Lynda continued her friendly chatter, watched Buenos Aires disappear beneath the clouds. Then she switched gears, brought up the case, and he started to listen.

Lynda told him that Brazilian trawlers off the coast of Fortaleza had first sighted the *Arctic Tern*. Fishermen were, by nature, a suspicious lot, and they took the boat for a competitor. She said they'd reported that the *Tern* was headed south. And she had a warrant for Aeneas's arrest.

"So what's your story with this guy?" she asked.

"I don't have a story."

"Then why are you here?"

"Ask Gordon."

"I did. All he told me was that you could I.D. him. Can you?"

Robert nodded.

"Well, that's a start. If all goes well, you'll be pointing him out by nightfall. Gordon pulled some strings with the Argentines. There's a naval cutter waiting for us in Puerto Madryn loaded with enough men and arms to invade Panama."

Everything was suddenly moving quickly, too quickly. The *Tern's* coordinates, the Argentine cutter. Success seemed inevitable, which would have been a good thing if they were chasing anyone else. But Aeneas in handcuffs seemed more dangerous to Robert than Aeneas on the run. The stories Aeneas could tell, once captured, to anyone within earshot. How Lynda would react if she learned the real reason Aeneas escaped under his watch five years ago. The new cases Gordon could open just as this one was being closed.

Robert began to imagine scenarios that would result in the use of lethal force. The images weren't hard to conjure— Aeneas raising a shotgun, Aeneas playing Kamikaze with his ship—giving Robert an excuse to react with a well-placed round, extinguishing, finally, the man and his stories. Extinguishing the memories, once and for all.

"You're not all that chatty, are you, Bobby?"

Robert turned away from the window. Lynda wore a sly grin, which pulled his mind back to the present. He forced a smile and shook his head.

"Like my husband," she said with a shrug. "We'll get along just fine."

As promised, the ARA *Roca*, a four-story gunmetal warship, was waiting for them when their taxi arrived at Puerto Madryn harbor.

"If only the Bureau moved this fast in getting me a raise," Lynda said as she and Robert hurried up the boarding ramp.

Robert looked up at the guns, at the men in uniform, and felt a twinge of embarrassment. He imagined what Aeneas would say at such a display of might—*All this, for little old me?*—and didn't know what bothered him more, the veritable army before him or the fact that he'd begun imagining what Aeneas would say.

Lynda stopped in the bridge, and Robert heard her talking to the captain in Spanish while he took up position outside on the wing deck, off the starboard side of the bridge, which gave him a panoramic view of the water below. He could still see Lynda inside, laughing at something the captain said. She was flirting with him—a short man in his forties, trim, with dark hair and the matching requisite mustache—and Robert felt his body begin to relax, knowing that she was taking care of things. It was nice, for the time being, to feel as though he were nothing but a passenger.

Within a few minutes, the boat was in open water, under

a cloudless sky. When Lynda joined him at the railing, Robert hoped that the stiff headwind, which made talking difficult, might keep her silent. But Lynda had a loud voice and stood extra close.

"Captain Zamora says we're not far," she said. "A fisherman sighted the *Tern* just an hour ago, not far from here. We should call Gordon and give him an update." She looked at Robert expectantly.

"What do you mean, *we?*" Robert asked.

"You've got the satellite phone. He's *your* boss."

"I'll call him when we've got actual news. What's the rush?"

"Look, Bobby, I don't know about you, but I've got to start scoring some points with upper management. I wasn't sent down here for my health, if you know what I mean. You do know what happened in Miami, don't you?"

"I read the report."

"That's the official story," she said. "Not the entire story." Lynda began to tell Robert about her attempt to capture Aeneas in the Port of Miami, much of it a rehash of what he'd already read. So he raised his binoculars, focusing more on the horizon than on her story.

She'd had only three agents to do a five-agent job— round-the-clock surveillance of the *Arctic Tern*. It would have been simple, she told him, if only she'd had the manpower: The Canadians had pulled the boat's registration. The FBI had obtained a warrant on the captain. The Coast Guard was on high alert. All they needed was a positive I.D. of Aeneas, and they would move in and make the arrest.

Then came the bomb threats, two of them, fifteen minutes apart. Two fully loaded passenger ships—one about to depart and one just arrived—had to be evacuated. More than seven thousand people spilled out onto piers, herded by SWAT teams, bomb-sniffing canines, and TV cameras. The next day, Lynda traced the calls to a cell phone on a ship that slipped out of the harbor during all the commotion—the *Arctic Tern*.

"Now for the part I left out of the report," she said. "You see, I was the only one on surveillance that afternoon. The only one. And I get this call on my cell. Franklin Bimler, he says his name is, out of Counterterrorist Operations. You know this guy?"

Robert shook his head.

"Of course not. Neither did I. Franklin tells me he's got urgent information, but he can't tell me because he thinks people are listening in via parabolic microphone—because I'm outside at the time. So I leave my post and get into my car, and that's when all hell breaks loose with the cruise ships."

"So?"

"So, there was no Franklin Bimler. Not on the phone. Not anywhere. I ran a search on the guy, and there's nobody by that name in the Bureau."

"Franklin could have been Aeneas."

"I considered that. I did. But how'd Aeneas get my number?"

"He's good."

"I don't know. How'd he even know I was working the case?"

"You think that someone in the Bureau set you up?"

"Crazier things have happened."

"You're getting paranoid, Lynda. Aeneas will do that to you."

"I suppose."

"Why didn't you put that in your report?"

"Because I left my damn post, that's why. I got duped. It was bad enough I let him get away. Would you have put it in *your* report?"

He wouldn't have. There were a lot of things he'd left out of his own report on Aeneas. He looked at Lynda, who was still watching him, and wondered how much she knew.

"It was Aeneas," Robert said, turning away and raising his binoculars again. "Trust me."

"*¡Ballenas!*" shouted one of the uniformed men standing below on the main deck. Following the man's pointed finger, Robert scanned the horizon, then broadened his viewing arc. He zoomed out, then back in, but he did not see any ships. He lowered the binoculars and turned to Lynda.

"Whales," she explained. "I think."

"You *think*? I thought you were fluent."

"I am. They speak a different Spanish here," Lynda said. "The double *el* has a *jha* sound. Always throws me."

Robert returned his eyes to the water just as the nose of a whale emerged, missile-like, off the right side of the ship. The gray marbled monster rose ten feet, twenty feet, angled, then fell sideways into the water.

"I was right!" Lynda reached into her backpack, pulling out a camera. Looking down, Robert counted five men in uniform doing the same, aiming their cell phones and pocket cameras.

"Five summers dragging my nephews into Boston Harbor," Lynda said, "and we never saw so much as a fin. They're not gonna believe this."

After getting her fill of photographs, she began to flip through a travel guide. "Must be a southern right whale," she said. "This is where they give birth and raise their young. And did you know there are penguin colonies along the shoreline? Along with elephant seals and blue-eyed shags. Maybe we can swing by there on our way back, hey, Bobby?"

"This isn't a vacation," he said.

She shrugged. "Might as well get something out of it besides frequent flyer miles."

Suddenly the ship turned sharply left and coughed up a thick blast of smoke. Robert grabbed the railing to avoid losing his balance. The two officers standing next to them began talking rapidly.

"What are they saying?" Robert asked.

"Looks like we've got a runner." Lynda raised her binoculars, and Robert followed where she trained them. He could make out three small ships on the otherwise flat horizon. The one in the middle, a medium-sized fishing trawler, appeared a lighter shade, possibly painted white. It emitted clouds of smoke, evidence that it, too, was in a hurry.

As the *Roca* began to catch up, Robert watched the white ship expand in size until he could count the number of decks (three) and estimate the length (150 feet). Yet he did not recognize the ship itself.

"That's it," Lynda said. "That's our ship."

Robert looked again and realized that he had been searching for something much smaller, the boat he'd sailed on five years ago. The ship ahead was larger, probably a recycled commercial fishing trawler with ice-reinforced hulls. Robert thought of Aeneas using a former fishing vessel to attack fishermen, and how much Aeneas would relish the irony. He'd probably acquired the boat from the Russians or the Norwegians—the fishermen thrown out of work by declining cod stocks or some other overfished species. *It's time someone put this boat to a noble use*, he would say.

The *Tern* ran for a few minutes more before slowing to a halt. Because Canada had pulled the *Tern's* registration, it was now a ship with no country, meaning it could be boarded by any nation at any time. Not that Robert needed an excuse. They already had the warrant. Still, he realized, this was all too easy. Aeneas would not have stopped running.

The Argentine captain radioed the *Tern* but got no response, and he began speaking to his officers in rapid-fire Spanish. As Lynda listened in on the chatter, Robert stepped outside the bridge to call Gordon on the satellite phone.

Robert paced the deck until he got a clear signal, then wrestled with an unresponsive keypad before giving up and tossing the phone back into his backpack. If they were chasing real terrorists, Robert would have the latest-generation satphone, plus a backup. But not here. Everything down here was old and used. Secondhand. Including him.

By now, they had pulled within a football field's distance of the *Tern*. The ship, painted white from mast to bow, looked like a U.S. Coast Guard cutter, with the exception of three large black letters painted on each side of the hull: CDA, for Cetacean Defense Alliance. The name RV *Arctic Tern* was visible in smaller letters, the "RV" indicating research. There was, of course, no research being done aboard the *Tern*, just as whaling ships claimed to be research vessels without ever publishing a single study. *If the Japanese are going to play the research card*, Aeneas always said, *so will we*. And on the side of the bridge were painted a dozen black checkmarks, one for each whaling vessel sunk over the years. Robert had been a witness to one of those checkmarks.

Lynda and Robert stepped into a lowered Zodiac, and a crew member ferried them over the chop, followed by a dozen men in uniform. Lynda was the first up the ladder on the side of the *Tern*. Robert held back, watching as the uniforms pulled themselves aboard, one by one, until he was alone with the driver.

He'd tried to brace himself for this voyage into his past, for the opening of old wounds, mostly his own. But now he could feel his body tensing, his heart accelerating. What if someone up there recognized him; what if some fragment from his past did emerge? More important, he didn't know how he would react once he came face-to-face with Aeneas after all this time, with all the history between them.

Robert heard a shout from above. Lynda, looking down at him, waved him up. He reached down and made sure his gun was holstered, safety off. Then he took a deep breath, slid on his sunglasses, and grabbed onto the ladder.

Assembled in front of him on the rear deck was what

looked like an Earth Fest crowd—about two dozen college dropouts, potheads, and tattoo addicts. A few wore white T-shirts with the CDA logo—a black silhouette of a whale fluke with the letters CDA superimposed in white. Most of the crew wore secondhand flannels and fleece, ripped jeans, flip-flops. As Robert reviewed the faces beneath the beards and piercings, he began to breathe more easily, thankful that the CDA did not pay a salary, ensuring a high rate of turnover. He did not recognize a single face, and he was growing optimistic that nobody recognized him—which was fortunate, as Lynda had apparently left the introductions to him.

"We're with the FBI," he said. "I'm Agent Porter, and this is Agent Madigan. We're here to execute an arrest warrant for Neil Patrick Cameron."

"Who?" asked a gangly, unshaven man standing in front.

"Aeneas," Robert said.

"Are you in charge of this vessel?" Lynda asked.

"In a manner of speaking."

"What's that supposed to mean?" Robert said.

"I'm the chef."

Muted laughter emanated from the crowd. For a ship that was on the run, these people appeared awfully relaxed. But perhaps they were bluffing; perhaps Aeneas was hiding somewhere below. But Robert had a feeling that he was long gone, that Aeneas again had managed to stay a few steps ahead. The only times he ever got captured were times he chose to be captured. Like in Iceland, during the CDA's first year. Aeneas sank three whaling ships and eluded a fleet of naval and Coast Guard ships for six months. Then, one afternoon in October, he sailed into the Reykjavík harbor and turned himself in. He'd wanted a high-profile trial. Iceland, fearful of negative publicity, stuck him on a plane to London and barred him from ever returning.

Aeneas was an expert in the game of cat and mouse, a

trait Robert envied when he was on the side of the mouse. Now that he was the predator, he felt predictable and slow. Yet he had little choice but to continue along this preordained path, go through the motions, search the ship, ask pointed questions, ignore the laughter.

Robert looked at Lynda. "You want to do the honors?"

"My pleasure." She said something in Spanish as she led the way into the ship, a few of the Argentines following her, a few heading for the bridge.

"You all stay right here," Robert told the crew on the deck. He knew that the faces staring back at him knew where Aeneas was, and he knew just as well that they would not give up their leader. As Robert paced the deck, he envisioned the uniforms below, opening doors, lockers, anything that might contain a heavyset man of just over six feet. They would, he realized, come up empty handed.

The chef stepped forward. "About how long do you expect this open house to last?"

"Until we find him."

"I've got food on the cooker," he said.

"It can wait."

"I am quite serious," the chef said. "We could have a fire in the galley if I don't get down there."

"Tell me where Aeneas is, and I'll let you go."

"I don't know where he is."

"Then tell me where you dropped him off."

"I work all the way down there. I don't know what goes on up here."

"Then tell me who does."

"I do." A tall woman in a red fleece jacket and wraparound sunglasses emerged from behind the crowd.

"Who are you?" Robert asked.

"I'm the captain."

"Aeneas is the captain."

"Aeneas isn't here."

The woman—somewhere in her thirties—had the hardened look of a triathlete, with close-cropped blond hair and dark skin blushed red from the wind and sun. Robert considered telling her to remove her sunglasses. He wanted to see her eyes, to know if she was hiding anything. But doing so would have only made him look desperate, which he wasn't, not yet.

"What's your name?" he asked.

"Lauren Davis."

"Very well, *Captain* Davis, tell me why you're headed south via Argentina instead your usual route via New Zealand?"

"You should already know that."

"Indulge me."

"So you can pass it along to the Japanese?"

"I don't work for the Japanese."

"You might as well."

"You haven't answered my question."

"If you want to catch a fish, go where the fish are; if you want to catch a whaler, go where the whalers are."

Robert felt blood rush to his face, not just because he recognized the line—one of Aeneas's many adages—but because of the way she delivered it. Knowingly. He lowered his sunglasses. He wanted her to see *his* eyes, to see that she was mistaken, that she did not in fact recognize him.

"Have the whalers moved to a different location?"

"Not yet. But they will," she said. "The Aussies are sending two naval ships to protect their waters. This will force the Japanese into the Amundsen Sea."

"Which is where you are headed."

"If you'll let us."

"All I want is Aeneas. Show me where you dropped him, and you'll be free to continue on, save all the whales. I'm not here for the ship. I'm here for him. But if I can't get him, I'll settle for the ship."

She removed her sunglasses. Her eyes, bright green in the sunlight, stared defiantly at him.

"Unlike you," she said, "we don't leave people behind."

She knew. Robert could see it in her eyes. She knew who he was, and she probably knew everything. Aeneas must have told her. Maybe he told everyone.

Robert turned and walked to the rear of the deck and leaned over the railing as if checking a possible hiding spot. He looked back at the Argentine ship, anxious to return to it, angry with Gordon for sending him here, angrier with himself for coming. He dug his fingernails into the railing, as if he could bore through layers of paint, peel away the history of the ship. He should have known better than to think he'd been forgotten just because a few years had gone by. A fresh set of faces didn't save him from the same collective memory. Now Robert had their ship, but they had—and always would have—his past.

Lynda emerged from below, followed by her Argentine escorts. When she saw Robert, she stopped and shook her head before joining him at the railing.

"You don't look surprised," she said.

"They dropped him off somewhere, not far from here. That's why they didn't run far when we chased them."

"They tell you that?"

"No," he said, "I just know."

"In case you're wrong, Sherlock, we should take the ship back to port and do another sweep. Get the dogs on here."

Robert knew she was right but was too weary to say anything, the jet lag catching up with him, the feeling that this short mission would not be so short.

"Hand me the phone," she said. "I'll call Gordon."

ANGELA

ZERO FOUR TWO TWO NINE.

Angela had tagged him during her tenth season at Verde.

At the time, the penguin had taken a liking to the old Toyota pickup that the researchers used to travel to town. He would belly up to one of the worn Goodyears and paddle it with his wings—the flipper dance. It was a mating ritual, one normally reserved for females of the same species. Clearly, he was not the brightest of penguins, but he was young still.

They named him Diesel.

Sometimes Diesel would offer up a flipper dance to a seated human. That's how Angela got to know him. She used to read in the early mornings, seated outside the cinder-block *cueva* that she shared with six other researchers, sneaking in a few moments of peace before the day ahead.

Diesel mostly spent his days on his stomach under the rear of the truck, watching the humans pass. But one morning he cautiously approached Angela and began to poke at her shoes with his beak. She put her book down on a cinder block and he pecked at that as well; then he stepped forward and began to flap his wings against her right leg.

"It's nice to get attention from a male once in a while," she later told Shelly, her boss. "I won't bicker over species."

Over time, Diesel spent more time around humans than with his peers, loitering around the camp, trying to push his way into the *cueva* or the office. They soon discovered that he wouldn't bite if touched, and he became more of a pet than a penguin, always nearby as researchers prepped for a day's census or as they walked among trailers and tents and the bathrooms. None of them thought Diesel was likely ever to find a mate.

He followed Angela into the public toilet one evening after the tourists were gone. She had to pick him up to get him out and was surprised that he didn't struggle at all and made no attempt to bite her. From then on, during her morning rituals, she would skip the book altogether and lift Diesel onto her lap, staring at him, eye to eye, his head turned so that he could see her more clearly.

What a sight they must have been to anyone who woke early—but Angela didn't care. Diesel was uninterested in his own species, and she was uninterested in hers. Two loners, sharing their mornings.

And just when the humans were sure Diesel was far too domesticated to take a mate, he found one. Or one found him, as was usually the case. One morning, Angela discovered Diesel under the Toyota with a partner on her belly next to him.

Angela felt somewhat abandoned when she first saw them together, but the naturalist within her quickly took over, and she spent the next two weeks deliberating with the others on how to remove the truck without disturbing this fragile relationship. They had to move quickly—once an egg was laid, any disruption could cause the penguins to retreat to the water, sacrificing the next generation. If Angela had had her way, the truck would never have been moved at all.

They spent a week constructing an artificial undercarriage out of leftover plywood, brass pipes, duct tape, two spare tires, and cinder blocks—such an odd contraption that the tourists actually began taking snapshots.

The switch occurred during the morning hours when the

birds were standing beside their nest, crowing to each other.

Stacy, a rookie researcher who was good with a stick shift, piloted the pickup; the rest followed closely behind with the contraption. The penguins watched this bizarre parade with interest, but did not seemed terribly alarmed. When the humans left, they returned to their counterfeit nest. The true indication of success came in the form of two eggs, which Shelly noticed three weeks later. The eggs were smaller than normal but still viable. Sometimes it took a year or two for young penguins to become successful breeding pairs. Diesel was just getting started.

Angela had already selected names for the chicks.

THE SKY WAS DARKENING WHEN ANGELA entered the dining room. She was too nervous to eat, with thoughts of a man off in the darkness, shivering and hungry. But she needed to make an appearance for the sake of continuity—humans being creatures of habit, too—and she needed supplies. The dining room had been a storage shed in its first life. Now it consisted of two long tables and a propane stove, four small windows covered in plastic. There were no overhead lights, but candles and portable fluorescents created a warm environment for the nine researchers—three men and six women, including Angela.

Shelly Sparks, the director of Angela's research camp, was a tall, trim woman in her late forties with long black hair. She always said that you could tell what month of the breeding season it was by the length of her roots. She dyed her hair before she arrived at Punta Verde in late August and not again until the last of the penguins had traded in their old feather coats for new and returned to sea. *We molt together,* she'd say.

Shelly could never resist making light of the scabs and

stitches and torn gloves that no naturalist escaped, and that evening she invited Angela to show off her new wound during the meal. Angela stood and waved her swollen hand like the Queen, which was met by cheers from the junior researchers who had long since forgotten that she, too, was human.

Angela caught Doug's eyes and glanced at the floor. She was avoiding him now. He had followed orders earlier and stayed close to the nest, but when she told him to fetch the first aid kit for her hand, he was incredulous. *Why don't we return to camp together?* he asked. One sharp glare from Angela had been all it took to send him off on his one-hour round trip. She got a secret thrill from putting him back in his place.

While Doug was gone, Angela had deposited her castaway in the northern reaches of Back Bay (Shelly had named parts of Verde after neighborhoods of Boston, her hometown). Angela assembled the man's waterlogged tent between bulbous Lycium bushes. He had a pronounced limp and was shivering.

"I need to get you dry clothes," she told him.

"I've been wet before," he said. "All I need is food. And liquor couldn't hurt."

Shelly was heading back to the States in the morning, to give exams to her Boston University students and to squeeze more money from donors, leaving Angela in charge for a week. Her departure gave Angela hope that she could keep the man hidden.

Angela folded a large piece of lamb into a napkin, no small feat, as she was a vegetarian. She excused herself from dinner and exited through the back door, by the storage room, where she grabbed a bottle of Malbec.

Outside, Angela peeked underneath the pickup truck, a ritual she now dreaded. The female was there waiting, her head swaying erratically from side to side, the chicks chirping loudly, calling out to be fed.

Diesel should be back by now. Back with a belly of food

to feed his chicks, to relieve his mate so she could go back to sea to feed herself, continuing the relay race of raising their young. Another day and this penguin would have no choice but to abandon her chicks.

Angela opened the creaky door of her trailer. Now that she was second in command, she no longer crammed into the *cueva*, and while an eight-foot, 1970s-era trailer that leaked wasn't exactly high living, it was a big step up. Mostly, it was privacy. It also came with its own penguin, Geraldo, who nested under the trailer, between its cinder-block foundations. In early mornings and late at night, Geraldo brayed loudly, calling out for any and all potential mates. Angela was long past being awoken by penguins, but she still liked hearing him flap his wings against her floor.

Unlike Diesel, Geraldo had at least selected a nest that was guaranteed to be around for awhile. But here at camp, these penguins were still a kilometer too far inland; the most desirable nests were nearer the water, closer to the swarms of anchovies, krill, and sardines the birds relied on. Penguins waddled to the ocean two or three times a week, and adding a kilometer of pockmarked land to the journey made these inland nests less desirable. But the younger males took what they could get, even if they ended up with "starter homes." Angela sighed as she entered her trailer, knowing that Geraldo would likely be single for another season.

A few minutes later, Doug knocked. "You look like you're going somewhere," he said when she opened the door.

"Just up the hill, like always."

"You need a companion?"

"I think I can manage tonight."

"You sure?"

"I'm quite sure."

She could tell that Doug was not accustomed to rejection, and he loitered around her trailer as she headed up the hill.

Fifty yards into the darkness, Angela heard movement and stopped.

It was Doug. "Centaurus is going to be brilliant tonight," he said, squinting as she turned her flashlight on him.

"Doug, go home."

She watched him sulk back to camp, then waited another fifteen minutes to be certain he would remain there. She knew that eventually she would have to humor him and take him along on a trip or two. How quickly the object of her affection had become one of annoyance.

Her mind wandered as she hiked through the darkness toward the tent, the moon not yet making itself known. Why was she harboring this man? Maybe it was transference, caring for this lost soul as a way of making up for another lost soul: Diesel's. Maybe it was the scientist in her, the opportunity to study a human for a change, instead of a penguin. Or maybe she simply found him too attractive to share with the others.

She opted for the scientific explanation. After devoting a lifetime to studying hundreds of thousands of penguins, her life had become consumed with numbers and averages. The average-sized penguin. The typical lifespan. The standard rate of reproduction. Statistical outliers were always left out of the calculations, as they should be. But now Angela found herself face-to-face with a statistical outlier. A human anomaly. Not average in any way. And not so easily dismissed as a number.

She found him standing outside his tent, looking back over the water.

"How long do you need?" she asked.

"A few days."

"You cannot leave this campsite," she said. "I will bring you food and water. But under no circumstances do you start a fire or draw attention to yourself in any way. And by no means do you set foot on the tourist trail."

"People will just think I'm one of you."

"You're not one of us. This is a provincial reserve, not a campsite, and it's surrounded by private land. If the *guardafauna* doesn't shoot you, the ranchers surely will."

He sighed loudly. "You're the boss." She handed him her flashlight and a large water bottle. When she offered him the lamb he waved her off.

"I don't eat meat," he said.

"You have to eat something."

"That will suffice," he said, pointing to the bottle of wine. Angela had forgotten a corkscrew, so he carved an opening with his pocket knife and took a long drink.

The moon was rising and, with it, the volume of the penguins around them. She studied his face in the dim light as he watched a penguin lean forward and let forth an escalating progression of honks.

"Do you have any earplugs?" he asked.

"You'll get used to the noise." Angela remembered a protein bar she'd tossed into her backpack last week and dug it out.

"Thank you," he said, tearing open the wrapper with his teeth. He sat on the ground and inhaled the bar. She sat across from him. Angela could tell the man was starving, and yet he'd turned down the lamb. Most of the other naturalists at Verde were meat eaters, and it always bothered her that they could devote their lives to protecting one animal while consuming another.

"We have something in common," she said.

"What's that?"

"I'm a vegetarian, too."

He took another swig from the bottle and studied her face. She averted her eyes, focusing on a penguin as it passed behind him, the bird's white belly glowing in the moonlight.

"How's your hand?" he asked.

"All stitched together," she said, holding it up as proof.

Despite being alone with a strange man in the middle

of the night, in the middle of nowhere, she was not afraid. She never really felt alone out here, surrounded by knee-high chaperones peeking at her from under bushes and within burrows. Some hovered nearby, cutting wide swaths around the tent as they trekked to the water.

Angela didn't ask the man who he was or what he was running from. There was something freeing about knowing nothing about someone, about him knowing nothing about you. Her research camp was a soap opera, one that grew more incestuous by the day. Everybody knew about her crush on Doug, including Doug. Angela never deluded herself. Although her body was slim and athletic, she did not display it in a way that that attracted men's eyes. She had a chest, she knew, that might catch an eye or two, if she hadn't tethered it under a sports bra that could be washed in a bucket and dried on a clothesline in ten minutes. She dressed for fieldwork, wearing cargo pants for function rather than fashion, layering on dusty shirts and sweaters in the region's dark green and taupe. She had always dressed to blend in with the landscape, not stand out.

Yet during those times Doug tagged along on her nightly trips up the hill—the closest thing to a date she'd had in years—Angela found herself wishing she'd packed something sexier. It felt almost romantic the way Doug, an astronomy major before switching to biology, pointed out the Southern Cross and the creatures of the heavens, like Leo and Pisces. Angela realized that she had been coming to Punta Verde for fifteen years, had identified every square meter, every bush, plant, bug, rodent, mammal, and moss, and yet she'd never bothered to tell one star from another. She spent her life looking down.

Doug got her thinking about children for the first time, simply by asking if she had any. But he was only a flirt, only interested in Angela for her knowledge and experience. Perhaps he was angling to co-author a research paper with her, to leapfrog the postdocs. Their profession could be as ruthless as nature itself; not everybody would get the research grants or the honorary professorships, see their names in news articles. With people and with penguins, scarcity drove them to do extreme things.

Even Angela was not immune. A month ago, she nearly flew into a fury when Doug and the others did not show up for an outing, until Shelly told her it was Thanksgiving and they were in town calling their families.

So Angela was glad for a new, albeit mysterious, companion. As they sat together in the dark, she found herself thinking of the body under her filthy work clothes, a body kept in camouflage suddenly yearning to be noticed. A body that had not been touched in a long time. A body that, just now, wanted to remember what it felt like.

She took the bottle when the man offered it to her. With each drink he became a bit more talkative, as did she. He asked for her name, and she told him.

"They call me Aeneas," he said.

"You're kidding."

"You've not heard of me?" He appeared surprised. "Surely you've read about me in the papers."

"We don't exactly get home delivery here."

He explained the name, an alias, and his pursuers— various coast guards, police bureaus, and intelligence agencies.

"I do battle with whaling ships," he said.

"Like Greenpeace?" Angela asked.

"They fight with words and water guns," he said. "We fight with the hulls of our ships. We ram them. We mangle their props."

"You sink them?"

"On occasion."

"Is that why you're here?"

"No."

Angela left it at that. She didn't want to know more, to find out anything worse.

"Are you married?" he asked.

"Do I look like I have time for a marriage? Out here attending to wayward men?"

A sneeze broke the silence that followed.

"What was that?" he asked.

"A penguin."

"Penguins catch colds?"

"They sneeze to exhale the salt from their beaks."

"I could probably do the same," he said, rubbing his nose. "I was married once."

"You?"

"She was a volunteer. Earnest. A scientist, like you. Told me I was full of shit one day, and I was hooked. We made it official in Ushuaia. Had the ceremony on the ship in middle of the Drake Passage. It's not easy saying *I do* with forty-foot waves lapping at your feet. That time of year, the sun never sets, the body never gets tired. There's a sense of collective euphoria. It's as if you've stepped outside of the world and none of the old rules apply. Eventually, however, you have to head north again. Where there are roads and traffic lights, yards that need to be mowed, bills to be paid. She traveled with me for a while after her tour was up, but I think she thought it was a phase I was going through. She went back to LA and waited for me to settle down, to return to her. I didn't. And she divorced me in absentia."

He took a long drink. "You find that amusing?" he asked.

Angela realized that she had been smiling. "No. It's—it's that word."

"What word?"

"*Absentia*. When I was a kid, I used to think absentia was an actual place. I even spent time looking for it in the atlas at the school library."

"I've been living in absentia for years," he said. She saw his lips curve upward, into a private smile, as if he'd forgotten she was there. And as the silence lingered, once again she felt left behind.

The bottle was empty, and reluctantly she stood to leave.

"Come here." In one smooth motion, he stood, grabbed her waist, and kissed her. She felt the scruff of his unshaven face bite her chin as she kissed him back. Then, remembering where they were, she pulled away. "Wait," she said.

"Wait for what?"

She didn't know. She was certain Doug hadn't followed her; they were as alone as any two people could be. And maybe this was the problem: that a wish, one she could barely admit she'd wished, was being granted.

She began to say something, but he grabbed her again, this time more tightly, and she responded by pushing against him so that he stumbled backward into a *quilembai* bush. A startled penguin emerged from under him and bit his leg.

"Ouch!" he yelled, flushing out several more penguins, sending them flapping away on their bellies.

Angela attempted to smooth down her jacket, her hair, before turning away. "Good night," she called out, walking off into the dark.

On the next hill, she stopped and removed her jacket. Her heart was pounding, and she looked back into the darkness. Despite his aggressiveness, she still did not fear him. Mostly, she feared herself, and how close she came to not pushing him away. Instinct served her well in self-defense. But now she was alone again, heading back to an empty trailer.

THE MORNING WAS DRIZZLY, the first rainfall in a month. Outside the office, Shelly gathered food requests from the

assembled naturalists—energy bars, Doritos, Red Vines—
and loaded her bags into the pickup truck.

Then she approached Angela. "Can I bring you anything?"
she asked.

"I think we're good here."

Such departures were frequent at the camp and did not
warrant hugs or other displays of affection. Yet Shelly seemed
to linger longer than usual. "I'll see if I can scrounge up
another satellite transmitter," she said, and Angela felt herself
wince before Shelly added, "As a backup."

"Right. As a backup." Angela forced a smile. Shelly
climbed into the car with Stacy, and they left for the Trelew
airport.

Now in charge, Angela sent the team, including a
reluctant Doug, south of the camp, and she headed north.
During the long walk alone, her mind turned to Diesel. It had
been Angela's idea to attach the satellite transmitter to him.

Using a blend of duct tape and superglue, Angela had
affixed the transmitter to Diesel's flank on a cold morning.
The yellow device was about the size of a deck of cards,
with rounded edges and a three-inch rubber antenna. Once
activated, for up to six weeks the device sent signals at five-
minute intervals to a satellite twenty miles above the planet. To
conserve battery life, the device shut itself off while the penguin
was under water and out of range. To a satellite, the path of a
penguin looked more like Morse code than a continuous line,
but Angela could decipher the data, connect the dots, learn
where Diesel traveled to fill his belly. The transmitters cost
$5,000 each, so it was very important to get them back. The
key to getting one returned was selecting a bird that had a
reason to return—in other words, a male penguin with a new
chick. Shelly had thought it was premature to tag Diesel. *Give
him another year*, she said. But Angela had insisted.

It was a two-hour procedure, and Doug had helped,

though he'd made it known he did not approve. Although each new generation of transmitter diminished in size, the devices still exerted a drag on a penguin in water, reducing its odds, ever so slightly, of out-swimming a leopard seal or an orca. Doug held Diesel while Angela attached the device. The procedure usually lasted up to an hour, and a penguin usually struggled during every minute. But Diesel was calm. He seemed to enjoy the attention.

It's a Southern Cross, Doug had said while looking at Diesel's belly. Angela looked at the dark smudges on his white feathers, how they did indeed form a cross, something she never noticed until now.

What's the point of tracking them, Doug added, *if the act of doing so reduces their numbers?*

Fishing nets do more damage than these devices will ever do, Angela told him.

This they knew from the dozens of flipper tags they received each year, mailed anonymously from the fishermen who obeyed the *Avise al* request stamped on the back of each tag. Some tags arrived carefully flattened out by hammer, easier to slip into an envelope; others arrived intact, little thin triangles. And Angela always wondered how many tags were left on those ships, or sank to the bottom of the sea.

Her life was consumed with attrition and its causes. The unreported oil spills, evidenced by the blackened, shivering birds that staggered upon the shores. The plastic six-pack rings that doubled as lassos. The baited longlines, meant for large fish but difficult for any species to resist. And the most acute and least visible cause of all—the food supply. Penguins depended on anchovies and krill, once abundant and ignored by fishermen, now in demand at salmon farms and for multivitamins. Like penguins, fishermen aimed for the food nearest to shore, and because they were more efficient and rapacious, penguins were forced to forage farther and farther from their nests, diminishing the odds of a successful return.

Still walking north, and fifteen minutes away from the research camp, Angela sighted a yellow jacket atop Beacon Hill. She rushed toward it to find Aeneas straining his eyes over the water. "I told you to stay at the tent," she said.

"I needed a higher vantage point. I thought I saw my ship."

But he did not see his ship, and Angela scolded him as she led him back to his camp. "Do you have to wear that jacket?" she asked.

"You don't like it?"

"It's not exactly camouflage."

"You should talk," he said.

"What do you mean?"

"With that red hair of yours, I could spot you a mile away."

Angela felt her face blush at the thought of him watching her, and she was glad for the biting wind.

She had work to do, and she decided that if she was going to harbor a fugitive, she would at least put him to work. She led Aeneas to the farthest reach of the colony, six miles from the park entrance. She could hear him breathing heavily behind her.

"You walk too fast," he said.

"And you walk too slow," she countered.

As they hiked along, she began to ignore his harmless taunts. But just as they'd reached the place where she wanted to begin the census, he gave a startled shout, and she turned to see him with one leg knee-deep in the ground. He had collapsed a penguin burrow, apparently twisting his ankle. She bent down to assess the damage—to the nest, not him— and was relieved to find the burrow empty.

"You ruined the nest," she said.

"This place is a mine field."

"It's not any easier for the penguins, but they manage. We're a mile inland, and look at all these nests. It takes a penguin two hours to get here. But they do it all the time, and they don't complain. And they don't collapse each other's nests."

Aeneas grunted as he pulled himself up. Angela ignored his grimace and his limp as she pulled out a five-meter length of rope, her notebook, and Shelly's map of the colony. By counting penguins within five-meter circular plots placed twenty meters apart, they'd get a reasonably accurate population estimate. And although Angela had been doing this on her own, finding the edges of a circle was best accomplished with two people. She stood Aeneas in the middle of one of Shelly's mapped circles, a measured piece of rope in one hand, her notebook in the other, while she walked the perimeter, holding the other end of the rope, calling out what she found: single male, active pair, one egg, two eggs, inactive nest.

"So is the colony growing or shrinking?" he asked.

"Shrinking. Though I can't say how much. That's why we're here."

"How many of these circles do we have to do?" he asked.

"You have somewhere better to be?"

"I'm just curious."

"A hundred or so," Angela said. "I could try calling your ship from our research station."

"They'll call me. Fortunately, my satphone is waterproof," he said. "Are you trying to get rid of me?"

She didn't answer him. He'd been there for two nights now, and Angela wasn't sure how long she could keep him hidden from the rest. At least keeping him close to her kept him away from the others. The circles would last for another day or so, and then what? He drank too much. He continued to reach for her, beginning with her shoulder, resting a hand, then two, massaging her neck. She no longer resisted. When he drank he also talked, and she found his stories exciting.

That night, she brought two bottles of Malbec. "To celebrate a hard day's work," she said. As they began to pass the first bottle between them, she asked him how he'd gotten his alias.

"When we sank this Icelandic whaling ship years ago, I spray-painted *Aeneas* across the hull," he said. "I figured it would confuse them. It did, for a period. But the name stuck."

"Why *Aeneas*?"

"Because he was fearless. Because he was a man without a country, a man without a port."

Aeneas stood and looked through the darkness toward the ocean. He looked anxious to return, and Angela felt bad for reminding him that he was not out there. She tried to steer him back toward land.

"Where will you go when the whaling season ends?" she asked.

"I'll head north. There's always a hunting season for something somewhere."

"Don't you have a home to return to?"

"My home is the ship."

"But don't you rest at all?"

"Do you?"

Angela smiled. "No."

"As long as there are fishermen out there, I'll be out there. Fishermen don't fish anymore. They obliterate, slaughter, expunge. They use vacuums, for fuck's sake. That's not fishing. That's extermination. When you raise cattle, you at least feed them. But fishermen don't feed fish. They just take. They even take the food the fish eat. Sheer avarice. I could kill them all."

He emptied the bottle.

"How'd you end up here, in Argentina?" Angela asked.

He paused, then reached for the second bottle. "A

few weeks ago," he said, "we came across a fishing trawler poaching in protected waters. I got in a Zodiac and started pulling in their longline. One of my volunteers was helping." He uncorked the bottle and drank before offering it to Angela. She shook her head.

"She was young, and it was her first season with us," he continued. "She was all fired up, and stubborn as hell. I had a difficult time saying no to that woman. I should have. I should have left her back on the ship."

He went silent, and Angela waited. She was learning that he tended to communicate in waves of dialogue, broken up by gaps of wind-blown silence. Initially, the silence made her nervous, and she filled the gaps with penguin trivia. But he wasn't really listening to her, so she eventually let the silence flow over the both of them. She came to enjoy the intimacy between people who were silent together.

"I was piloting the Zodiac, she was hauling in the line. Dangerous work. Every fifteen feet there's a razor-sharp hook the size of your index finger. Anyway, the trawler saw what we were doing, and they ran right at us. We should have tossed the line and got out of there. This trawler was huge—about twenty times bigger than us. But I thought I could dodge it and keep on pulling in the line. I cut across the front of their bow, too close." He took a long drink. "I should have left her on the ship," he said again.

"Did she drown?"

"No. She got caught up in the longline. Pulled into the water. She was sucked into the props."

"Oh my God."

"We never found the body. In all my time doing this sort of thing, from the Arctic to the Antarctic, we've never lost a life. Came close plenty of times. But we always were a bit luckier than we deserved. Until that day. I only wish it was me who went into the water."

"I'm sorry."

"One wrong move, and I'm no longer an activist," he said. "I'm a terrorist."

"What about your crew? Won't they be arrested?"

"The ship will be boarded, if it hasn't already happened. But it's me they want."

THE NEXT DAY, THEY MADE GOOD TIME on their circles. Aeneas was a reliable partner, quiet and focused, but always quick to make a joke when the opportunity arose. Angela could see why a woman married him. Yes, he belched and cursed like a sailor, but he also listened like a therapist as she rambled on about oil spills and overfishing. She told him that she hadn't dated a man in three years and not many men before that. But he didn't judge her, or if he did, he kept his thoughts to himself. For lunch, they sat on a berm overlooking the beach, not far north from where she first discovered him. They watched the wind blurring the tops of the folding waves, blowing spray into the air.

"Did you always want to protect penguins?" Aeneas asked.

"I used to think I was going to study the albatross."

"Makes sense."

"How so?"

"The albatross keeps to itself." He stopped, but she knew where he was headed, and she resisted arguing. He was right, after all; she, too, was a loner.

"Actually," she said, "my vision isn't all that good, so my professor at the time told me to focus on birds that I could get a bit closer to."

After lunch, he helped her attach a satellite transmitter to a male penguin. He had an impressive grip that held the bird steady as Angela applied the device.

"Since we started using these transmitters five years ago," she said, "the penguins have been traveling farther and farther away from the colony. Some travel more than a hundred miles each way."

"One hell of a commute," he said.

"It's because of the fishing trawlers. You know how they operate—they take all the fish close to shore. And we can only measure distance. We can't measure the fear these penguins feel when the fishing grounds they have known their entire lifetimes disappear overnight. Or the stress a female with its young undergoes because the male must travel farther and farther out. All we can measure are the paths they travel. We need more measurements. We can watch them around the clock when they're on land, but we know so little about their lives out there. And the more we know about penguins, the more we will know about the oceans. If the ocean is healthy, they are healthy. And if the ocean is dying—"

Angela stopped herself. She was rambling, her voice shaking, and she did not want him to see her so upset. She'd finished attaching the transmitter, and she released the penguin and watched him scurry off toward the water. Aeneas was silent. She was thankful until she raised her eyes and realized that he was not watching the penguin but was watching her.

"The Romans used to believe you could tell the future by studying birds," he said. "They looked for omens, good and bad, in their flight patterns. Wars were waged based on whether or not a particular bird passed by. One might say it was an absurd religion they followed, the leaders relying on augurs to tell them what the flying gods had in store for them. I don't agree. Nature *is* a god. And you, Angela, are its augur."

She didn't know what to say and was grateful when he changed the subject. "What're those?" he asked, pointing toward three rabbit-like creatures in the distance.

"Those are maras. They're unique to Patagonia."

"Do you count them too?"

"No. But they could certainly use an advocate because they're endangered. They're strictly monogamous. The ranchers used to say that if you kill one mara, you have to kill its mate as well, because it will never breed again."

"Romantic, in a ruthless sort of way."

"Penguins are also monogamous, but practical. If they lose a mate, they'll rebound quickly. Not maras. They mourn for years, some forever."

"How long will it take you to get over me?" he asked, a smile on his face.

"Why don't you leave, and we'll see?"

He laughed so loudly the maras scattered. And she realized how long it had been since she'd made a man laugh out loud.

"You want to switch?" he asked as they stood to return to their census taking.

Angela was pleased, if a little surprised, to see him taking an interest. And so she taught him the difference between *quilembai* and Lycium bushes, how to guess a penguin's age by the dark rings in its eyes, how to spot flipper tags from twenty yards. She enjoyed watching him grunt and curse as he crawled on the dirt, straining to see into the burrows. A man of the water, he was far removed from his element, and he lumbered about like the penguins. During lunch, as they sat on the rocks of a dry riverbed, a harmless snake made him spill his water bottle. He made her laugh as well.

During the circles, occasionally she would notice him looking eastward, toward the ocean, even if it was hidden behind the hills. She pretended not to notice, feeling a slight ache in her chest. She wanted to read his mind, to know how he felt about her, but men were a species she'd never understood; she had not been with enough men to draw statistically valid findings.

That evening, she took him to a spot she usually visited alone—the edge of a red cliff that looked out over the water. The wind was so loud they just sat there, sandwiches in hand, as the penguins emerged in herds from the water. She took him there because she knew what he wanted, but as he scanned the horizon she hoped there would be no ships today. She wanted to shave his beard, see his face in full, smooth and warm and up close. Then she caught herself and turned to thoughts of the remaining nests to be counted.

ROBERT

THE SUN WAS SETTING as Robert climbed the ladder to the roof of the harbormaster station, a one-story structure at the foot of the cruise ship pier, where Lynda sat on a folding metal chair behind an air-conditioning unit, binoculars on her lap. From the roof, Robert had a clear view of Puerto Madryn, a modest resort town lining a three-mile crescent of sand and sidewalk. On the other side, at the far end of the pier, was the *Tern*. Robert wanted it closer, but the other spaces were reserved for the 3,000-passenger ships that kept the town's economy running. Fortunately, those ships were absent today, giving Robert and Lynda an unobstructed view.

After they'd documented every crew member and searched the ship—again, and with dogs—they'd continued their surveillance in twelve-hour shifts. It was now day two, and Robert knew they couldn't keep up this pace. While staring at a ship sounded simple enough, fighting boredom and sleep was hard work. Robert's mind wanted to wander and usually succeeded.

The harbormaster had volunteered to help, and while Robert didn't trust him, he wasn't going to turn down another set of eyes. For all of Robert's lobbying, the only help the navy had offered before exiting the harbor was to leash the *Tern* to the pier with a three-inch-thick chain, which, as Robert could see through the binoculars, still remained intact. Although an arc welder could slice through it in an hour or so, anything that would slow them down was worth using.

Robert had called Gordon and asked him to pull more strings with the Argentines, but Gordon told him they were out of strings and low on agents. When he added *Merry Christmas* just before hanging up, Robert remembered that the holiday was just a few days away.

He could smell the harbormaster's cigar smoke wafting up through the downstairs window as he handed Lynda a soda from the bag he carried. He picked up her binoculars to take a look. "Did I miss anything?" he asked.

"A produce delivery. A few games of Hacky Sack. The chef waved at me a few hours ago. I waved back. Then he brought me a tofu and tomato sandwich. It wasn't bad."

"You need some sleep," he said.

"Easier said than done. I'm covered with bedbug bites. Is your room as bad as mine?"

"Why do you think I took the night shift?"

Lynda grabbed her binoculars back. Robert was warming up to her, beginning to relax again, to put this mission in perspective. In the end, this was just another job; he was just another government employee. He needed to stay focused on the smallness of his life, even when he suspected the stakes were not quite so small.

"Maybe Aeneas really is gone," Lynda said.

"No. Here's around here somewhere. He won't leave his boat behind. He's just waiting for the right moment to sneak onboard."

"Suppose he does sneak onboard, and they torch through the chain and tear ass out of the harbor. Then what? It's not like we can pull them over."

"I know that. You know that. But they don't know that. For all they know, the navy is waiting for them just off the coast. I expect them to pull a stunt similar to what they did in Miami. Create a disturbance. Or catch us off guard. Unless, of course, we happen to catch them off guard, which is what I expect to do. Which is why you need to get some sleep."

"Okay, okay. If you need me, I'll be at the Ritz." Lynda grabbed her backpack and descended the ladder. Robert watched her walk along the main street, then turn right at Nuevo de Julio. He welcomed the solitude. Alone, he could let his guard down, enjoy a few hours free of probing questions.

Robert raised his binoculars. The windows of the lower decks glowed, but the bridge remained dark; perhaps they were up there watching him. A part of him wanted to sneak down and unlock the chains, let them slip away, along with the past. Call Gordon and tell him he had failed. It would not be the first time.

ROBERT SNAPPED AWAKE to the cool spatter of rain on his face. He blinked the sleep out of his eyes to find a leviathan of a cruise ship towering over him like an office building, blocking his view of the *Tern*. He stood up too quickly, then fell back onto his chair, his mind hazy.

He glanced at his watch: 6:15 a.m. On the cruise ship's dock below, crew members in light blue jumpsuits were scurrying about, dragging ropes, shouting back and forth in an Asian language; the ship had arrived only moments ago, and he'd slept right through it.

Robert slid down the ladder and sprinted across the concrete embarcadero, bracing himself for a view of an abandoned pier, pieces of chain scattered about. But when he cleared the cruise ship, he saw the *Tern* anchored at the end of the pier, right where he'd left it.

He stopped and caught his breath. He leaned against a nearby bench but didn't sit; he couldn't risk nodding off again. He needed to remain on his feet until sunrise, until

Lynda returned. Through his binoculars, the chain that stretched from the *Tern* to the pier appeared untouched. The windows along the hull and upper decks were dark. Then he noticed a pulse of light on the observation deck above the bridge, and he adjusted his focus. It was the light of a small phone, bathing Lauren's face in a pale yellow glow. Robert assumed she was talking to Aeneas, based on her animated expressions, the way she paced the deck.

Suddenly conscious of eyes upon him, he gazed up at the white steel ship, with *Emperor of the Seas* emblazoned across the bow, and noticed silhouetted bodies in windows several stories up. They seemed to be watching him with the same curiosity with which he was watching the *Tern*.

ANGELA

FOR THREE DAYS Angela and Aeneas circled and counted nests. Long enough to develop routines, long enough for her to begin wishing his ship would never return.

But Shelly would be back any day now, and her arrival would bring Angela's secret field trips to an end. Other naturalists had started to question why they couldn't attend to nests up north. People, like penguins, had their territories and rituals, and Angela had disrupted them. Penguins, at least, didn't nag.

That morning, after sending the teams yet again to the south, Angela returned to the office and pored over spreadsheets of satellite tracking data. Rows and columns of times and transmitter I.D.s and coordinates. She leaned over a large map of the South Atlantic and cross-checked every coordinate, every I.D., hoping for a number out of place, a false positive, a statistical outlier.

Doug entered and hovered over her shoulder.

"Still no sign of Diesel?" he asked.

She wanted to elbow him in the stomach but instead kept her eyes on the charts. "Shouldn't you be in the South End by now?" she asked.

"I'll catch up. I needed to talk to you. Privately. You see, I had a rather strange sighting yesterday evening," he said. "What shall I call this one—a yellow dot?"

Angela spun around. "What did you say?"

"I was looking for you. We finished up early, and I

thought you could use a hand with your surveys. When I got about a mile up north I discovered why you didn't want me tagging along, and how you were to able to cover so many circles so quickly."

"Who have you told?"

"Nobody, yet. Who is he?"

"I can't say."

"Why not?"

"I just can't."

"You'll have to report him."

"There's no need. He'll be gone soon."

"Angela, people know something's up. And if I don't say anything and somebody else sees this guy, which is bound to happen, they're going to think I was in on it, too."

She could see it in his eyes—he had moved on. He'd found some other naturalist to shadow, and his allegiance would now shift as well, even as he tried to conceal it under that handsome veil of enthusiasm. If he turned Angela in, it would demonstrate his loyalty to the camp, to the penguins. Not to her.

"And there's no chance you would risk anything on my behalf?" Angela asked.

"It's not personal, Angela. I'm new here—and I'd like to be invited back next year. If you don't do it, I will, if for no other reason than to preserve what's left of our Malbec supply."

THAT DAY, FOR THE FIRST TIME, Angela did not visit Aeneas. Instead, she escorted Doug and the others to the South End, where they spent the afternoon weighing and measuring chicks in two dozen flagged nests, nests they'd monitored for more than a decade. She had told Doug that she needed one more day before turning in her companion, and he reluctantly agreed to stay silent. But her one day was passing much too quickly. She needed more time. More time with Aeneas.

"I have to return to camp," she told Doug, avoiding his eyes. "You work on the nests over by the point."

Walking the north line, she encountered a penguin dead in his nest. She saw the teeth marks and could tell that a culpeo fox had killed him the night before, not for food but to mark territory. Nothing more than a thrill kill. Bycatch.

Angela looked at the female—sitting on her eggs, eggs that would be abandoned soon, and weaving her head from side to side—and felt herself beginning to cry. She held it in, surprised that she had turned so emotional. The female penguins were never single for long; males in the surrounding bushes were already eying the empty nest. But what Angela had once seen as instinctual head movements she now saw as a creature in mourning.

In the distance, she noticed clouds of dust forming a trail, the sign of a fast-moving vehicle. She made a mental note to remind the *guardafauna* to post speed-limit signs. Taxis lately had become reckless, trying to squeeze in additional trips before the gate closed. But when Angela mounted the last hill before camp, she saw the source of the dust wasn't a taxi but a speeding police car, lights flashing.

The police car skidded to a stop at the *guardafauna*'s gate but only for a second as the *guardafauna* waved it through. Angela picked up her pace, and then she started running.

The car was going too fast to stop for penguins, and she prayed that no birds were crossing the road as the car crested the hill. She lost sight of it through the brown dust, but she stayed on the road, dreading the thought of trying to rescue an injured bird or, worse, having to put one down, which had happened last season.

But either the police were more careful than she thought or the birds more cautious; she didn't find any injured penguins along the way. Relief turned to fury as she saw the empty police car ahead, its blue lights echoing off tour buses and the darkening hills. Intending to teach the officers a lesson, she began practicing her faded Spanish in her head: *Se ponen en peligro los pingüinos. Contacto con sus jefes.*

She pushed her way through the crowd. It took her only a moment to ascertain what had happened. There'd been a fight. A tourist, with a bleeding face and hysterical wife, required medical attention. The perpetrator had taken off into the bushes. Police had already begun scouring the colony, disregarding the warning signs and ropes. Penguins on the trail panicked and flapped about.

Angela had a bad feeling, and as the police reviewed tourists' cell phone footage, she stood close and watched. She caught a glimpse, on a tiny sun-bleached screen, of man punching man, bloody faces, dust. And one of the men wore a bright yellow jacket.

SHE FOUND HIM ON BEACON HILL.

"What the hell happened out there?"

"I was looking for you," he said. "I thought you might be on the trail."

"You assaulted a tourist?"

"He nearly stepped on a penguin, Angela. He was completely off the trail, trying to take a close-up photo. I kindly asked him to step back, but he refused. I even said *please*. But my recidivistic instincts got the better of me."

"You have to leave."

"That's what I was coming to tell you. My ship is on its way. They're sending a Zodiac. I'll be gone in an hour."

She looked out over the water, her mind desperately trying to process everything. The chaos in the camp behind her. This man about to leave her. The anger inside, causing her hands to tremble—or was it fear? She didn't know what she was feeling anymore.

"Come with me," he said.

"What?" She turned to face him.

"I said, come with me."

"Where?"

"To the ship."

Angela looked into his eyes, wide with excitement, alluring in their depth. She felt her heart stutter as she considered the invitation, the madness of it all. Running away. Freeing herself of Doug. The gossip. The camp. Perhaps it was time to leave it all behind. To start over. To fight a new battle. To have a man in her life instead of more birds.

Then reality sunk in. Penguins in need of counting. A Ph.D. not yet attained. People who depended on her. How could she leave now, after so long? And for this man, this capricious, unreliable drunk of a man?

"We'll get a new ship," he said, as if reading her mind, sensing her hesitation. "A ship that patrols only these waters, keeping the trawlers out of the penguin feeding areas. Angela, you'll do more good for those birds out there than you could ever do counting survivors here."

"Is that all you think I do, count survivors?"

"Of course not. But at some point you have to ask yourself what's the good of counting penguins when they're going extinct."

"I'm a scientist. I'm not some warrior."

"You're wrong. You are a warrior. And this is a war. Only the battleground has shifted. Those hundred thousand tourists each year are protection enough. If a bus runs over one penguin, you researchers will turn it into a provincial disaster—you said so yourself. Out there, the fishermen kill a thousand penguins a month, and nobody hears a word. You could change all of that. They need someone out there doing what you've already accomplished here. Protecting them, instead of counting them. You can't tell me you're not weary of diminishing returns."

"Just leave."

"I'm going to," he said.

"I mean now. I don't care if you swim out of here!"

She was not aware she was shouting, until he got closer to her and she could hear her voice echoing back. For so much of her life she'd kept an emotional distance to prevent exactly these moments—an arm's length, to prevent getting bitten. She pushed him away, but he resisted. She slapped him, but he kept coming. He grabbed her and hugged her tight until she began to sob. Until she told him about Diesel.

Zero four two two nine.

A number in a log book that would never receive another notation. A number gone dormant, like most of the log book itself, and the story of her life. Numbers upon numbers of birds that one day left shore and never returned. Diesel had grown into so much more than a number. He'd become a husband and a father; he'd remained her friend. And now he was gone, like all the others.

Aeneas listened patiently, until Angela's face was dry. She stood back, feeling embarrassed.

"Zero four two two nine," Aeneas said, quietly, almost like an invocation. And she knew that he understood, that his whales were so much more than numbers to him, too—and at the same time she realized she'd found the one person in the world who understood her, who could read her mind, and he was about to leave.

She stepped forward and kissed him before she could talk herself out of it, until he pulled away. She watched him, with blurry eyes, as he limped away, crested the hill, and disappeared toward the sea.

ROBERT

"It's like an invasion," Lynda said.

She and Robert watched the tour buses arrive at the pier, one after another, and empty their cargo. Passengers, eyes squinting, shuffled single file down the steps and up a ramp back into the ship. It was late afternoon, and the *Emperor of the Seas*'s restless engines signaled an end to its brief visit. Robert sat on a bench, coffee in hand, watching over the circus of street vendors and pedicabs, desperate for last-minute business.

"Looks like they're preparing for departure," Robert said.

"I pity the next port of call."

"For someone from Miami, that's really saying something."

Robert should have been sleeping now, while Lynda stood sentry, but he couldn't sleep without dreaming, and his dreams were more stressful than being awake or suffering sleep deprivation. He drained his coffee and stared out at the *Tern*.

He knew the crew was getting ready to make a move. Earlier that day, they'd let a fuel truck through, as well as deliveries of food and water. Robert considered preventing the supplies from arriving but realized that this would only prolong the waiting. Not only was he tired of it, but he knew that each passing minute felt like an eternity to Aeneas, with the Japanese already prowling the Southern Ocean, harpooning whales without resistance. Time, Robert realized as he yawned again, was working against the both of them.

He heard the brief *whoop* of a siren and looked back at the

63

tour buses. A police car had snaked its way through the crowd. Two officers got out and approached a tour guide, a hot little number in tight khaki pants. She pointed them toward a few passengers who held up their cell phones for review. A crowd began to gather.

"What's going on over there?" Lynda asked.

"I don't know."

"Has the makings of an international incident, I'd say."

"Stay here and keep an eye on the ship." Robert approached the huddle and pushed his way through. He looked over the shoulder of an officer at a cell phone video. Nothing more than tourists and penguins. Penguins on their bellies. Penguins walking. Penguins flapping wings. A woman posing in front of penguins. Then shouting from off camera. The woman pointing at something, the camera following, refocusing on two men arguing, one in a yellow jacket, the camera too far away to make out faces. The man in the yellow jacket throwing a punch. The camera zooming in, freezing on the man's face.

ROBERT DROVE WHILE LYNDA monitored the phone. The rounded gravel road was surrounded by chaparral and low-lying hills, and if it weren't for the steady stream of dust-covered vehicles headed in the opposite direction, Robert would have thought they were lost. The angle of the road kept their rental car in a persistent state of sliding off, like a boat heading into the wind, forcing Robert to right the ship every few seconds. But that wasn't what bothered him at the moment; it was the fact that only one windshield wiper worked, the one on Lynda's side. Every ten minutes Robert had to stop to wipe off the dust.

"I thought you asked for a new car."

"I did," Lynda said. "I didn't think we'd be off-roading today."

The phone rang. Lynda answered it, listened, then dictated. "Gordon says a cruise ship reported a fight at Punta Verde between a passenger and an unidentified gringo," she said. "The man was described as large, heavyset, hostile. And American."

Robert sped up until the car began to shake. Going to Punta Verde together was a calculated risk. Lynda had volunteered to stay behind, but she would be more valuable here, helping him track down Aeneas, allowing him to cover a larger swath of land. Lynda had instructed the harbormaster to keep an eye on the *Tern*, to call them in case of any activity. The fact that the phone had not rung yet was a positive sign. And if by chance the *Tern* did make a run for it, at least Robert knew where it would be headed. If he moved quickly enough, he stood a chance of catching Aeneas on the shore.

After they passed a sign indicating they were ten kilometers from Punta Verde, the passenger's side tire blew, sending the car veering off the road in a cloud of dirt, rear first, into the bushes.

"Lynda." Robert tried to cough away the dust. "Lynda, you okay?"

"Yeah, yeah."

Robert punched the steering wheel, got out, and surveyed the damage. Except for the tire, the car seemed drivable—but Robert suddenly felt too tired to rise up from his knees.

"You need a hand?" Lynda asked.

He stood. "What I need is a decent fucking car—one that would have had me there by now."

"Well, Bobby, they were all out of time machines at the rental lot. So you're going to have to make do with this one." She paused. "You want me to get the jack out, or do you want to do it?"

Robert felt as overheated as the car's anemic engine; he needed time to cool down. Without speaking, he walked into the brush, until he was hidden behind a wall of it. He took a deep breath and looked out over the undulating panorama of scrubland. Not a tree in any direction. For a moment, he thought he might get lucky and see Aeneas somewhere, anywhere. He was due for a break. But as always, time was working against him, so he turned to walk back.

Then he heard a noise behind the bushes, the sound of movement, something large. He froze, then pulled his gun. He took a step toward the sound, then another, then he pointed his gun at the source and waited. Ten feet away, a cat emerged, about the size of a bobcat, with a smaller head and a coat streaked white and brown. Robert lowered his gun, and in a blur the cat was gone again, a large tail disappearing into a bush.

Robert holstered his gun and returned to the car. Lynda had the car up on the jack.

"Need a hand?" he asked.

"No," she said. "I need a time machine."

BECAUSE IT WAS A TOURIST ATTRACTION, Robert expected the entrance to Punta Verde to be grander. But it was just a gravel road that culminated at a cinder-block tollbooth with a manually operated, rusted steel gate. To the left of the booth, three single-story concrete buildings bordered a parking lot occupied by half a dozen cars and four large tour buses. Beyond the gate, the road turned to dirt, narrowed, and wound up a large, dun-colored hill.

"Where are all the penguins?" Lynda asked.

"Maybe they're taking a lunch break."

Robert pulled into the lot. Lynda got out and knocked on the door of the largest building, which turned out to be the park ranger station, and she interviewed the man in charge while Robert jogged to the top of the nearest hill. He could see a slice of ocean about a mile away, but no ships. No people. Just dirt and bushes, interspersed with patches of pale green grass.

And penguins. He didn't notice them at first, but now he could make out little specks of black and white—huddled under the bushes, walking in pairs or small groups in the direction of the water. It was surreal to see penguins here, without a blanket of snow or ice under them. He was tempted to stay longer, but the sun was beginning to set.

He headed back toward the parking lot and noticed a small building a few hundred feet behind the ranger station. He peered inside a window and saw a darkened office with no signs of life. Twenty feet back was a cinder-block hut, and he knocked on its door, but nobody answered. He opened the door and stepped inside: a row of cots, clothes scattered about, two large plastic water jugs propped on cinder blocks.

He returned to the office, where this time he detected movement inside. Moving closer, he saw a young man leaning over a map. Robert tapped on the window with his handgun, displaying his I.D.

The young man's name was Doug. He was a naturalist in training. And he knew all about the man in the yellow jacket.

ROBERT SAW HER A HUNDRED YARDS AHEAD, seated between bushes. Her short, messy red hair matched Doug's description, and her face was windblown to a nearly matching shade. She was oblivious to Robert, and as he got closer, he saw why—she was coaxing a penguin out of its nest with some sort of hook. Then she gripped its head tightly, as its wings flapped and it bit at the air; it looked as if the bird would either fly away or take off her index finger. But the woman did not seem at all bothered by the commotion. With one hand holding the bird, she used the other to scribble notes in a journal.

"Are you Angela?" he asked.

"That's me," she said, not bothering to look up. She straddled the bird, silencing its wings, returning a sense of calm to the scene. Yet whatever she was trying to do next, the bandage on her left hand was clearly causing her problems.

"You need help?" Robert asked.

"Ever handle a penguin before?"

"No."

"Then I don't need help."

"I've got two good hands, at least."

She sized him up, and he felt oddly insecure that she paused for so long.

"Okay," she said finally. "Come over here and position yourself next to me, just like this. Now, I'm going to get up and you're going to slide over and hold her between your legs just like I'm doing. I'll keep hold of her head."

He did as instructed.

"Now, see how I'm holding her. First put your left hand over my right, just like that. Now your right. Hold firm but not too tight. Do *not* let go."

The bird between his knees was stronger than he expected, and the feathers were not smooth but finely knit, like the exterior of his synthetic jacket. Angela held the caliper to the penguin's beak and feet, and Robert felt a sudden childlike excitement come over him. The penguin raised its head with an almost human look of indignation, and he couldn't help but feel sorry for it.

"You can let go now," Angela said.

Robert released his hands and widened his knees, and the penguin scampered back into its nest. Robert stood, brushed the dirt off his pants, then slowly circled one of the bushes, looking at birds crowded underneath, in distinctly separate cubbyholes, like some thin-walled tenement, so many eyes and beaks following his movements.

"I had no idea there were so many penguins here," he said.

"There used to be more."

"Why do they move their heads back and forth like that?" he asked.

"They're trying to frighten you away."

"They think I'm a predator?"

"Worse. They think you're a tourist."

Robert looked up at Angela, with her backpack on, notepad in one hand, staring at him impatiently. He suddenly remembered why he was there.

"Actually, I'm an FBI agent."

"Looking for a missing bird?"

"I'm looking for the man involved in the altercation this morning. I believe you know him."

Angela began scribbling something into her notebook as she spoke. "As you can plainly see, I spend too much time with penguins to notice every tourist who passes through."

"That's not what Doug tells me."

She stopped writing and looked up at him—just the response he'd hoped for.

"So what has Doug been telling you?"

"That you recently adopted a fugitive, someone who looks strikingly similar to a man we're pursuing."

"Doug can't tell the difference between a Magellanic and a Humboldt, so I wouldn't put much faith in his ability to identify anything."

"Where is this fugitive he mentioned?"

"Gone," she said sharply. "He left a few hours ago."

"On a ship?"

"I couldn't say. I didn't follow him."

Robert studied her eyes more closely, the redness around the edges, perhaps not the result of the wind after all.

"Was his name Aeneas?"

"Yes, his name was Aeneas. And as I just told you, you're too late. Now, if you don't mind, I've got penguins to count."

She turned and started off down the hill, toward the research station. Robert considered chasing her. But what would that accomplish? If Aeneas were still here, he would be in the opposite direction, along the coastline. The sun was already behind the hills, turning the sky into reds and oranges, like the skin of a mango. And Robert needed more time—time to watch Angela from a distance, time to gather more resources. He walked to the water's edge and scanned the length of the beach, as if he might find Aeneas. He saw only penguins.

Lynda approached. Her dour expression matched how Robert felt. "He's gone," Robert said.

"So's our ship."

"The *Tern*?"

"What else?"

"When?"

"A few minutes after we left."

"Why didn't the harbormaster call us?"

"He's been trying. That crap phone is acting up again."

"The chains should have slowed them down."

"He told me the chains had already been sliced through, or he would have tried to stop them himself. They must have accomplished that little task when we weren't looking. I'd love to know how we missed that one."

Robert thought back to the night he nodded off, how the cover of a cruise ship would have given them the time they needed to torch through the chains, at least enough to easily break free when the opportunity arose. Aeneas was one step ahead even then. Or, more accurately, Robert was one step behind.

"That's it then," Lynda said. "He's gone. Headed south." She pulled a camera out of her shoulder bag, crouched, and focused on a pair of penguins under a bush.

"You don't seem all that disappointed."

"Sure, I'm disappointed. I'm spending my Christmas vacation standing around here with you instead of being at home with my old man. But I'm going to make the best of it." Her camera flashed.

"Don't you think it's odd how they always seem to know what we're doing before we do it?" Robert asked.

"Maybe they're just good," Lynda said, now taking a picture of Robert.

He held a hand in front of her lens. "A little too good."

"What's that supposed to mean?"

"You tell me," Robert said. "I'm not the one who suggested there was someone working on the inside."

Lynda lowered the camera and studied him. Her eyes narrowed. "Oh, I see. I'm the mole, is that what you're implying? I let Aeneas slip out of Miami. I tipped him off before we boarded the ship. Maybe I even helped out with the chains during my shift yesterday. And let's not forget that flat tire I engineered. You know, Bobby, I wasn't going to do this to you, but you leave me no choice."

Lynda moved toward him then, quickly, as if preparing to strike, and Robert took a step backward. But instead of punching him, she held a photograph up to his face. It was badly faded and creased down the middle, but Robert recognized the two people standing in the frame. A woman and a man, both in their twenties, sunburnt and smiling, standing on the rear deck of a ship, holding the tattered remnants of a fishing net.

"Care to tell me what this is about?"

"Where'd you get that?" Robert grabbed the photo.

"Where do you think? On the bulletin board in the bridge of the *Arctic Tern*. Back when we boarded her. Now, I may not be smart enough for the D.C. office, but I know when *I* smell a mole."

"I was undercover."

"And I'm Mary fucking Poppins."

"I'm serious. How do you think I know what Aeneas looks like? I was working undercover as a deckhand."

"Why were you there?"

"We were looking for someone who had been torching animal testing labs and factory farms. Someone on Aeneas's crew. Went by the name of Darwin."

"But you let Aeneas get away," she said.

"I wasn't after Aeneas. I was after Darwin."

"So I take it, by the rather stunning lack of documentation in your report, that things didn't end so well?"

"You could take it that way."

Robert looked out over the water. A row of five penguins stood on the hill below, single file, looking up at him. He must have been standing in their path, and they appeared content to wait him out. In that moment, he was a tourist, another human just passing through.

"I wasn't accusing you," he said to Lynda. "I'm just frustrated. Thinking aloud."

"Careful. Think too loudly, and you might offend someone."

Robert nodded. He was being too hard on himself—a recurring theme of his life—and too hard on Lynda, too. But he felt as though he were caught on one of those long fishing lines, that he was being pulled along slowly, inevitably, to some horrible conclusion.

"Look, Bobby, don't sweat it so much. I know you want to catch Aeneas, and so do I. But it's not as if we're getting a hell of a lot of support from the mother ship, you know?"

Robert glanced at the photo again before folding it into his pocket.

"By the way, who's the girl?" Lynda asked.

"I don't remember," he said.

ANGELA

Six hours had passed since Aeneas left.

That night in her trailer, Angela imagined that she had said yes. That she had followed Aeneas to sea, that she was now high up on a deck, looking back at Punta Verde as penguins porpoised around her. The researchers would have their theories as to why she left suddenly. People who did not know her would say she'd been kidnapped. People who did would say she was in love. But she was neither. Aeneas had been right. She was tired. Tired of watching trawlers pass at night, their multitude of nets and longlines and vacuum hoses sucking the life from the ocean with GPS-enabled precision, with her penguins as bycatch. Tired of days spent holding on to the ends of ropes, walking in circles. Tired of counting survivors.

In the morning, she woke earlier than usual. She went to Aeneas's empty camp, broke down the tent, packed up the trash and wine bottles. Later she asked Doug to help her carry the bags back to the station. He seemed happy to be in her good graces again. That evening, he offered to show her Neptune, but she declined.

The next day, Shelly returned, and they all settled back into their old routines. The chicks were fledging. The breeding season would be over in six weeks, and the penguins would waddle their starved bodies back to sea to drink deeply, to follow the fish, to elude the predators that waited just below the waterline.

Tourist buses gridlocked the parking lot and dirt road, a convoy of idling engines and exhaust. Angela skipped dinner that evening, knowing that Shelly would be there, that by then she'd know about everything that had happened while she was away. Angela knew she had to apologize, but she didn't have the strength for it yet. She retired to her trailer alone.

Later that night, a noise woke her, and she rushed outside, hoping it was him. Instead she found a pair of dueling male penguins. As she watched them, she cursed Aeneas for ruining her home. For half her life, this had been the only land that mattered, the only place she truly called home. Now the entire landscape felt barren and lonely.

The next morning, a penguin was run over as it tried to scurry between two buses. Angela pleaded again with the *guardafauna* to shut down the road and make the tourists walk the last half-mile uphill to the trail. He said he would ask the provincial administrator when the man arrived in two months. It was too late, she tried to tell him; by then, a dozen more penguins could get hit.

No one seemed to understand that the penguins had a tight schedule to adhere to and could not wait patiently for buses to pass. That penguins weren't comfortable walking through throngs of people to get to the water, to their food source. That these human obstacles could mean life or death for their chicks. Once, Angela remembered, a penguin had died of heat stroke waiting for tourists to let it pass. He'd died right there in front of them, surrounded by flashing cameras. For the birds, the tourist trail was a gantlet, one that grew more dangerous every year.

The tourists are loving them to death, Shelly once said. But Angela didn't detect much in the way of love. Tourists didn't come to sit and observe. They didn't come to learn and appreciate. They came to turn their backs to the penguins, to pose for photographs, to prove that they'd been here. The penguins were nothing but a backdrop to them.

Angela wandered off toward the water, aimless. She stared at the ocean until the sunlight faded, watching penguins fall into the crashing waves, drink deeply, shake the land from their feathers, and finally disappear below. It was so much easier, she realized, to be the one who left than the one left behind.

Angela walked to Diesel's nest, now empty. She got on her knees and lifted out the bodies of the chicks. She buried them behind her trailer.

ROBERT

WITH AENEAS GONE, Robert and Lynda retreated to Trelew, the flat inland town they'd flown to from Buenos Aires just a week ago. Robert drove around the town square looking for a place to stay overnight. Lynda pointed to the Hotel San Martin, which had a faded sign that read "historic," and they checked in. His room was stiflingly hot, with an AC unit that was apparently only good for white noise. Fortunately, the bar downstairs was air-conditioned, and he met Lynda there later that evening.

"I read that Butch and Sundance stayed here," she said.

"And they haven't renovated since."

Robert looked around the dark but expansive room. The crowd was a mix of well-dressed locals and tourists in jeans and baseball caps. A Christmas tree in the corner gave the room a festive air. Robert tried to imagine this place in older days, when there were no cars and no roads and the only tourists in town were a couple of young Americans on the run from the law. He could see why characters like Butch and Sundance would end up in these parts—Aeneas, too. The desolate prairies of Patagonia remained one of the last frontiers on a shrinking planet, and it didn't seem like such a bad refuge.

"So what did Gordon say?" Lynda asked, gesturing at the satellite phone on the bar. Robert, ignoring her, waved the bartender over.

"You haven't called him yet, have you?" she said.

"What am I going to say, Lynda? 'Mistakes were made'?"

"Of course. Isn't that what we always say when we screw up?"

Robert turned away to order a drink. When he turned back, Lynda had left her barstool, and he could see her through the window—she'd grabbed the phone and stepped outside into the burnt orange light of sunset, her shadow stretching out of view. Robert watched her grimace at the phone and hold it away from her ear. He was glad Lynda was the one telling Gordon that Aeneas had escaped yet again.

Now, he just wanted to go home, and maybe they would. There wasn't anything more they could do without a ship of their own, and even if they found one, they would be a good day or two behind. Robert should have been relieved; Aeneas getting away meant he took with him Robert's past. And there was so much in his past that he did not want to revisit.

Lynda returned and dropped the phone back on the bar. "Coward," she said.

"I saw him yelling at you."

"No, it's the damn volume control. It went into speaker mode right in my ear. Nothing like sharing government secrets with half the town."

"So what's the verdict?"

"We're heading home. First thing tomorrow." Lynda finished her bottle of Quilmes and stood. "Gotta call the hubby. Tell him Santa's coming to town."

Robert watched her leave, then emptied his glass. He had no one to call. Tomorrow was Christmas Eve. If they were lucky, they would be home Christmas Day. For Robert, this meant only that the stores were closed and he'd have a hard time finding someplace to eat.

Robert was trying to catch the bartender's eye when he locked eyes with an Argentine woman seated by the glowing fireplace. She held his eyes dangerously long before looking back at the couple seated across from her. She was dark skinned and wore a black skirt and white blouse that hung open when she leaned over for her martini.

He ordered another glass of whiskey and held it to his nose. The smell of hard liquor alone was often enough to put his shoulders at rest, erase the lines from his forehead. Foreplay for his nerves. His mind returned to the woman near the fireplace, and he glanced back in her direction, as if meaning to watch the bodies passing outside on the sidewalk.

Robert didn't want to spend the night in his cave of a room. He thought back to college, when he and two buddies drove to Padre Island for spring break without any money or anyplace to stay. The rules had been simple—if you wanted a hotel room, you needed to find a girl. That week, Robert hadn't spent one night in the car and became a celebrity back at college.

A tap on the shoulder brought him back into the present, the bar, the empty glass in front of him. The Argentine woman was now standing next to him.

"Do you speak English?" Robert asked.

"*Sí,*" she said. She turned to him and smiled. "*¿Habla español?*"

"Yes," he said.

Her room was on the top floor. The sheets were clean. And the room was air-conditioned.

THE CLOCK READ 3:27 WHEN ROBERT STUMBLED through the dark to retrieve the nagging phone. It was Gordon, with a new assignment.

Robert had the front desk wake Lynda, and he waited for her out front, in their still-sloping car whose tire they hadn't bothered to replace. She was quiet as he drove through the dark to Puerto Madryn, half an hour away.

They arrived at the harbor to find the cruise ship fully

loaded, glowing from every orifice, idling loudly as anxious officers and security guards paced about under the lights. It was not the first time Robert had been sucked into a maritime missing persons case. This was one of the higher-profile responsibilities of the Bureau, and also the most frustrating and fruitless. If a person fell off a ship at sea, or jumped, or was pushed, that was that. Without evidence of foul play, which there rarely was, the ship continued on, and the widow or widower returned home. Bodies were rarely found, questions rarely answered. About half a dozen people went missing each year from cruise ships, which wasn't many compared with the millions of passengers who returned home safely. But this was of little solace to those left behind, who would plead with him to make it all better, to bring back the past.

Robert had mentally rehearsed his lines: *The ship is bigger than a city, and how many people get lost in cities every day? More people get temporary amnesia each year than fall off boats. Don't worry. Don't worry.*

Three Argentine cops were talking to their ship-bound equivalents, and a half-dozen crew members with name tags gathered around as well. But there was no crying spouse, no significant other. The purser, a portly American in khakis and a blue polo shirt, filled him in: A male passenger in his early thirties had taken a day trip to see the penguins, then returned to the ship. The man's I.D. card affirmed him getting off the ship that morning and back on after the field trip. But then the man had left the ship again, less than two hours before it was due to depart.

Robert listened to the chatter of the *policía*, though he couldn't understand them. *Desaparecido*, they repeated to one another.

"Disappeared," Lynda translated. But he pictured the word "desperate," which was how he felt right about now, with another missing man on his hands and little else to go on.

79

"Who was he traveling with?" Robert asked.

"No one," the purser said.

"Alone on a cruise? How often does that happen?"

"About five percent of our cabins are single occupancy," the purser replied. "But what was odd about this passenger was that he had booked the captain's suite. A thousand square feet, large balcony, hot tub."

The purser handed Robert a photograph—a digital print of the photo taken for the I.D. card. White male in his thirties, dark hair, medium build, sad eyes. Not the look of someone on a vacation but more like a mug shot.

"My captain says we are free to proceed since the incident occurred outside of the vessel," the purser said.

"Tell your captain to cool his heels," Lynda said.

Robert and Lynda walked down the pier, to where the *Tern* was once docked. A fishing trawler had taken its place; men hosed down its decks, and the water fell onto the pier and over the few charred links of chain that remained.

"I think he jumped," Lynda said.

"And the I.D. card? How do you explain him checking off the ship that last time?"

"Those cruise ship cops are covering their butts. Who travels alone on these ships?"

"Someone who wants to off himself in a romantic fashion?"

"Exactly."

Robert sat on a bench overlooking the water. The lights of the fishing vessels twinkled on the horizon.

"So what do you want to do then?" he asked.

"I don't know. Let 'em go, I guess." She sat next to him and voiced his own thoughts: "We're losing men right and left these days."

Everybody thought the FBI could punch a few keys on a laptop and bring up the latest tracking data on a suspect. If only finding people were that easy. Lynda was right; this man was dead. Officially, missing. But, practically speaking, dead. Robert knew this already. He knew the odds.

If by chance the media got wind of this story, Robert would tell them the FBI was using all available resources. He would lie. The man would receive no search and rescue effort—no search and recovery effort, for that matter. He was gone, and here sat Robert, the common denominator of lost men.

A flashlight caught his eye, out in the water, near the mouth of the harbor. He heard shouting. A fishing trawler at the end of the nearest pier put its spotlight to work, illuminating a tiny yellow lifeboat overloaded with passengers. He glanced at Lynda. If he were in Miami, he might think it was a boatload of desperate fugitives. The voices grew louder, but Robert could understand none of it. Lynda, however, was listening intently, and she got up to move closer.

Robert followed her to the end of the pier. The boat had pulled parallel, and the men climbed out. They looked Argentinean, with calloused faces, stout bodies, wearing worn dark clothes and hip waders. They were shouting up at the men onboard the trawler.

"They're fishermen," she said.

"I gathered that."

"Someone stole their boat. Stuck 'em in the raft. About fifteen miles offshore." She walked a few steps closer, listening. When she turned around, she wore a grin. *"Pirata."*

"Pirate?" Robert asked.

"Not just any pirate."

"Aeneas."

She nodded. "Get Gordon on the phone."

ANGELA

Two DAYS HAD PASSED since Aeneas had left. No, a day and a half. Actually, twenty-eight hours, to be precise.

Angela used to find comfort in being precise, methodical, unemotional. But that was before Aeneas. Before he filled her head with passion, with talk of battles on the high seas, with ideas for making a difference. She used to be numb—able to stare at a penguin carcass, still warm in her hands, and think only of the cause of death, of when and what it last ate. She could weigh it and measure the feathers around its beak. She could glance at her GPS and note the coordinates. Finally, she could unfold the old pocket knife she kept in her backpack, calmly saw through the fibrous left wing of the bird, and pocket the stainless steel tag.

But this was all before Aeneas. Now, every penguin she measured had the saddest of eyes. Every dead chick nearly brought her to tears. Just a day and a half. Two nights. And now it was morning again, and the pain of his absence, like a migraine, had not subsided, blurring the terrain.

In her backpack was a new satellite tracking device. A wealthy supporter had recently "adopted" a penguin with a generous donation. Shelly had selected the penguin to be tagged. She had a knack for selecting males who would return, a feat that Angela had not yet mastered, with penguins or men.

Angela hiked alone to the nest in the north, at the very

edge of the colony. She tried to ignore the fact that it was not far from where she'd first found Aeneas. At the nest, the penguins crouched defiantly in their burrow, guarding their young, heads waving. Angela did not want to bother them this morning, to tear them apart from each other even for a moment.

For now, for once, she would let science wait. She sat down and stared off into the hills. Then she heard a voice.

"Angela."

She turned around. It was Aeneas, in his yellow fluorescent jacket.

She blinked, doubting her eyes. But he was still there, watching her. She stood and smiled, but he did not smile back. Slowly, he approached and pressed a shiny steel penguin tag into her tattered, bloodstained glove. She held it up and read the numbers.

Zero four two two nine.

"I am sorry," Aeneas said.

He had remembered Diesel's number. The only man who probably ever would. He told her that he'd boarded two fishing vessels before he located Diesel's body. He terrified the men with a squarely aimed shotgun that had never been fired. The crew resisted him, so he stuck them on lifeboats and sunk their trawler, the trawler that took Diesel's life. But it was worth it, she thought. He brought Diesel home to her. He could have sunk them all, every last one.

She pressed the metal hard between her fingers. The indentations of each digit. She could feel Diesel now, on her lap, the raspy purring noise. Gazing into his reddish-brown eyes. Imagining the thousands of miles he had traveled to be there, right there with her. This tag was all that was left.

"I can't stay," he said. "They know I'm here."

Of course they did. She told him about her visitors. She could picture Aeneas cutting through the feathers and cartilage and cold blood. Sawing the tag free to return it to her. To return Diesel to her, in number only, something she could feel with her fingers and her eyes. Numbers did not lie.

She grabbed his jacket by the sides and pulled him to her. She kissed him, his beard sanding her lips. She smelled salt air and his hands were cold but firm. She held him tight, as she would a penguin beak.

She took him to her trailer. She lit a candle she had been saving in the sink with the drain to nowhere. The wind picked up and the walls began to vibrate. They made love as Geraldo brayed, calling out to the female he had yet to find, or had yet to find him.

IN THE MORNING, WHILE AENEAS SLEPT, Angela slid out of their cramped alcove and stared at him. Though his face and neck and arms were tanned dark brown, his body was as pale as a polar bear. He snored. He rolled away from her, eyes closed.

She stepped out the trailer door and down the cinderblock steps. She peeked underneath to find Geraldo blinking at her, still alone. She blinked back and smiled. In the office she hung Diesel's tag on a chain around her neck. She looked down at the latest satellite tracking logs, more out of habit than hope. Outside the office, researchers had gathered, some with coffee. Backpacks and teams assembled. She abstained.

"I'm not feeling well," she said, and no one objected. How could they; she had never before called in sick. Shelly gave her a knowing look; Doug had probably told her everything by now. A day ago, Angela might have turned red and lowered her eyes. But not now. She was already somewhere else.

She retreated to the trailer and found Aeneas seated outside on a cinder block, tying his shoes. "Love 'em and leave 'em?" he said.

84

"Something like that."

She waited for him to ask her to come along. She pleaded with her eyes for an invitation, even though she knew she could not say yes.

"You are always welcome on my ship," he said. "Always." He noticed the tag around her neck, and he held it and kissed her forehead. "Now you're a known-age bird," he said.

He left the trailer, and she waited a few minutes, but he did not return. When she poked her head out the door, she saw a small canvas sack on the ground. She remembered him carrying it the night before so she looked around but did not see him. She picked up the bag, and it jingled as if full of bottle caps.

She kneeled and opened the bag to find penguin tags. Nothing but penguin tags. She ran her hands through the metal and held up one after another. How many of these were her birds? So many mothers and fathers caught up in nets. So many abandoned chicks. So many red dots. She turned the bag upside down and spilled them out. She felt rage building inside of her, the need to fight back. Perhaps she was a warrior after all.

She returned to the office, finding it empty. She grabbed her backpack and wrote Shelly a note. She began walking up the hill, toward the water, then picked up her pace until she was running. Tourist buses passed her, coughing dust. She could feel the eyes and cameras upon her. But she no longer cared. From the distance came the sound of a boat engine. There was still time. She crested the hill, leaping onto soft dirt and patches of grass, hopping the prickly *quilembai* bushes. She could feel Diesel's tag around her neck, reminding her that he was now looking over her, tracking her movements. In places cold and always blowing. In sickness and in health. In absentia.

PART II

ETHAN

WHEN ETHAN FIRST SET EYES on Annie Miller, he thought he'd made a mistake. She was far more attractive than the other women he had been paired with. Her short spiked hair drew attention to her blue eyes, skin browned from the sun. And though her face exhibited eight piercings—three on each ear, a silver ring on her upper right lip, and a tiny stud through the left nostril—they did nothing to reduce her appeal. If anything, the perforations only illustrated just how durable her beauty was. She could change her hair color, pierce her nose and lip, tattoo her forehead if she wanted—and Ethan still would have been seduced by her.

He was at work when he first encountered Annie. She was one of the three million members in the eCouplet.com database, and he was the programmer tasked with improving the member search engine. Every search engine ran on algorithms—lines upon lines of a language that was indecipherable to most humans but was poetry to a computer. Ethan's algorithms parsed each profile—the favorite movies and foods and colors, the income levels and hometowns—all toward that goal of pairing one person with another.

Ethan sometimes used his own profile for testing. He had developed an entire stable of artificial member profiles that he would insert into the pairing engine, but these were not real people. His, on the other hand, was an authentically average profile, representative of so many millions of people who joined these websites—people who did not stand apart in looks or career.

Ethan was taller than most men, with a runner's build, but he was not an athlete in the organized-sports sense of the word. And though his height gave him every right to an extrovert's personality, he was shy around women. His photo worked against him. Though his face compared favorably with those of his fellow programmers, he was competing in the gene pool of San Diego, competing against surfers and skateboarders who wore their free spirits in their tanned faces and sun-bleached hair. Ethan was pale, his body artless. He had a full head of dark hair, but the cut was conservative. He intended, one of these days, to visit a salon instead of a barbershop. He intended to take his well-meaning sister's advice: Get his teeth whitened; work on his posture; begin, finally, to look women in the eyes. He'd intended to make numerous self-improvements over the years, but he never followed through. He blamed the job, the long hours, the crunch time leading up to a new software release. But the truth was, good intentions were no match for his periodic but extreme bouts of insecurity.

Fortunately, insecurity did not come across in a search query—which was how Ethan and Annie met.

When he saw her photo, his initial reaction was to close the search window and start over. When her face came up a second time, he clicked on her profile. She was twenty-four to his twenty-nine. She was an environmental activist. She had been in jail half a dozen times for various protests. She was a college dropout. She bagged groceries at the health food co-op in Hillcrest. She didn't eat meat.

Ethan suspected a bug in his code. An if/else statement gone awry. A poorly defined algorithm. A memory leak.

Memory was like oxygen to a computer—and every piece of software required memory to function. Elegant software recycled memory after it was used. Poorly written software progressively consumed more and more memory until there was no oxygen left, and the system crashed. One sign of a memory leak was software that acted unusually or, in this case, a search engine that returned odd results.

Ethan returned to the code and meticulously scanned every line for a missing semicolon, a recursive loop, anything that would have paired a geek with a beauty, a meat eater with a vegetarian, a jailbird with someone who'd never gotten as much as a speeding ticket.

He re-compiled the code, ran the search again, and again her smiling face greeted him. He knew better than to believe the numbers could lie—and yet he wanted to believe that the code had functioned correctly, that he and Annie could be a match. That perhaps, for once in his life, destiny and data were in sync.

THIS WAS NOT A DATE, ETHAN TOLD HIMSELF. This was work. Fieldwork.

He would meet Annie for an innocent meal. He would get to know her better. In doing so, he would diagnose why that search engine of his had placed them together. An hour in a restaurant would be far more effective in solving this mystery than another week spent debugging. This was what he told himself, and no one else.

He wasn't allowed to date Annie. Company policy forbade it. Last year, a competitor came under fire for pimping out its employees on dates to improve member retention rates. But these were details Ethan found easy to overlook; he had not been on a date in more than a year.

He arrived early at the Italian restaurant in Hillcrest and ordered a beer. Annie had suggested the place when she responded to his e-mail; he'd been careful not to use his work account. Her e-mail voice was bright and succinct. He appreciated the absence of emojis and exclamation points. As he sat at the table sipping his beer, he began to wonder why she'd agreed to meet him so readily. Surely she'd read his profile; what was the appeal? Unless, perhaps, the search engine was working as intended, had detected something between the two of them that Ethan had not, something that would lead to romance. Ethan's over-clocked brain began to imagine an evening turning into morning turning into happily ever after.

But this was not a date, he reminded himself.

If this were a date, he would have been visibly nervous. His forehead would have glistened. Words would have collided with one another on the way out of his mouth. The menu would have flapped like a bird's wing in his hands. But because this was not a date, he was calm. Work was the one area of his life in which he felt completely confident.

He watched her enter the restaurant and pause as her eyes adjusted to the darkness. At first glance, she was wildly contradictory. She wore a blue fifties-style poodle skirt cut a few inches too short for that decade. She wore a white-and-yellow plaid sweater that barely covered the tattoos on her arms. The tattoos on her legs emerged from her bobby socks, winding up her thin legs.

Ethan stood and waved her over. "Annie?"

"Hi, Ethan." She shook his hand and they both sat down.

His confidence began to vanish, and Ethan looked around for their waiter, feeling the pressure of silence building. When he turned back to Annie, she was extending a clipboard towards him. "Since we've got a moment, I was hoping you could sign something," she said. "It's a petition to ban foie gras."

He looked at the clipboard and then at Annie. "I'll bet you say that to all your dates."

"You can sign right there." She handed him a pen and pointed at the bottom of the page, oblivious to his attempt at humor.

Ethan took the petition and squinted at it. The candle at their table didn't provide enough light to make sense of the fine print. Again he looked for their waiter. He knew he should just sign it and get on with the date—except that it wasn't a date, and he didn't like to sign petitions, even for causes he agreed with.

"Do you think we could eat dinner first?" he asked. "I promise not to order...faux..."

"Foie gras."

"Right. To be honest, I don't even know what foie gras is."

Annie gave him a sympathetic smile. The waiter finally arrived, and she ordered a beer. She told Ethan, in surgical detail, about foie gras: the restraining cages, the metal tubes used for ritual force-feeding, the way the ducks would cry to one another at night.

"I have videos," she said.

"I'll take your word for it."

"My goal is a thousand signatures. We need more than a quarter million to have a shot at getting this on the ballot. Which is why I'm doing everything short of blocking intersections to get them."

"Is this date one of your signature-gathering strategies?" Ethan asked.

"Of course not. I'm just here for a free meal." She smiled.

Ethan assumed she was joking with him, but he could not be sure. While he could always tell what was going on inside of a computer, people were more of a challenge. He was a terrible judge of emotions and other human subtleties, and he knew it but couldn't seem to solve it. He spent a lot of time over the years asking "what?" as those around him laughed at some inside joke or sexual euphemism that he apparently missed altogether. He was on the outside of most conversations, looking in, trying to see what everyone else saw so easily. He tried not to let it bother him. He was smarter than other people in so many ways, and he contented himself with that knowledge. But he could not help but struggle in moments like this, not knowing if a girl was smiling because she was happy or because she was inwardly laughing at him. At times like this, Ethan often assumed the worst and responded defensively.

"Annie."

"Yes?"

"I can't sign your petition," he said. "It's not because I don't agree with your cause but because as a matter of principle I don't sign petitions."

"You don't *sign* petitions?" She stared at him.

"Petition drives have gotten out of hand in California. And the only way to fight back is to refuse to sign them altogether. It's been years since I last signed one."

"You trying to win a medal or something?"

"Do you realize there were seventeen propositions on the ballot last year?"

"Yes. One was a proposition that I helped get on the ballot."

"Oh?"

"Proposition 3. To expand the size of battery cages for chickens."

"I thought you didn't eat meat."

"I don't eat meat, or any animal product. But even those on death row deserve humanity." Annie stood and reached for her backpack. "Look, Ethan, if you're not going to sign it, that's fine. It's your choice. Give me my clipboard."

As Ethan handed it back, the waiter approached with Annie's beer, and she held the clipboard out to him. "Would you like to sign a petition banning foie gras?"

"Sure thing," he said. "We don't serve it here."

"And you don't have any principles against signing petitions?"

"Why would I?" he asked. Annie looked down at Ethan, and he wanted to jump to his feet, grab the clipboard back, and start again. But it was already too late—he had gone from first impression to last impression in record time.

"Nice to have met you, Ethan," she said.

He nodded, avoiding eye contact, then stared at her back as she left the restaurant. He paid for the beers, and as he walked home he tried to convince himself that he'd done the right thing. She was trying to use him, and he had held his ground. Back in high school, the only pretty girls he'd gotten close to were those who needed help with their homework. He was branded a computer nerd, and even the emergence of fabulously rich computer nerds did not seem to brighten his prospects. He had come to assume the worst of beautiful women: They wanted something from him. How could they not? What good was he but for a late-night computer question, a reinstalled operating system, a signature?

He had been accused by previous girlfriends—all three of them—of not talking enough. The last one—the one with whom he could see a real future, even marriage—told him he was emotionally distant. She was probably right, but he did not know how to rectify the situation. He was fluent in any number of programming languages, but these were foreign tongues to the women he most wanted to be with, and plain conversational English often seemed foreign to him. Over the years, he'd made significant upgrades to his repertoire of small talk. He could banter about the weather in San Diego (or lack thereof) and the best beaches to surf (though he didn't surf). But small talk only delayed the inevitable. Eventually a woman wanted more. Eventually, in quiet moments together in cars or in elevators or at home waiting for the toaster to pop, he would have nothing more to say. She would ask what she had done wrong. He would tell her that everything was fine. And eventually she would see him as mute, paralyzed, useless. And she would leave.

When Ethan returned home, he logged into eCouplet, telling himself he needed to check his work e-mail, though he only wanted to see her face again. And then he realized his hypocrisy. He had accused Annie of using him for his signature. But he had been using her, too, manipulating a search engine, asking her out under cowardly pretenses. And neither had gotten what they wanted.

When Ethan went to look up her picture, he was denied access. She had blocked him from viewing it.

If he'd only signed that silly sheet of paper, just signed it. She would have put the clipboard away. They would have had a fantastic meal. They might have made the perfect match. Instead, she had dumped him, after only one date.

And it wasn't even a date.

JAKE

FIRST, JAKE GAVE UP FISH. That was easy. It was a chore of a food, and he'd eaten it only because it was supposed to be healthy. He never could tell the difference between halibut and scrod, and he didn't care if salmon came from a farm or the inland waterways of Alaska. It all looked and tasted pretty much the same, and it all left him feeling hungry.

Then he gave up pork, also not much of a sacrifice. He liked bacon, but he rarely had time for breakfast. Chicken he would miss. Wings, fajitas, all those pasta dishes that used chicken like croutons. Chicken-salad sandwiches. Chicken soup. Rotisserie chicken from the neighborhood grocery, warm and golden in its clear plastic container.

Then there was beef. Jake wouldn't miss steak so much as the steakhouse—the dark paneling and green-shaded lamps, the stiff whiskey taken neat, the garlic mashed potatoes and the white-aproned waiters who spoke of cuts and aging. But as much as he liked the experience, steak was always a bit too highbrow, a bit too theatrical; he was a true connoisseur of the hamburger. In every new town he visited, he would seek out the best burger joint. Mr. Bartley's in Cambridge, Massachusetts, where burgers were named for political figures and served with thin, curly fries. Booches in Columbia, Missouri, where palm-sized cheeseburgers were served on sheets of wax paper and could be paid for only in cash. Two Bells in Seattle, where the French baguette that served as a bun attempted to belie the dive-bar atmosphere. But now there would be no more field trips, no more research, no more late-night visits to In-N-Out.

He was now a vegetarian.

He was one of them. Earth-conscious. Crunchy. Cruelty free. Instead of deciding between rare or medium rare, his decisions consisted of tofu: medium or firm. His days began with soy sausages and ended with bean burritos. And though he had accomplished the expeditious transformation from carnivore to vegetarian, he was still only halfway toward his goal.

The 2001 Rights for Animals Conference was a week away, and if he wanted to pass his audition and get on that ship, he had to go all the way. As in vegan.

So Jake gave up cheese and butter. Then he gave up milk. Then he gave up eggs. He worried about losing muscle mass. He worried about starving. He worried he wasn't going far enough. But then he learned that with veganism, you could never go far enough. Animal products were everywhere—in soap and in toothpaste, in gelcaps, in chewing gum. When he visited an online message board and asked about a brand of vegan cheese he was considering, Alex2000 wrote back: *When the chief selling proposition of the cheese is "it melts," then you can bet it doesn't taste good.*

It didn't.

Conference attire was another challenge. He wanted to look young but not immature, dedicated to the cause but not crazy. He was thirty, but with a tight shave and shaggy hair, he could pass for twenty-five, and he thought that would be good enough to the impress the captain. He wore a used pair of Converse sneakers, old jeans, and a faded black T-shirt. At the last minute, he bought a wristband with the word PEACE imprinted on it.

The conference was held in a large hotel next to LAX,

and Jake's room overlooked one of the runways. As planes descended past his window in sixty-second intervals, Jake sat on the bed and prepared himself. Originally from Austin, he was fresh out of grad school. He was committed to direct action. He could fix any engine, tie any knot. He didn't get seasick. And, if necessary, he would mention the helicopter.

He took the stairs to the lobby. To his left, down a long hallway, he saw the welcome table. He completed a registration form and handed over his credit card. The woman at the table, a ponytailed redhead with a pierced nose, looked up and smiled. "Is this your first RFA Expo?"

"As a matter of fact, it is," Jake said.

"Awesome. Most of the sessions are in those rooms over there and on the second level. There's an orientation session in Room 105, and the exhibition hall is directly behind me."

Jake studied the schedule. From *Activism Against Vivisection* to *Blood on the Ice* to *Free Trade Kills Animals,* the following two days would be packed with every animal atrocity he'd ever imagined, and probably more he hadn't. He began by wandering the exhibition hall. A hundred tables and booths were assembled along eight narrow aisles. He took his time circumnavigating the room, watching people while trying to look as if he wasn't watching people. Dogmatic T-shirts were ubiquitous: I DON'T EAT MY FRIENDS. I THINK, THEREFORE I'M VEGAN. EAT LIKE YOU GIVE A DAMN.

He chatted with the eager faces at each table. The woman who founded an Iowa dog-and-cat rescue organization. The editor of a start-up vegan magazine. The Chinese man who set moon bears free. Dogs in Ethiopia, Cape fur seals in Namibia, kangaroos in Australia. The biggest draw in the exhibition hall—and the reason for his attendance—was the Cetacean Defense Alliance. People crowded around, three deep, blocking the aisle. Jake wanted to approach the table and begin his audition, but his nerves got the better of him.

Instead, he entered one of the lecture rooms and took a seat near the front. He wondered if the people seated around him could tell that he was an imposter, a carnivore among vegans. Could someone tell that he had only recently stopped eating meat simply by looking at him? Was there a residual smell?

A somber young man stood at the front and introduced a video his group had taken while working undercover at a slaughterhouse in rural Ohio. The lights dimmed to show a video of the men who worked there, punching birds on conveyers as they hung there, strung up alive by their fragile legs. If a turkey came loose, the men kicked it around like a soccer ball. One man reached into the female birds, searching for eggs to hurl at co-workers.

Jake could hear a woman crying behind him, and he fought back the urge to duck out of the room and away from those images. But he remained in his seat, watching the tortured birds conveyed through a machine that in one quick motion stretched wide their necks, ran them by a spinning blade, then released them to bleed to death as their bodies continued along the line, their flapping wings eventually going motionless. And then he could take no more.

He hurried out of the room into the main hall, stepping straight into a dark-skinned woman in a long madras skirt and a white Kiss me, I'm Vegan tank top. She grabbed his arms for balance, and he grabbed her waist. After an awkward moment, a moment that lasted a half-second too long, a half-second he would replay forever, she pulled back. Or he released his hands. How was it that this innocuous invasion of personal space had become so intimate? When their eyes met, he smiled and she wrinkled her brow. Then she began to walk away.

"Do you get many takers?" Jake asked.

She stopped and turned around.

"Your shirt," he said.

She eyed him suspiciously, studying him from head to toe. "You're vegan?"

"Of course," he said.

"Then how do you explain that?" She pointed at his wristband, the wristband that Jake suddenly realized was made of leather.

He smiled sheepishly. "I don't eat it; I just wear it."

"Perhaps you should visit the orientation session. Room 105. And take notes." She shook her head and walked off. She had seen right through his disguise, though—he hoped—not far enough.

Jake watched her disappear around the corner, wanting to follow her, to run into her once again. But he turned and made his way to Room 105.

AFTER A DAY OF VIDEOS AND LECTURES and no sign of the woman in the tank top, Jake returned to the exhibition hall. The scrum around the CDA table was as dense as before; Jake had no choice but to plow through. At the main table he purchased a book—*The Anti-Whaler*—from a young woman wearing a beret. The cover was a photo of the bearded man now standing off to the right of the CDA table, signing each book as it was handed to him.

Jake thought it odd that the man was standing instead of sitting. Yet he looked perfectly at ease, legs apart, solid as a statue. Perhaps after years spent standing in the bridge, he no longer felt the need to sit. As Jake studied him, the man seemed to sway ever so slightly, as if he were still at sea. Or maybe it was Jake who was swaying, now feeling his stomach tighten. The moment he had prepared for was now seconds away. His audition.

Now next in line, his mouth had gone dry. He could feel

his hands trembling. He forgot what he had planned to say.

"Whom shall I make it out to?" the man asked.

"Jake."

"Does Jake have a last name?"

"No, I mean, it's for me. Jake is fine."

The man took the book and pried open the cover. Jake had to move quickly. "Do you have any spots left on your next voyage?" he asked.

"Voyages are for tourists."

"What I meant was that I'd like to volunteer. On your ship."

"The ship is full."

"I can fix any engine, diesel, gas, you name it."

The man handed the book back. "As I said, the ship is full. But we always need volunteers on land. Most of our crew members began right here behind this table."

Jake left his name with the girl in the beret and walked off. He looked back at the CDA booth and watched the man signing books, occasionally pausing to look up and scan the hall—as if he were looking out over the water and the people were nothing more than waves to him, to be sailed past on his way to the next battle.

Jake opened the flap of his book.

Jake —
Fortitudine Vincimus.
　　　— Aeneas

That night, in his hotel room, an Internet search deciphered the message: *By endurance, we conquer.*

Endurance. Jake didn't have the luxury of time to volunteer, to work his way up the CDA ladder, to wait until next season. He needed to be on that boat now, or give up entirely.

He stood at the window and looked down on the airport

runway lights, then up at the approaching planes. On this remarkably smog-free evening, he saw the lights of three, then four of them, one after another, stars dropping from the sky. He thought of his father, who spent most of his life as an airline pilot before dying of a heart attack three years ago. *Every landing is just a controlled crash,* said his dad, who was a navy pilot before joining the airlines. He taught Jake to fly a Piper Warrior two-seater when he was seventeen, and a helicopter not long after. The helicopter was the most challenging—it was unstable in every direction. But Jake mastered the controls quickly, brought order to chaos. He didn't know that those skills would play such a large role in his life, for both good and bad. He'd just been trying to please his old man. Those hours in the cockpit were the only hours Jake still remembered about his father. They'd moved a lot, renting houses in nice neighborhoods, and Jake had idealized that existence, crediting the many schools he migrated through for his ability to assimilate anywhere. And still he was unable to assimilate here, at Rights for Animals, still unable to become one of them. But having a pilot for a dad was a surefire ingredient to a peripatetic life, to the life that Jake was living—one controlled crash after another.

ETHAN

ETHAN FOUND ANNIE working the register in aisle three of the health food store. She didn't notice him until after he had unloaded his basket onto the conveyor belt.

"What are you doing here?" she asked.

"Just shopping."

He watched her scan the vegan cheese and tofu hot dogs. She glowed in her bright green apron, her hair pulled back into two small ponytails, like one of those perfect actresses who attempt to dress down to play a certain role.

She held up a carton of almond milk. "This is for *you?*" she asked.

Ethan nodded.

She scanned a packet of fake chicken. "I thought you ate meat."

"I'm cutting back."

He handed her the reusable cloth sack he'd purchased the day before. "I even brought my own grocery bag."

She eyed him suspiciously, then looked in the bag. "There's something in here," she said.

"That's for you."

"What is it?"

"You'll see."

Annie rolled her eyes and reached in and removed a paperclipped batch of signed petitions, twenty-six pages in all, representing most of his colleagues at eCouplet.com, six residents from his apartment building, and the bartender at NuNu's.

"How many?" she asked.

"Two hundred and fifty-five."

"Including yours?"

"Including mine."

She leaned toward him and he leaned forward to meet her, but the conveyer belt kept them apart. Ethan wanted to climb over and embrace her but he could sense impatient bodies to his left, mounting pressure to pay up and leave her for the next person in line.

"There's hope for you yet, Ethan," she said, ruffling his hair.

That night he logged on to eCouplet.com to find that she had removed the block on his account.

ANNIE SUGGESTED A MEXICAN RESTAURANT on Banker's Hill. They each ordered black bean tacos (no cheese) and margaritas, his with salt, hers without. When they'd first met, Ethan noticed that Annie always seemed to be looking off to one side, as if her mouth were gently caught on some invisible hook, and he'd assumed she was bored with him. But now, as he studied her, he realized that it was just the way she was. Knowing this gave him hope that she would not walk out, or toss her margarita into his lap, when he told her the truth about how they met.

"I have a confession to make," he said. He told Annie that he worked for eCouplet.com, about his blatant manipulation of algorithms and, indirectly, of her. And then she laughed.

"What's so funny?" he asked.

"You must be one hell of a computer geek," she said.

"What do you mean?"

"Because whatever you did with that algorithm, it must've worked," she said. "You're my one and only eCouplet success story."

"I am?"

"Success is relative, I suppose. But my dates don't usually make it through to dessert," she said. "Either I walk out, like I did with you, or they come down with a sudden case of the flu."

"Why?"

"I come across as a bit, I don't know, *abrasive*. Like when I told you I despise anyone who eats meat, fish, or cheese."

"Oh." Ethan had never considered that she might have difficulty meeting men. Nor had her activism struck him as offensive. Perhaps it was because her animal-rights narratives and environmental vocabulary were as exotic to him as his technical skills probably were to her. They were like tourists from two different countries: There was no pressure to get along because they weren't supposed to have met in the first place.

WHEN ANNIE'S ROOMMATE GOT A JOB in Seattle, selling her condo and leaving Annie without a place to live, Ethan offered up his apartment. "You can stay as long as you want," he said.

She moved in, and they made love that first night in the bathtub. She floated up and down on his arms, weightless. He watched her eyes close and her head fall back. She moaned, louder and louder, and he nearly lost himself listening. Afterward, they dripped over to his bed and he massaged her body dry with a towel, meticulously following the flowing lines of her tattoos, ending at her feet. He kissed her toes and her ankles and worked his mouth back up her body, until he reached her eyelids, closed again. He wanted to say right then that he was in love with her, but she was somewhere else. He often lay awake watching her sleep, wondering where her mind was, wishing that he could be there, too.

She said from the beginning that she didn't want a

relationship, that they were only "roommates with benefits." Ethan was happy to abide by her semantics, just as long as she returned to him each night. Ethan thought he could convert her, make her fall in love with him over time. It did not occur to him that she might also be trying to convert him.

"I signed up to volunteer with the Cetacean Defense Alliance," she told him one evening over dinner. She told him about their anti-whaling battles down in Antarctica. The ships they had sunk during the five years since they began their missions. The larger ship they had recently purchased. "It's called the *Arctic Tern*," she said. "And if I'm lucky I'll get to join the crew someday."

"Going to Antarctica?" Ethan asked.

She nodded, then invited Ethan to volunteer with her.

"Does the boat have Internet access?" he asked, half joking. But this wasn't the answer Annie wanted, and Ethan spent the rest of the evening alone at his computer. He wanted to be as free as she was, and he didn't want to lose her, but he wasn't quite ready to join up with a bunch of outlaw activists, to plan on leaving his job for months at sea.

Since meeting Annie, he had returned to his algorithms with renewed energy. He developed an *opposites attract* feature, which matched people with their apparent opposites. He named it Antipodes. And when he told Annie about it, he thought she would see that she was the inspiration, that she was needed here, here with him in San Diego. But she didn't seem to care. She was too busy organizing another environmental event, a whole weekend of events taking place throughout San Diego County. She had invited the über activist Adam Cosgrove to deliver the keynote at the Hillcrest Community Center. She pointed him out in an issue of *Vanity Fair*—a tall, scruffy blond man standing topless on a black-sand beach. He had served time in Oregon for burning down an animal-testing lab. He had been interviewed by *60 Minutes*. He had dated Hollywood celebrities.

Ethan asked her if she had a crush on Adam.

"Of course," she said. "You would, too, if you were a woman—or a true activist."

Ethan shouldn't have let her comment bother him, but she was right; he wasn't a true activist, and it was just a matter of time before Annie left him for someone who was. Ethan began to imagine the many ways that she could exit his life. He worried about the men who paused by her register. She was the prettiest clerk in that store, and men would surely go out of their way to be in her line. They would talk about vegan foods with genuine knowledge and interest; they would make her laugh. And she would forget about him.

He asked her to quit the job. But she refused. He asked where their relationship was headed. "There is no relationship," she reminded him. "Just two people sharing an apartment, taking it one day at a time."

In a parallel universe, Ethan told himself, Annie was his girlfriend. She had decided to settle down, had decided that she wanted children after all. A programmer always considered multiple outcomes for every scenario, and Ethan stayed focused on the outcomes that favored his dreams. The challenge was in knowing how to effect this change. Annie's mind did not work like any algorithm he had known, and every day his mind kept busy trying to debug it.

In the absence of clues, Ethan figured his best strategy for winning her over was plain old proximity. He attended all of her protest events and fundraising drives. He joined activists holding angry signs at busy intersections as drivers honked at them. And he sat next to her the evening that Adam Cosgrove delivered his keynote speech at the Hillcrest Community Center. The room was crowded with people who looked and dressed a lot like Annie and Adam—hemp clothing, long hair, tattoos; Ethan felt like more of an outsider than ever before. Physical proximity alone, he had begun to realize, was only making him feel more distant from her. He needed to go further if he wanted to be a part of her world. His mind whirled as Adam spoke about protests and animal rights, his battles with the law and his time in prison. And when he asked for questions from the audience, Ethan was the first to raise his hand.

"How would one go about building an incendiary device?" Ethan asked. "Like the one you used?"

To answer, Adam demonstrated. He picked up an apple-juice container from the potluck table. You needed only to fill it with fuel, he said, then to shove an old cotton T-shirt into the top and insert a slow-burning fuse. He held up a cellular phone and his iPod. He explained how to set the device off remotely, at a precise time.

Ethan had no idea how soon he would regret asking that question, how soon he would be running the scenario through his head over and over again, as if it were an algorithm he could go back and fix—the if/else equation that worked reliably in computers but always led to surprises in real life.

If Adam had not answered the question. If Adam had not provided such detail. If an unfinished condominium development in La Jolla had not been set on fire later that evening by a similar type of device. If Ethan had not raised his hand, none of these things would have happened—and Adam would not have been arrested by the FBI the following morning. And Annie would not have left Ethan to run to Adam's defense.

So many ifs, all set in motion by one question. Ethan had always lived in a world of undos, of parallel universes. But he could not undo what he said. He could only watch as Annie slipped out of his universe and into someone else's.

JAKE

UNWILLING TO ACCEPT DEFEAT, Jake remained at the conference through the bitter end, lingering in the halls. He never saw Aeneas again. He watched as tables were drained of books and signs, as people packed up displays. He paced the hallways, then circled back into the main hall once more, finding it empty. The vegan T-shirts and tattoos had disappeared, replaced by suits, rolling luggage, and a full-color sign announcing a radiology conference.

He sat at the hotel's bar, ordered a Guinness, and stared up at the baseball game on the television.

"Where's your bracelet?"

Jake looked over to see the woman he'd bumped into yesterday, or who'd bumped into him. She was wearing a white T-shirt and a wraparound skirt, a small pack slung over one shoulder.

"I must have lost it," he said.

"I'll bet you did."

She took the seat next to him and ordered a vodka on ice. She didn't look at him.

"I wasn't being completely honest with you earlier," he said. "I only recently became a vegan."

"If only there had been some clue."

"Now you're making fun of me," Jake said. "I guess I deserve it." He held up his beer. "At least this is vegan."

"Barely."

"What do you mean?"

"Guinness only recently became vegan. They used to use isinglass, which comes from fish, to remove the excess yeast. Any longtime vegan would've known that." She smiled and downed her drink.

He suspected by the way she let her shoulder rub against his as she rummaged through her bag that his lapses might be forgiven. He bought her next drink before she could find the money she was searching for. She bought the next round while he was in the bathroom. They did not talk of food or animals or each other. They watched the baseball game; she rooted for the Red Sox, and he rooted for the Dodgers. When the Dodgers lost he drained his beer. She wiped the foam mustache off his upper lip and licked her finger.

"What's your name?" Jake asked.

"Noa," she said. "What's yours?"

"Jake."

"It's a good thing you're a vegan, Jake."

"Why's that?"

"I don't sleep with carnivores."

Jake followed her to her room. There was a large nylon backpack in the corner, a rainbow-colored Tibetan prayer flag draped across the TV.

"What are you praying for?" he asked her as she removed his shirt.

"Peace." She removed her top. "Love." She untied her skirt and let it fall to the floor. Jake cupped her breasts in his right hand and kissed them.

"And happiness."

No more words were spoken that night. The sex felt at times angry and at other times playful. She giggled when he licked her calves. He squirmed as she took him in her mouth, and she gave him a look that said *relax,* and he let go and let her take charge. She wanted his body, and he gave it to her and gazed up at her as she writhed on top of him, eyes closed, grinding, arched back, grabbing him at his base, to feel him and her as one.

The next morning they made love again until the bed was stripped of sheets and pillows and he had collapsed onto her. He fought back sleep as she kissed his chest.

He awoke while she was in the shower and stared at her backpack. Something told him that it contained most of what she owned, and he felt intoxicated all over again—not only by Noa but by her lifestyle. He imagined leaving his own life behind, following her and her Tibetan flag. He could see them hitching through Russia, sleeping under the stars in New Zealand, tending bar in some Caribbean country. Off the grid.

Then he remembered who he was and what he was doing here. And Gordon. What would he tell his boss? That circumstances had changed? Priorities had shifted? He could hear himself talking like an agent, hiding behind third-person sentences, euphemisms, excuses. But the truth was that he had failed. He hadn't gotten the access he needed, and now it was too late. Maybe it was time for a new career. Or no career at all.

Right then he wanted nothing more than to leave Jake behind—but more than that, he wanted to relinquish Robert, too, before he got completely lost in bureaucracy and undercover assignments, before he lived so many lives as other people he would no longer be able to tell the difference. Noa was real, genuine. He wanted to follow her, and her Tibetan flag, wherever she was headed. It would surely be more exciting than where he was headed.

Noa entered the room, towel hanging from her breasts.

"Where are you going from here?" he asked.

"I'm catching a boat to Norway."

"Can I come?"

"You serious?" She cocked her head to one side.

"Of course I'm serious."

"We've got a full crew, but I could squeeze you on. We'd have to share a bed."

"I think we could manage. Do I need a ticket?"

"No. You'll work for your passage." Her towel dropped as she walked toward him. "We all work for our passage."

"We?"

"The Cetacean Defense Alliance. CDA. We're a new anti-whaling group. Only a year old. Ever heard of us?"

She kissed him on the lips and then began working her way down. A flash of light caught his eyes—a reflection from a descending plane. And he realized that now he, too, was back on course. Despite himself, he had achieved his objective. It was a sign, he realized, not only that he—Robert—was back on course but that Jake was meant to live just a little while longer.

"CDA," he said, closing his eyes as Noa's tongue reached his navel. "I think I've heard of them."

ETHAN

ETHAN GLANCED ACROSS THE COURTROOM from his modest perch on the witness stand. He'd expected a larger venue for a federal trial: wooden floors and wrought iron railings, like in the movies. But the San Diego federal courthouse was a low-rise office building, and the courtroom had a conference-room feel—the faded carpeting and low ceilings, the knee-high glass barrier separating the actors from the gallery. There were few seats in the gallery, as if to discourage spectators, and Ethan scanned each one in hopes of seeing Annie. He touched the envelope in his pocket, the one from the travel agency, and felt foolish for bringing it. She was not there.

It had been six months since Annie moved out, soon after he was called to give a deposition. She'd blamed him for Adam Cosgrove's arrest, he knew, but at least she'd stood by him, though not as closely as she stood by Adam. She spent most of her days working in Adam's defense—but at night, it was Ethan she came home to, and because of this he allowed himself to hope they might still have a future together.

Until the deposition. *Just lie your ass off,* she'd instructed him, and he intended to do just that. But when the prosecutor stared him down and threatened him with perjury, Ethan ended up telling the truth. Because of Annie, it had still felt like a lie.

Not long afterward, Adam was charged with one count of distributing information on explosives with the intent of inciting others to commit acts of violence. And not long after that, Annie packed her things. Ethan knew what he'd done wrong, but he didn't know how to fix it.

He hoped to see her here today, at the trial, thinking that maybe he would do now what he had failed to do before. He wanted to start over. And although he did not see Annie in the gallery, perhaps it was that urge to begin anew that compelled him to respond the way he did—to say, when the prosecutor asked him to repeat what Adam had done that evening in Hillcrest, that he could not remember. Even when the prosecutor repeated himself, asked him the same question in three different ways, each time Ethan told him that he could not remember.

The prosecutor's voice grew louder, the judge chimed in, the gallery began to applaud—then came the pounding of a gavel, and, mercifully, a recess.

Ethan stood alone at the far end of the hallway, looking out the tinted windows. He didn't want to be near the activists who clotted together at the other end of the hall talking in whispers, or near the government agents, the men with close-cropped hair, checking e-mail on their phones.

"Ethan."

He turned to see Annie standing behind him. He leaned toward her, but she backed up a step.

"Hi."

"That was a brave thing you did," she said. "There's hope for you yet."

"You were in there?"

"I heard."

"It was nothing," he said, and decided to take a chance. "Come home with me tonight."

She smiled. "I think it's time I leave San Diego. I've been holding out for a spot on the CDA ship. I should know next week."

Ethan reached into his pocket and held out the envelope.

"There are other ways to get to Antarctica."

"What's this?"

"It's a cruise ticket."

"A cruise?" She wouldn't take the envelope. "Ethan, I'm trying to *protect* the environment, not *pollute* it."

"You always wanted to go to Antarctica, right? We could go together. I know going on a cruise isn't the way you wanted, but at least it's a ride down there."

She looked at him sadly. "If the CDA doesn't work out—" She stopped. "I don't know. Maybe."

"That's a start." He pressed the envelope into her hand. "The ship leaves in three weeks. The trial will be over, we'll both be free. Just think about it."

"Ethan—"

"Don't decide now," he said. "I'll be on the boat, waiting for you. Just two people sharing a cabin. Roommates with benefits."

She gave him a quick smile, and in the end, she accepted the envelope. As she walked away, she looked back at him—briefly, but it was enough to give him hope.

MEMORIES FADE WITH TIME. Unless, of course, they are captured on tape, digitized, transcribed. Like an audio recording of the lecture, submitted anonymously to the judge, and entered into evidence. When Ethan returned to the witness stand, ready to forget everything that happened that night, or any night, the prosecutor handed him a transcript. He then pressed a button on a laptop connected to a speaker.

Ethan's heroic act was nullified by a tape recorder. Ethan could fault his brain for forgetting, but how could he argue with his voice on an MP3 file? And how could Adam Cosgrove argue with Ethan's testimony?

After the guilty verdict was delivered, Ethan tried to reach Annie. He left voice mails, sent e-mails. He told her of the guilt he was feeling—the one thing they now had in common. Eventually, she sent him an e-mail. She said she needed time to sort things out, that she would get in touch when she was ready. He sent her one last reminder about the cruise.

The best he could do would be to leave her be and meet her on board the ship. There was nothing more left to do but wait. And he now knew that, faced with a life without her, he would wait as long as necessary.

JAKE/ROBERT

DURING THAT FIRST WEEK on the boat with Noa, somewhere in the North Atlantic, Robert spent most days on his knees at the toilet. When he wasn't there, he was alone in bed, wishing he had never come aboard, never joined the FBI. His body heaved with convulsions, as if trying to repel some strain of virus, in vain.

Noa took pity on him, this runt named Jake who should never have been on the ship to begin with. She promised that he would adapt, that his body was only reacting to a force it did not understand. Eventually it would make peace with the motion, she told him.

She wiped his forehead with a sponge, cleaned his face. She gave him a fresh T-shirt. She forced him to drink water every two hours. In the dark, she was a soothing voice, a warm hand on the back.

She still believed he was nothing but a young idealist, a twenty-five-year-old with a passion for animals and the planet, and for her. At least that much was true: That first night, in the cramped bunk, legs intertwined, he threaded his fingers through her thick, dreadlocked hair and wished he never had to leave their bed. In her arms, his body found its peace, though he knew it couldn't last.

When he awoke the next morning, he wondered how he'd suddenly grown so frail. A man trained to kill other men, laid prone by a few waves.

When he was Jake, his life was simple, and once his stomach stabilized, he found that he liked it. He was traveling to Norway to do battle with whalers—a crew member on the *Eminence,* the CDA's first ship, financed by wealthy donors and outfitted with a helicopter to harass the whalers from above. As soon as he felt better, he joined the other five deckhands, all younger than he was. There was Tommy, a brooding, bearded loner with a smoker's voice. Brandon, a carpenter and boyfriend of Carrie, the chef. The other three were buddies from the University of Illinois whom Noa called the Three Amigos, freshly graduated and looking for an adventure, or maybe an excuse not to get real jobs. She was the boss of all of them: Every day, she told them which decks to scrub, which walls to repaint. Once the others learned about Jake and Noa, they ribbed him every chance they got. And as Jake, he didn't care. At night, under damp clenched sheets, her hips and back salty to his lips, he didn't care about anything else.

But when he was Robert, life was not so simple. First, there was his assignment—identify and arrest Darwin, an alias for the terrorist who had torched three mink farms in Idaho, after releasing the farms' unwilling inhabitants. Dry winds had turned one of the blazes into a 500-acre firestorm, taking down an entire subdivision and nearly killing two firemen.

His boss, Gordon, was certain that Darwin had been a crew member on the *Eminence*—they had tracked an e-mail linked to Darwin through a satellite data network—and he hedged his bets on Darwin sailing with the *Eminence* again. Norway was prepared to fast-track Darwin's extradition to the U.S. on arson charges; all they needed now was a face to go with the alias, a body to go with the handcuffs.

Robert had traveled light: his thrift-store clothes, a handgun hidden in his army duffel along with Jake's authentically phony passport. The night before he boarded the ship, he'd contacted Gordon for what would be the last time in weeks. Gordon didn't ask exactly how Robert got into the CDA, and Robert was not about to volunteer it. The Bureau did not permit agents to become intimately involved with those they were charged with investigating, although he learned years later that this rule wasn't always enforced. The more close-knit the organization, the more difficult it was to infiltrate, and tactics were localized to the situation.

To be an undercover, you must be good at telling lies, Gordon always said. And Robert was good, perhaps too good, especially when it came to lies of omission.

Noa was not his usual type. Robert had grown up dating blond cheerleaders, prom queens. The ones who knew their way around the cosmetics counter at Nordstrom. But he was not Robert on this boat. He was Jake. Jake the vegan. Jake the nonconformist. And Noa was Jake's type. She wore tunics and loose-fitting hemp dresses, the swaying fabric encouraging Robert's imagination. Dreadlocks falling past her shoulders. Her skin a light brown and without defect, the skin of her mother, she said, who was from India. She'd been with the organization since its founding, and had made every mission once it acquired its ship: traveling to Iceland to battle the whalers, to the Galápagos to battle the longliners. She oversaw the deckhands, from menial chores to raising anchors to dropping Zodiacs in the water. She had the toughest job on board. While the bridge officers and engineers worked in shifts, the deck was always on call, and people always called on Noa first.

She was as strong and sturdy as anyone on the ship, and bore all the stubbornness of her father, a onetime professional hockey player from Montreal. She drank and smoked, as comfortable at sea and with the crew as if she'd been born on board. Jake would have followed Noa to every corner of the Earth she planned to visit.

But Robert had a job to do, and once he gained his sea legs, he reluctantly went to work. He narrowed down his list of suspects: the mechanic, Randy; the first mate, Hudson; and Tommy, his primary suspect. Tommy was the explosives expert at the CDA, and, after a long night of drinking, he told Robert why.

"I was in charge of the Iceland operation," he said. "We snuck on board and deposited Molotov cocktails in the storage holds of the four largest whaling vessels while the ships were in harbor and their crews asleep on land. By the time the Coast Guard arrived, it was too late. In one hour, we had taken out a third of the fleet."

Right then, Robert could have arrested Tommy, called the Norwegians, and gone home. But he wanted to be more certain that Tommy was Darwin; he wanted more evidence. At least, this was what he told himself. In truth, Robert didn't want to go home. Not yet. And it wasn't as if Darwin was going anywhere either. What would be the harm in waiting?

Most of all, waiting meant a few extra weeks with Noa. Robert felt himself steadily, inevitably slipping deeper and deeper into character. One evening, Aeneas joined everyone in the galley with a bottle of whiskey. Until then Robert hadn't seen much of Aeneas, but he could tell that he was in a mood. Their helicopter pilot, Aeneas grumbled, had the flu. "Guess I'll have to take her up," he said.

"Like hell you will," Noa said. "You can't fly that thing."

"I can fly it," Robert said.

"You?" Noa asked. "Where did you learn to fly?"

"My dad was a pilot. He taught me years ago."

Aeneas squinted at him. "Did he teach you how to land on the back of a galloping ship in thirty-knot winds?"

The next day, the crew gathered around the upper deck to watch Robert's audition. The bird was an aging Robinson two-seater, suitable for covering traffic in LA, but highly questionable for navigating the high seas of the North Atlantic. But Robert had little trouble lifting off the deck and landing again—and days later, he was the one, on a clear windy morning off the coast of Spitsbergen, who sighted their first Norwegian whaler, the MV *Nørstad*. The ship, loaded down with two whale carcasses, one hanging from each side, appeared to be close to killing a third.

The crew went into battle mode and quickly caught up to the whalers. Although the *Nørstad* was twice their ship's size, Aeneas brought the *Eminence* diagonally in front of its path, both ships blaring horns. As long as the *Nørstad* changed course, there would be no collision. But the *Nørstad* did not change course.

The moment of impact seemed to happen in slow motion, with the deck of the *Eminence* heaving to the left as the *Nørstad* ground into it. Tommy manned a water cannon and drenched the *Nørstad*'s bridge while Robert and the others tossed smoke bombs onto their deck. The *Nørstad* veered right and pulled away, taking along with it an indentation and blue paint chips from the hull of the *Eminence*. The *Nørstad* fled at full speed, and the chase was on.

Tommy lowered a Zodiac into the water. His goal was to toss a length of barbed wire in front of the *Nørstad*, disabling its propellers. The idea of attacking a three-hundred-foot ice-strengthened vessel with an inflatable boat and some sharp wire seemed nothing short of martyrdom. Yet Robert was first in line to man the bow and toss out the prop fouler. At that moment, he wasn't sure whether he was simply authenticating his role, or whether the adrenaline he felt was due to something else. The more time he spent with Noa, the more blurry the lines between crime and mercy became.

Robert held the heavy gauge, razor-barbed wire in his gloved hands as Tommy piloted the Zodiac. They careened off the wake of the *Nørstad*, but Tommy kept the nose on target.

They soon pulled parallel with the ship. Water drenched them from above; the *Nørstad* also had a water cannon. When Robert looked up he saw the whale, dangling by a chain around its tail, its nose underwater, blood streaming from its belly and jaw. Its eye was still open and a flipper trembled.

"They let 'em bleed out first," Tommy said.

At that moment, everything disappeared: the FBI, the job he had to do, even Noa—everything but the whale struggling before him. Robert wished he had his handgun on him; he wanted to put this poor animal out of its misery, and even take a few Norwegians with it.

Tommy swerved the Zodiac into the path of the ship, and Robert threw out the prop fouler. They followed the ship for a few minutes, but the *Nørstad* continued on without pause. The device had failed.

And when Robert returned to the ship, he was no longer playing Jake, the environmental activist; he *was* Jake, the environmental activist. He climbed up onto the helicopter pad, put on his helmet, and started the engine. He could see Noa waving him down from the lower deck. She would be saying that it was too windy, that the waves were too high to land safely, and she would be right. But before she could get to him, Robert had cranked up the blades until the helipad shook. The noise was deafening. He had taken up the helicopter just twice on this trip, in calmer waters, but he could not let that whaler alone. He waited until the *Eminence* crested a large wave before pulling off the pad, careful to ascend quickly.

It took Robert just a few minutes to catch up to the *Nørstad* by air. He circled the ship like a hawk, looking for a weakness of some kind, trying to figure out what he could do to slow it down. He moved up a few hundred yards ahead of the ship, descended, and then ran straight for the bridge—as if he were on a suicide mission.

As he got closer he could see the men in there, mouths

shouting, eyes wide. For a second Robert considered following through, taking this dicing blade right into that bridge and taking as many bodies and arms and legs as he could—fitting retribution for their torture of that whale. But then he thought of Noa, and he veered right at the last moment. And even as he returned to the *Eminence*, even as he struggled to land while the ship bounced over strong waves, he could see only the whale's large unblinking eye gazing at him.

Once Robert was back on board, they tried to return to the *Nørstad*, but the whaling ship had disappeared, and its size and speed were no match for the *Eminence*. Aeneas tried for several hours to locate it again, to no avail.

So they headed farther north, well past the northern reaches of Norway, hoping to locate other whalers, to interrupt another hunt. They circumnavigated the islands of Svalbard without any luck, refueled at Longyearbyen, Svalbard's only port, and continued north, with nothing but ice between them and the North Pole.

The journey was long, and in the rare moments when neither of them was working, Robert and Noa would escape to her cabin, stay naked in bed for as long as they could, slivers of the midnight sun breaking through the porthole.

"You're kissing infinity," she said when he placed his lips on her right wrist.

"Why'd you get this tattoo?"

"To remind myself every day that anything is possible," she said. "It's so easy to be depressed when you see the things we see. You can be a vegan to save the world, or you can be a vegan to make the world a less sucky place to live."

It was moments like these in which Noa talked the most. She told him everything about the CDA, about the crew, about Aeneas. Robert worried that the FBI agent in him was all too obvious as he asked question after question: What were the histories of the first mate, the second mate, the chief engineer, the head chef, the nurse? Yet Noa must have seen all his questions as innocent curiosity, or passion for the cause; she answered every one.

Robert had begun to hope that Tommy was not Darwin, that Darwin was not on board at all. If Darwin were revealed, Robert would have to make the arrest, turn the boat around— and Noa would exit his life as quickly as she'd entered. So many ifs, with seemingly no way to avoid the inevitable, the heartbreaking inevitable.

"What will you do after this trip?" he asked her.

"Find a job for a few months," she said. "Until Galápagos. You want to come?"

He moved his face toward hers, pulled back the worn sheets, and kissed her olive skin from the base of her breasts to the infinity sign and back again.

ONE NIGHT, WHEN THINGS WERE SLOW and Robert was waiting for Noa to join him on the rear deck to look at the stars, he heard a noise and looked up. Aeneas stood there, a half-empty bottle of bourbon in his hand. The ship was cruising along at a steady pace, the seas calm, the polar ice cap less than twenty nautical miles to the north. He sat next to Robert and extended the bottle. "Join me in taming the sea."

Robert obliged, then handed the bottle back. Aeneas poured a good amount of liquor down his own throat, then stared out at the water, eyes glazed, appearing lost within himself. Noa had said once that Aeneas was best avoided in times of heavy drinking, when his anger toward the world, usually so well directed toward its intended targets, spilled over onto anyone within range. Last year, near Heard Island, south of Australia, Aeneas had been drinking when the *Eminence* drew alongside a pirate fishing trawler that was pulling in longlines studded with a bycatch of sharks and penguins. Aeneas boarded the ship and grabbed the longline, sending one of the three-inch hooks through the captain's right hand. The pirate fishermen made a quick and silent exit. Now, Robert could smell the alcohol wafting from Aeneas's pores and glanced around to make sure there were no sharp objects within reach.

"You need me to do anything else?" Robert asked.

"Tell me what the hell you're doing on my boat besides banging Noa."

"I'm just a volunteer."

"And I'm just a sailor."

"I'm not sure what you want to know."

"I want to know what a helicopter pilot with the nerves of a marine is doing on my ship. And don't give me that wanderlust crap you fed everyone else. Every person on this boat has a reason for being here. Maybe they're running from something, or maybe they're running toward something. Maybe they're trying to make amends. But nobody is here by chance."

Robert took another drink and handed the bottle back to Aeneas. While Aeneas sucked down the last of the bourbon, Robert's mind raced, desperate for an authentic-sounding story, something to get him out of this situation before it turned dangerous. But he wasn't prepared, so he found himself resorting to a worst case scenario: the truth.

"Does guilt count?" Robert asked.

"Guilt? Guilt makes the world go 'round."

"You want to know why I'm here. When I was a senior in high school, I lived alone with my mom and our two dogs. One night, the dogs cornered an opossum in our basement stairwell. The dogs scared it into this coffee can–sized drain at the bottom of the stairs. Only the drain had a cap on the bottom, which left the opossum stuck there with his angry hissing head sticking out. It was late, and the dogs were waking up the whole neighborhood, and here I was trying to play man of the house. I poked at that animal with a stick, then a steel rod, then a sharper stick. Then a knife. I stabbed it three times in that thick back, until blood began to leak out. Nothing worked. It would not move. I should have let it alone and it would have gone on home. But the dogs were driving my mom insane, and I was cursing this thing now, getting angrier and angrier. And then I got this ridiculous idea. I figured that animals were scared of fire. I poured a tiny amount of lighter fluid on its fur and I had the hose all ready to go and I tossed a match."

"What happened?"

"He didn't move. He just stayed there, on fire. He sat there, ignoring every instinct, burning to death. Perhaps his fear instinct was stronger than his fire instinct. I rushed to douse the fire but by then half his fur was gone, and the whole place smelled like burned flesh. He was hissing and he looked up at me and he turned his head from side to side in slow motion. I kept yelling at him because now he was dying on me and he still wouldn't leave. I should have put him out of his misery right then. But I didn't have a gun, and I didn't have the heart to stab him any more. I found an old trunk in the basement and I put on some old winter gloves and I picked him up, what's left of his fur still smoldering, the poor thing hissing, and put him in the trunk and put it in a dumpster in an old industrial park near my house. For weeks I had nightmares. I could see him still, hissing, alone, in that trunk, that poor animal. What did I do to him? I tortured him, and I didn't have the courage to put him out of his misery." Robert felt tears welling up. "But he had courage," he added, thankful for the darkness. "He never stopped hissing at me."

Aeneas reached into his jacket, removed a flask, and handed it to him. Robert took a long drink. "I never told anyone that," he said.

"Your secret's safe with me," Aeneas said. "I am not one to judge. I am the son of a fisherman, raised in Port Townsend, grew up working the coasts of Alaska. My father once said I had two options in life—the military or the sea. And when I said none of the above, he punched me in the face. He didn't believe in the belt—he was a hands-on parent. I'm a pacifist compared to him. But I used longlines once. I understand fishermen. They live in the past because the past tells them where the fish are. They are a tragic lot. They take from the sea, but what do they give back? The Greeks made offerings to the gods. But not my old man. He looked at the sea like an ATM with no limit. All you can eat. When I was young, I thought those fish they caught were so big. As I got bigger, the fish got smaller. But they kept shrinking even after I stopped growing. He took to crab fishing late in life when the salmon stocks dropped, got caught up in a line and was pulled overboard. And I got his boat. So in the end, he gave back to the ocean. That counts for something."

Aeneas tucked the flask back into his jacket. "Enough about me. The purpose of my impromptu visit was to tell you that we are heading for Antarctica in December for our inaugural battle with the Japanese. There's a spot open for you, if you're up for more abuse."

"Why me?"

"Why not you, Jake? You have other plans?"

"No."

"Perhaps this is your purpose in life, to join us. To fight for those whose instincts alone cannot save them. To make reparations."

"Is Noa going?"

"Is Noa going?" Aeneas laughed. "Why do you think I invited you?" He got up and stumbled his way back across the deck and up the stairs to the bridge.

Robert debated whether to share the news with Noa but

decided that he had to, in case Aeneas mentioned it. He told her the next evening, when they were alone having a smoke on the top deck. She lit up with a smile he'd never seen before.

"Think about it," she said. "Bipolar sex."

Right then, he wanted to become Jake for good. To accept the invitation because Robert could not accept it. Because Robert was about to arrest a member of Aeneas's crew. Because he was a member of the FBI and had now developed a detailed breakdown of the organization and how it functioned—not to mention that he was not a vegan and was never much of an environmentalist.

So why was he so happy? Because he'd been accepted into the group? Was he really contemplating joining them? The last time he'd felt this way was the day he got accepted into the Bureau. Yet acceptance by the CDA seemed more significant because of the odds stacked against these people; because most of them were there as volunteers, sacrificing jobs and relationships; and because of Noa.

She lit another cigarette using her Zippo lighter, with its peace symbol inscribed on the front. In part to change the subject away from the future, Robert reached over and took it from her hand, then held it up. "That's an odd location for a peace sign," he said.

"Because fire isn't peaceful? That's what everyone says. But fire can lead to peace. It clears away the old growth and man's mistakes."

"Like what?"

"Mink farms, for example," she said.

He looked at her. "What do you mean, mink farms?"

"You know, the places where they pen up innocent—"

"I know what it is," he interrupted. "I meant—are you saying that you actually set fire to a mink farm?"

She nodded and leaned in. "You have to swear not to tell anyone. What's wrong?"

"Nothing," Robert said.

"You sure? You look like you saw a ghost."

"I'm just a little surprised. I wouldn't have pictured you doing such a thing."

"That's the whole point, silly. If Tommy had torched the place, he'd be serving time right about now. He just looks guilty. But not me."

He listened as she recounted the Idaho burnings in great detail. She made it look as if a man had done the damage, by creating a fake alias for the guy on the web, a guy who posted angry messages in all the right places, sure to confuse the law. The only flaw she made was in posting to websites that were popular among the CDA members. She didn't notice it. No human would have noticed the connection, but pattern-matching software did notice it. A machine had made the connection, and Robert was sent to make the arrest because machines could not do that, not yet.

Duty now required him to function like that machine, to do as he'd been programmed. To arrest Noa, a.k.a. Darwin; to contact the Bureau, to turn the ship around and get on with his life.

But he was not a machine. And he was in love with Noa.

Maybe he would not arrest her. He would return home from a failed mission, hardly the first in the history of the Bureau. Maybe his career would stall; he would be transferred to some desk job that everyone feared. Hell, maybe he'd even be promoted.

Or maybe he would quit and run away with Noa. He could marry her, right now on the ship, have Aeneas make it official. Husband/wife privileges would protect her from the stand. His colleagues would forgive him for losing his head over a woman.

This was the outcome he dreamed of when he went to sleep that night, Noa in his arms, the constant hum of the engine lulling them to sleep.

ETHAN

AFTER SEVEN DAYS AT SEA, Ethan was no longer exploring the *Emperor of the Seas* but pacing it. Annie had not boarded in San Diego, as he'd hoped. Yet he stayed on the cruise ship as it made its slow passage down the Chilean side of Patagonia and through the Strait of Magellan. With every new port came renewed hope that she might join him. Perhaps she'd missed the boat back in San Diego and had planned to meet him in another location. Or perhaps she'd gotten a job on the CDA boat—which allowed him to believe that he might see her along the way. He'd been spending a lot of time on the CDA website and had learned that Ushuaia was a port of call for all vessels heading to Antarctica. It was a place where an anti-whaling boat like the *Arctic Tern* could pull up next to a cruise ship like the *Emperor of the Seas*.

A part of him knew that the odds of either scenario coming true were incalculable. But another part reminded himself that random things happened every day. That he and Annie being matched up in the first place was one of those random things.

After pacing the upper deck until well after dark, he returned to his cabin. He'd left the sliding balcony door open, and the room was freezing. He walked outside and blinked into the darkness. Whitecaps reflected the moon, and the ocean looked like static on a black TV screen. Ethan closed his eyes and rested his head on his arms, and he could see her again, sleeping next to him. Her tiny shoulders. The light tufts of hair on the back of her neck.

He opened his laptop and checked his e-mail again. He scanned the subject lines, the e-mail addresses, but she had not written back. Perhaps she wanted to surprise him or, more likely, the CDA boat had no Internet access. Eventually, however, she would be in port and would find her way to an Internet café. She would write to him and apologize for not being there, for all the money he spent on the cruise, for the cruise-issue parka he'd mailed to her last available address. But his efforts were not in vain, she would say. She would greet him when he returned, and they would give it one more try.

ROBERT

ON THAT LAST DAY on the *Eminence*, high in the Arctic Sea, Robert awoke alone in bed to voices outside his porthole. At first he thought he was dreaming. Then, as he emerged further from sleep, he thought the boat had docked somewhere and the noises were from the pier. Then he realized that this was not possible, that the boat was still moving, and when he stood and looked out the porthole he saw that the boat had pulled alongside a fishing trawler. Two men stood on the deck, their rifles pointed at the *Eminence*. At their feet were hooked fish and the coils of longline they were apparently in the process of reeling back in. Aeneas had interrupted their work, and the fishermen clearly were not happy.

As Robert turned away from the porthole, he heard a gunshot.

Quickly he reached under the bed and extracted the handgun he'd kept hidden in his bag. He ran upstairs in his bare feet, gun held behind his back. He exited on the opposite side of the deck and made his way carefully around to where he would have a clean view. One of the fishermen had already boarded the *Eminence*, and the CDA crew were scattered about the deck on their stomachs, arms behind their heads. The fisherman waved his shotgun above their heads. He was yelling something in Russian to the other, who was still on the bridge of the fishing boat.

Robert had to decide what to do, and fast. He could

remain undercover and take his position facedown on the deck. Or he could take the Russians down, blow his cover, and risk something else entirely.

Just then he caught sight of Noa, facedown near the gun-waving man's feet. She looked up at him, and he knew what he had to do. He turned the corner quickly, gun extended.

"FBI," he said, loudly enough for the fisherman to hear, not that he would understand.

The man smirked and without hesitation swung his rifle to aim at Robert. But Robert was already in position to shoot, and he had ample time to pull the trigger before the fisherman had a chance.

Robert fired three shots, watching as blood from the fisherman's head spattered onto the crew members spread out below. Robert turned the gun toward the man on the other ship, but he'd already dropped his rifle and had started the engine. Robert held his gun on him, letting him pull away. It had all happened in less than a minute.

When Robert turned back, the crew were on their knees, looking up at him. Despite the fact that he'd announced he was FBI, he was tempted to make up some story about being a drug dealer or former cop—any excuse to explain away the gun, to go back undercover. But he was tired of lying, and none of it would have mattered.

"I'm an FBI agent," he said. "My name's Robert Porter."

Noa approached, spots of the fisherman's blood dotting her neck and shoulders.

"I'm sorry," he said softly, but she continued past him and into the ship.

Robert scanned the faces of the crew, wondering whether he needed to fear them now. He saw Aeneas standing at one side of the bridge, looking down on him.

"Everyone just stay where you are," Robert said, trying to keep his voice from trembling. "I'm not here for you."

"Of course not," Aeneas said. "You're here for the camaraderie. The sea air. And let's not forget the romance."

Robert raised his gun at Aeneas, then lowered it. He tucked the gun into his pants and retreated into the ship.

He found Noa in their cabin, where she had turned his bag upside down and was shaking it frantically.

"What are you looking for?"

"Aeneas wanted me to search your bag when you came on board. I didn't. I told him I did, but I didn't. I vouched for you."

"I'm sorry."

"Was fucking me part of your mission, Jake? Or should I call you Robert?"

"No, of course not. My mission—I was sent here to arrest Darwin."

"Congratulations, Robert. You got your man." She held out her arms, wrists up. He grabbed them and raised her right wrist to his lips and kissed the infinity sign.

"I won't arrest you," he said. "I can't. I'm going to call Washington and tell them to get Russia on the horn because I just killed one of their citizens. That's it."

"Are you going to arrest Aeneas?"

"No."

She stared at him, and he could tell she didn't believe a word. "How can I trust you?" she said.

"Because I'm quitting. This is my last assignment. I'll follow you wherever you want to go."

Her eyes narrowed. "You'd follow me anywhere?"

"Anywhere."

He reached out and hugged her, hoping for a similar embrace. But she stood immobile in his arms. He didn't know how to act or what to say, now that his personas had collided, now that Robert and Jake were one. And he didn't know how to explain his actions to either of his two bosses, Gordon or

Aeneas. Either way he had failed.

"Let me clean up the mess up there, okay?" He pulled away and looked at her, hoping to get a response from her eyes. Even anger would have been a start. "Then we can talk. We'll figure everything out."

But Noa kept staring out the window, and finally Robert put on shoes and a jacket and went upstairs. On the deck, he found Aeneas standing over the body.

"I'm sorry this had to happen," Robert said.

"Are you?" Aeneas asked. "Someone is going to take the fall for this, and something tells me it won't be you."

"Just tell your crew to remain calm. I'm not going to hurt anyone unless they give me a reason to."

As Robert went through the fisherman's pockets looking for identification, he heard an engine come to life off the port side of the ship. He walked to the railing, and as he looked down, a Zodiac sprinted away from the ship with Noa at the helm. He shouted her name into the wind. She looked back at him just long enough for him to know exactly what she was doing. He said he'd follow her anywhere, and he knew that's what she was betting on—luring him off of this ship, away from Aeneas and their mission. They were alike that way, and she, too, had a mess to clean up.

Robert heard footsteps behind and he spun around, reaching again for his gun. Aeneas froze. "Where is she headed?" he asked, and Aeneas didn't answer. "*Where?*"

"By the looks of it, north."

Robert pointed his gun at Aeneas. "Tell her to turn around."

"With what? She isn't wearing a radio."

Robert glanced back at Noa, looking for the black nylon strap that would indicate she wore a radio. He couldn't see it, but he wasn't about to believe Aeneas. In the end, he knew he couldn't let her go. But he wasn't about to let Aeneas go either.

Then he remembered the helicopter.

He held his gun on Aeneas until he was strapped into the passenger side, then he fired up the propellers, keeping his gun in his left jacket pocket. He couldn't trust Aeneas, but he also knew that Aeneas couldn't fly this contraption on his own.

Once they were airborne, he relaxed. Aeneas would mind his manners, and having Aeneas with him guaranteed that the ship would be waiting when he returned. With a brief glance down, he saw that the crew was already scrambling to get the boat moving again, to follow as best they could.

Heading north, he kept Aeneas busy with the radio, making him call Noa, despite Aeneas's insistence that she had no way of responding. "Keep in touch with the ship so they stay close," he added.

Robert stayed close to the water, mindful of the automobile-sized icebergs that dotted the surface. In the distance he could see the ice blink, a crystal-white shadow in the sky reflecting the ice below it. Soon he began to see the mush of undulating ice that edged the polar cap. He began to run parallel to the ice line, looking for a point of entry.

"There's a trail," Aeneas said, pointing.

Robert circled around what could have been an opening through the slush cut by Noa's boat. He could see that she wouldn't get far. The sharp chunks of ice would inevitably puncture each of the Zodiac's six inflatable sections.

"Do you see her?"

"Not through this fog," Aeneas said. "Can you get any lower?"

The cloud layer had merged with the ice, forcing Robert to decelerate and stay as close to the ice as possible while still trying to avoid any spiked bergs. By then Noa's trail had sealed back up, and the slush turned to whiter chunks—solid ice.

"I'll double back."

"I see something," Aeneas said. "Circle around."

Robert banked, and Aeneas pointed below at what appeared to be the Zodiac, pinned sideways between two chunks of ice.

"See her?"

"No."

"I'll expand circles," Robert said.

"Wait, I see her."

Then Robert saw her, too, waving at them. Her red parka glistened with water, not a good sign. Robert began descending.

He looked for a stable place to land but saw nothing wide enough. Perhaps she could grab his strut and climb in. Looking down through the floor window of the helicopter, Robert descended over her—her hair flying everywhere, face ascendant and bright.

"Stop! You're shredding the ice."

Robert glanced down. Noa was no longer looking up at them but down at the ice crumbling under her feet. Robert ascended as quickly as possible and began to scout out a solid place to land. But with each second he slipped further away, until he lost sight of her completely. He spotted a wide slice of ice and dropped down hard; he could feel the ice bobbing under them.

"I'll get her," Aeneas said, stepping out.

"Not without me."

"If this ice begins to give, who's going to save the helicopter?"

Aeneas was right, and Robert reluctantly let him go alone, disappearing into the mist. Robert stepped out and circled around the helicopter, making sure the struts weren't perforating the ice. He leaned in to check the fuel gauge; they had just enough to make it back to the ship, assuming Aeneas returned with Noa within the next few minutes.

He tried to listen for voices in the whiteness surrounding him, but the steady throbbing of the blades kept him deaf. He felt time slipping, fuel expiring. He debated shutting down the engine, but what if the ice began to break? What if the engine refused to start again? And what if Aeneas had fallen into the water trying to reach Noa?

He didn't know how much time had passed, but it felt like too much. He began shouting their names. He walked to the edge of the ice floe, straining his eyes. He shouted again, then felt the ice pull out from under him like a rug.

He collapsed as the ice split in half, his toes on one piece, his hands on the other, holding his body above a widening pool of subzero water, frozen in a push-up position. He arched his back and slowly, steadily, carefully pulled the pieces back together, then rolled over onto a larger piece of ice.

Shaking, disoriented, he stood and searched the emptiness. He saw a shadow ahead and ran toward it. But it turned out to be a seal, poking its curious head out of the water. The sight of Robert scared him back under. But Robert, too, felt a jolt of fear, realizing that there were also polar bears out here, and they would not be nearly as easy to spot against the ice.

Following the sound of the engine, he made his way back to the helicopter, hoping to find both of them seated inside in the cockpit. But it was empty.

On the radio, he called to Noa, Aeneas, the ship. Nothing but silence. Was the radio broken, or were they ignoring him? He knew that if he waited much longer he would not have enough fuel to make it back to the ship. But he couldn't bring himself to engage the throttle, to raise the helicopter from the ice.

If he could find her, if she could hang on a little while longer, he could make it to the ship, refuel, and return to her. Another minute more and there would be no return, no chance of rescue. He lifted off. Below him, everything was slush. The fog was beginning to clear as he left the ice behind, but as he backtracked—or thought he did—the ship was not where he left it. He flew farther, in broad circles, but the *Eminence* was nowhere to be found. And now the helicopter's dashboard was beeping at him. Out of fuel, he had no choice but to return to the ice.

With the fog cleared, he found the overturned Zodiac. He landed as close to it as he could. The helicopter hit hard, piercing the ice, and Robert jumped out, scurrying away as the ice fell away under his feet. He heard the propellers slam into the ice and felt shards of glass and water rain on him from behind. He made his way to the Zodiac and struggled to turn it right side up. When he finally did, he pushed it into exposed water and scrambled in.

When his breathing calmed, he shouted for Noa. Then Aeneas. He shouted until his voice grew hoarse. Once, he thought he heard an engine, and he stopped and leaned into the mist, searching until his eyes blurred and the sound faded away.

Noa was gone. Aeneas, too, most likely. And Robert himself was soaked through, his fingers and face numb, a hundred miles from land. If he were to save himself, which was looking less and less likely, he had to start moving, but he couldn't bring himself to leave. He would rather perish out here on the ice than be proscribed to some sterile office in Washington, to live out a half-life of bureaucracy and paperwork. To live without Noa.

In the end, that was why he started the engine and began to scrape his way back through the ice, forcing open a passage a few feet at time. To return alone, if he returned at all, would be his purgatory, a fitting punishment, exactly what he deserved. Eventually the cracks began to give way to rivers, then to slush, then to open water, as if the ice were spitting him back out into the ocean.

The blue sky had been replaced by high clouds, and the

wind pushed the waves nearly seven feet high. Perhaps he would drown after all, he thought, and he began to welcome the idea all over again. Even if he did make it a hundred or so miles south of the ice cap, finding Svalbard would be no easy task. If he veered off only a few degrees in either direction, he would be out of fuel in the middle of the Arctic Ocean.

When he saw a plume of spray in the distance, just above the water, his ice-numbed mind focused on it, and he was surprised that with this sudden hope, his instinct to live was stronger than his desire to die.

But as he drew closer to the source, he saw a flipper slice the surface of the water and realized it wasn't another Zodiac but a whale. As he watched it—a humpback, as Noa had taught him—he grew so mesmerized by its graceful meandering that he began to trail after it, following its long pectoral fins, their jagged edges breaching the water every now and then.

As Aeneas had once said, the whale was the only mammal that had emerged from the sea at one point in time, taken a look around, and gone back. And in that moment, Robert felt as though he, too, were turning his back on dry land forever.

He followed the whale until he could no longer see it through the ice on his eyelashes, until his frozen hands could no longer control the Zodiac. He didn't remember losing consciousness; he only remembered waking much later, a Zodiac pulling up next to his, the crew of a tourist vessel helping him up, ushering him on board. A hot shower, a doctor, a private cabin.

He returned to the States, his mission a failure, as many missions were; agents learned to get past them and move on.

But Robert knew his failures went far beyond the mission, and there was no one he could tell. Aeneas, he learned, had survived; months later, the CDA announced a new mission, this one to Japan.

For more than a year, Robert looked for news about

Noa—anything. She was no longer a part of the CDA, but she didn't seem to be a part of any other organization either. There was no announcement of her death, no obituary—but Robert also knew that if she'd died on the ice, Aeneas would not want the bad publicity. His crew members, as he'd always said, came second to the cause, and no matter what happened, the CDA would persevere.

ETHAN

In Puerto Madryn, while most of the passengers were off at Punta Verde taking pictures of penguins, Ethan was in his stateroom lacing his shoes. He needed to take a jog, to clear his head, to get back to his old rituals. He needed to prepare for a life without Annie.

He'd been on the ship for more than ten days, and Annie had not shown up. And Ethan had not seen the *Arctic Tern* at any of their ports of call. Despite this, his mind had been relentlessly occupied with Annie, and he was now making an effort to empty the cache. He had to, if he was ever going to move on. He stopped checking e-mail, stopping using the search engines. He picked up a book on programming to give his mind something else to process.

There were still two hours before the ship was scheduled to leave. He didn't bother with stretching. He was anxious to escape the masses of people milling about on the pier, browsing the tourist stalls. He swiped his I.D. card and began jogging down the gangplank. The street was an obstacle course of tourists—cameras, a child on a leash screaming wildly, strollers, pedicabs, bicycles. Two miles later, Ethan reached the end of the Puerto Madryn harbor, stopped, and turned around. Even from a distance, the cruise ship loomed over the harbor. The thought of boarding it again made him cringe.

He made his way back to the ship, unintentionally scanning the face of every young woman he passed. As he neared the ship he began dodging people again. It wasn't just the passengers lining the sidewalk but people walking dogs, riding skateboards. It reminded him of the coastline back home—wherever water joined land, it seemed, humans fled toward it, as if there were some inexorable pull toward the water's edge.

Or maybe, Ethan wondered, it wasn't that people were drawn toward the water but that the water was holding them in. After all, they reached the edge, then stopped. At least, most people did.

Somehow, standing on the pier in Puerto Madryn, Ethan began to remember a frigid day in January, when he was thirteen and his dad had taken him to the St. Louis riverfront. The wind off the water was brutal, but he'd been young enough not to care. Back then, the riverfront was little more than cobblestones and mud, along with the skeleton of a tug boat that had sunk a long time ago. Ethan used to scan the shoreline for gold doubloons, remnants of the old riverboats that went down regularly in the 1800s. The old Eads Bridge stretched overhead, thick with brown stones and rusting iron. Casinos and condos were a good thirty years away still.

That day, Ethan noticed an old lady in a black overcoat and purse walking slowly to the water's edge. But this lady did not stop. Ethan watched her descend into the water as if walking down a flight of stairs, until her coat floated up around her like a lily pad. She continued down the stairs until her head disappeared in the brown water. Ethan looked over at his dad, who had just realized what was happening. His father ran into the water, dove down after her, and pulled her ashore.

People emerged from cars and the steps of the Gateway Arch. The lady was crying and shivering. The ambulance driver gave his dad a blue blanket with a red cross on it that ended up in their family room. His dad's picture was in the paper the next day.

It turned out that the lady had lost her husband three months before and was trying to join him. Ethan spent days and months wondering how she overcame her body's instincts to stay safe and warm and dry. How she stepped into that water so casually and with such purpose. He never had more respect for his father than that day—his father having thrown himself into the water to save an old lady, without hesitation, without fear. Yet it was the lady herself Ethan could not stop thinking about. The way she'd just kept going.

Now, his T-shirt drenched with sweat, Ethan approached the *Emperor of the Seas*. The lines to reboard were so long that he walked to the end of the pier to stretch. He noticed a much smaller ship docked at the end of the pier, a ship that seemed familiar. As he looked more closely, he felt his pulse quicken, as if he were still running.

He had seen this ship before. In the magazine Annie had left behind. Its picture on websites and brochures and news articles. Ethan had tracked it for months over the Internet but had never seen it in person.

The *Arctic Tern*. A three-story ship painted white. Antennas all over, like thorns from a cactus. A quietly spinning radar dish. A blue-and-white mural of a whale on each side. And a long ramp that reached down to him, inviting him in. People his age and younger rushed up and down the ramp, ferrying boxes and plastic cartons of vegetables. It was a chaotic scene, as if they were trying to beat a deadline.

He looked for Annie. She was not on the pier, nor on any part of the deck he could see. But there was so much he couldn't see. He would have to go inside. There was no such thing as randomness in computers, no such thing as luck—but life was a different matter. Was this where luck ended and destiny began?

Ethan picked up a crate of potatoes. He took a first step, without hesitation, without fear. Then another. His mind flashed back to that day on the banks of the Mississippi. Up the ramp he walked. Onto the deck. Into the ship. With purpose, like that old lady, like his father.

He just kept going.

PART III

ANGELA

THE WAVES CAME TO HER IN A DREAM. She felt her body, buoyant and lithe, pulled over them, floating just above the water, like a wandering albatross, her wings spread wide. Then she felt herself lifted up high on a burst of air until she was riding in the crow's nest of an ancient schooner. Dark clouds obscured the sky and sank so low she could almost touch them. She looked down and watched waves breaching the deck of her boat, until it was consumed entirely, the mast disappearing into black water. Penguins porpoised over the waves surrounding her, hundreds of them, circling in formation. She could feel them watching her. She wanted to dive in, to follow them to wherever they went when they left her shores. She was not afraid of the darkness, not afraid of drowning. She was ready to be with them, at last in their world, just below the waterline.

When Angela opened her eyes, she was in a dark room, alone in a single bed. She turned her head to the side. The bed across the narrow aisle was empty, the sheets twisted in knots, remnants of her first night aboard. The night before, Aeneas had paraded her through the ship's hallways, lined with crew members greeting him like a hero returned from battle. Angela felt like Aeneas's trophy, or his captive; all eyes were upon her, curious and probing. Back at Punta Verde, she'd always dressed to blend into the landscape; here, there was no blending in. As she watched the crew members study her, she realized how difficult it would be to fit into shoes that she'd rarely worn—she wasn't accustomed to the role of girlfriend or lover, let alone the girlfriend or lover of an eco-terrorist. And yet by association she had now become one of them—an activist and a pirate, on a wave-tossed descent to the bottom of the planet.

They had lingered in the galley after dinner, celebrating Aeneas's return over glasses of vodka. Angela sat next to D. J., the second mate and ship navigator. A clean-cut man in his thirties, he spoke quietly about coordinates and dates, and Aeneas assured him they would make up for lost time.

But it clearly wasn't meant to be a working evening. By his third glass of vodka, Aeneas's voice and mannerisms amplified; he grew more animated, holding up his penguin-scarred hands for all to see, standing to recite a poem:

> Will ye come down the water-side,
> To see the fishes sweetly glide
> Beneath the hazels spreading wide,
> And the moon that shines full clearly.

As his words segued into song, members of the crew joined in, as if this were a longtime family ritual. Eventually the entire room echoed with melancholy voices, and Angela was the only silent one, made even more self-conscious by Aeneas's eyes on her as he sang.

> While waters wimple to the sea,
> While day blinks in the sky so high,
> Till clay-cold death shall blind my eye,
> Ye I shall be thy dearie.

Song had followed song until the bottle was empty, and Aeneas led her again through the maze of narrow hallways, rooms, and stairways to his cabin—to *their* cabin, he called it.

"I don't even know your real name," Angela said.

"It's Neil Cameron," he replied. "But few of us go by our real names, particularly those of us with names on wanted lists. It's safer that way, for everyone."

"What about my name?"

"How about we call you *pingüina*?"

Just then she'd wondered what she'd gotten herself into, and the fear must have shown up in her eyes because Aeneas pulled her to him and hugged her tight. "Don't worry," he said. "You are safe here, and I am not leaving you. We're a team."

When he kissed her, she could forget the chaos and doubts of the last twelve hours, the momentary panic attacks about having abandoned her one and only career. His lips were warm and they relaxed her, and she had not felt relaxed for many years. How could she when a half million penguins needed to be protected? How could she waste a moment on a kiss when there was tagging to be done, data to gather? The few old friends who visited her at Punta Verde used to tell her how they envied her simple life, as if it were a vacation. But not once in her fifteen years at Punta Verde had she ever taken time off to read a book or spend the day in town or sleep in. Maybe if she had, she wouldn't be here now.

The bed was small, but they made the most of it. His back against the wall, sideways across the bed, feet propped against the other bed across the aisle. Her straddling him. Their noises camouflaged by the engine below. The movement of the ship bringing them together, then apart, then together again, in a slow rocking unison that made her forget everything else.

But this morning, the waves were no longer so generous. Angela sat up and looked out the small window and saw a clear sky, wind-blown waves—no land. Suddenly the boat dropped beneath her, and she fell back into bed and pressed her eyes shut.

Humans may have come from the sea, Angela reflected, but that was a long time ago, and bodies have a short-term memory. It wasn't her first time on open ocean, and she knew her body would resist the motion, in vain, before finally adapting. But this time, it was not only her body that would have to adapt. She found herself listening for the sound of penguins calling out to one another, for the gentle scratching of wings against the floor below her feet, for the steady drumbeat of wind against the single-paned window of her trailer. Now she could hear only the straining roar of the ship's engine somewhere far below.

She stood, uneasily at first, and emerged from her room, arms held up to brace herself against the doorframe. She squeezed past a large cluttered map table and an array of radios and terminals. Maps carpeted the linoleum floor. She stepped over them and through a doorway, then pulled herself up a flight of stairs to the bridge.

In the middle of the room was a chest-high control console, and to its left stood Aeneas, his face pressed to the glass. He seemed lost in the tempest of white-capped waves ahead of him.

D. J. stood behind the controls at the wheel. To his right, another crew member, a young man wearing a baseball cap and a tattoo of a skull and crossbones on the back of his neck, studied a radar screen. Angela considered introducing herself, but she didn't want to break their concentration.

"Steady one five," Aeneas mumbled.

D. J. repeated the command rapid-fire, hands loose on the small wooden wheel, so tiny in comparison to the ship that it looked almost ornamental.

Angela took a few tentative steps toward Aeneas, not wanting to disrupt the quiet, the sense of peace that filled this warm windowed room overlooking a wild sea. "Morning," she said softly.

Aeneas turned and winked. He did not make a move toward her, so she followed his lead and stayed where she was.

"We're well into the Drake Passage now," he said. "You're holding up pretty well."

"It's not my first time across."

"Oh, yes. I forgot. You were once the entertainment on a cruise ship."

"They use the term 'naturalist.'"

"Of course they do." He arched his eyebrows, and she couldn't help but smile back. She approached the window so she could stand next to him, her left arm touching his right. They looked out over the madness of water, and as sheets of rain began to pelt the windows, she imagined them as an old married couple, silent and calm. She wanted to hold his hand, to reach out and stroke the soft skin of his neck, but she did not. This was his place of work, his office, and she was only a visitor.

Aeneas mumbled something, and his mumble was echoed by D. J. Angela realized then that these two were more like a married couple than she and Aeneas were—they were the ones who spoke a secret language, who read each other's minds.

Aeneas reached into one of the bulging pockets of his jacket and pulled out a Blow Pop. He offered it to her, and she shook her head. "One of our supporters works at this company," he said as he unwrapped it. "Sends us a case of them before every trip. Lauren won't touch them because she doesn't believe they're vegan."

"Are they?"

"Of course."

"Who's Lauren?" Angela asked.

His eyes scanned the horizon, binoculars in one hand, Blow Pop stick in the other. She wasn't sure whether he hadn't heard her or whether he'd ignored her. For the first time it occurred to her that he now had the advantage that she'd so comfortably held on land. Now he was back in his element, and she was as lost on his turf as he'd been on hers.

"What are you looking for?" she asked.

"Icebergs. It's premature, probably, but I prefer that we see them before we hear them." His eyes remained focused on the outside.

Angela felt hunger growing within her and asked, "Have you eaten already?"

"I don't eat breakfast. But there's food in the galley." He glanced down at her, as if just remembering that she was new to the ship. "Want me to show you the way?"

"I can find it. Better that I get lost than we hit an iceberg."

She slid open the door and exited the bridge, where a burst of cold air slapped her fully awake. She stood at the rail for a few moments, watching the waves, catching the eye of a wandering albatross gliding past. It had been years since she last made this passage, and seeing the albatross felt like greeting an old companion.

She climbed down the stairs, back into the ship. She could hear music playing in the cabins as she passed, young voices talking and laughing. It reminded her of a college dormitory, and she felt stuck on the outside looking in, as she always had back in school. Those awkward years were nothing she wanted to repeat, but the feelings were still so vivid, those situations in which she'd always existed on the periphery.

In junior high, she'd lost herself in books, in backyards climbing trees. Most afternoons she hiked through a small patch of woods near her house, surrounded by industrial parks and divided by railroad tracks. She was too stubborn to worry about the risks of a young girl alone in the trees. She was invisible there, watching the older kids smoking pot in a clearing, imagining herself climbing aboard the trains that passed. While other kids were memorizing their lines for *Arsenic and Old Lace* or tossing a basketball around a humid gymnasium, she was watching squirrels bark at one another and hide acorns under leaves, or sometimes just pretending to hide things, to throw the other squirrels off. She had watched the birds, learned their names and voices: the cardinals calling to one another with their unmistakably sharp lyrics; the blue jays gathering on the tree limbs to harass a migratory Swainson's hawk, nipping at its feet in flight. Now, looking back, it was clear that she'd been on a path to becoming a naturalist. Perhaps if she'd had a boyfriend in school, he may have distracted her from her journey. But she was too busy nursing chicks that had fallen from nests back to health.

She passed by the closed cabin doors and found her way to the galley, a cramped room with four tables of various makes and sizes, each half-occupied. She felt eyes upon her as she navigated between the tables to a stainless steel counter that held what looked like breakfast. A man stood behind it, preparing coffee. "Hello, Angela," he said.

She recognized the face and smiled, wishing she could remember the name that went along with it.

"Garrett," he reminded her. "The chef."

"Yes, right."

"We've got pumpkin scones, Tofurkey sausages, the usual fruits and cereals. There is always plenty of everything when we're in the Drake Passage, with so many of the crew forgetting to take their meclizine tablets."

A tall blond woman brushed up against Angela and reached for an apple. Angela took a step back and offered her hand. "Pardon me. I'm Angela."

"I know who you are," the woman said, without looking up. She grabbed her apple and left. Angela turned to Garrett with a quizzical look.

"That's Lauren," he said. "Not exactly the warm and fuzzy type."

"What does she do?"

"Keeps the ship fueled, running, on time. We're off schedule, incidentally, which she's none too happy about."

"And I'm the reason why."

"Please. We've *never* been on schedule. Not with Aeneas at the helm. Every day's an adventure with our dear captain."

Garrett guided Angela around the room, stopping at each table and offering up names, too many to memorize. She focused on three at a time, the friendliest faces so far: Maggie, Hedley, Ben. Maggie, young and fresh-faced, wore a wrinkled CDA T-shirt. Hedley looked his role as first engineer, his long hair dirty and frayed as if from long hours in the engine room. Ben seemed to have more tattoos than skin to hold them; flames crawled up his neck and circled his ears.

Angela sat down next to Hedley with a scone and a mug of coffee, listening to the group banter over who clogged the toilet next to the meeting room, over why Maggie hadn't been in her bunk earlier that morning. And then Angela's mind returned to Lauren, to that stoic Roman face, devoid of emotional crevices and flaws, and she wondered how Lauren fit into the social structure of this mostly volunteer crew. Angela realized that this ship likely suffered from many of the same dynamics of her research base, and she wondered whether she'd simply traded a soap opera on land for one at sea.

"Is there a restroom on this level?" Angela asked.

"Down the hallway, on the left," Maggie said.

Angela thanked her and stood. "I think those waves are taking their toll after all."

"Or Garrett's cooking," Ben said.

They laughed, and Angela left, her breakfast uneaten. She didn't feel seasick; she simply needed to get out of there. She walked to the end of the hall, down a flight of stairs and then another, until there was nowhere else to go. The hallway was uncarpeted and dimly lit. She saw a room marked STORAGE and entered. The room, piled high with boxes, was lit by a tiny porthole. She approached the window and felt at first as if she were looking into a washing machine, eye level with the white tips of waves, dousing the glass, leaving streaks behind only to be erased again by the next wave.

Alone at last, she leaned her head against the thick glass. This was not how she imagined her voyage would be. Eyes following her every move. Not knowing where to turn for a moment alone. She'd never considered that she was stepping not only into Aeneas's life but into the lives of so many others—people who may not want her here, or at best, didn't care. At Punta Verde, escape was always just a hill away. On a boat in the middle of the Drake Passage, she had no refuge.

She looked at her watch. Though she felt as if she'd been awake for days, it was still only mid-morning. She imagined her camp, a few hundred miles to the north. It was Tuesday, which meant Shelly would be checking on the chicks in Back Bay. Doug would most likely be assisting. Others would be scattered north and south of the research station. And Shelly would have been the first to have read the hastily scribbled note in the office:

Leave of absence. Left by boat. Please forgive me.
—Angela

Would Shelly have been surprised? Would they now be missing her, as much as she was missing them?

She heard a noise behind her. Heart jumping, she whirled around to see a large cardboard box fall from the top of its stack, revealing a man in a white T-shirt that read CREW. Angela tried to step back and found herself pressed up against the porthole.

"I'm sorry," the man said. "I didn't mean to frighten you."

He was soft-spoken and sounded harmless, but she noticed that he didn't look quite like the other crew members.

Maybe it was the absence of tattoos on his arms, or the fact that his dark hair was short and neatly trimmed. He was tall, though slumped shoulders belied his height. And he looked away as she stared at him.

"I don't believe we've met," she said.

"Oh, no. I'm Ethan."

"Angela."

He locked on her eyes for a moment, then looked down.

"Is everything okay?" she asked.

"Yes. It's just that, well, I'm new here."

"That's refreshing. So am I." She smiled, but she wasn't sure he noticed; he didn't hold her gaze for more than a couple of seconds.

"No. I'm *really* new."

"I boarded last night," she said. "I'll bet you can't beat that."

He looked at her, surprised. "Last night?"

"Yes."

A weight appeared to lift from his shoulders, and though he didn't smile, she could see his chest moving again.

"I boarded in Puerto Madryn," he said.

"Oh?"

"To be honest, I'm not supposed to be on board at all."

"That makes two of us."

"No, I mean"—he paused and leaned forward—"I'm a stowaway."

Angela laughed and waited for him to join in, but he only looked at her. "You're serious?" she asked.

He nodded. "I'm afraid so."

"What about your uniform?"

He looked down at his CREW T-shirt and laughed awkwardly. "This? I just needed a change of clothes. I found a whole box of these in here."

Angela studied him, not sure how to respond. What she

knew she *should* do was leave the room and report him to Aeneas—but she didn't relish the idea of returning to a room full of strangers when she could stay down here with only one. And Ethan certainly didn't look dangerous; she'd probably handled penguins that could put up a better fight than he could.

"Please—don't tell anyone," he continued, as if sensing her unease. "I don't mean any harm. I was planning to get off the ship before it left, but the next thing I knew, it was pulling out of the harbor. I planned to turn myself in. I honestly did."

"Then why didn't you?"

"I was about to, but when I went up to the deck to find the captain, I saw him pointing a gun at this fishing boat. I figured it would be wise to lay low for a little while longer."

Angela felt a pang of guilt, knowing what drove Aeneas to board that fishing boat: the pursuit of a penguin tag, the one now dangling around her neck. She had never paused to think about those fishermen. But now that she was here, having left her anger behind on the shores of Punta Verde, she realized that she was as complicit as Aeneas. A pirate by proxy. She told herself that the fishermen were okay, that the sunken ship was insured.

But now she faced Ethan, another victim, albeit indirect. "So why'd you come on board in the first place?" she asked.

"I'm looking for someone. My girlfriend, Annie Miller. Do you know her?"

Angela shook her head. "But I don't know everyone yet. Are you sure she's here?"

He nodded. "She invited me to come along, but I was—well, the timing wasn't right. That is, until I came across this ship in Puerto Madryn. I thought I'd try to find her."

"Then why are you hiding?"

"I'm not hiding from her. I'm hiding from that crazy captain."

Angela sighed. "That crazy captain is my boyfriend." She watched his eyes expand.

"If I find Annie, she'll vouch for me," he said. "I'm just not sure how to do it without getting caught first."

He had a sad look about him, the look of someone left behind or lost, a feeling Angela could identify with, now more than ever. It made her feel sympathetic toward him, even though she wasn't sure what to do with him.

"Let me find her," Angela said. "Stay here, okay?"

Ethan nodded. She could only imagine how Aeneas would react if he knew she was hiding a stowaway. But a part of her enjoyed having a secret of her own, knowing that there was one person on this boat more lost than she.

She went out to the side deck for some air. The sun was still hidden by clouds ahead, but the horizon was outlined in a brighter, almost silvery shade. The waves were high—sea spray moistened her face, and she had to grip the railing to stay upright. They had to be close to the Antarctic Convergence, she realized—where the oceans of the north met the Southern Ocean, warm waters colliding with icy cold, a wild roil that made her wonder what other conflicts awaited her. Again she felt a twinge of regret for having left, but perhaps it was inevitable, part of the natural cycle of her existence, that she would one day leave her penguins in the same fashion they had, for years, left her: an awkward, hurried dash into an unpredictable sea.

ETHAN

ETHAN WATCHED ANGELA shut the door behind her, then closed his eyes. He pictured her ascending the ship, floor by floor, entering each room, asking for Annie. Could it be this simple? A human search engine, operating on his behalf? He smiled at the idea that Angela might accomplish in one afternoon what had eluded him for days, months. He imagined Annie's face as Angela delivered the news, those crystal blue eyes framed by ever-widening eyelids. She would hurry down the stairs and burst through that metal door to find Ethan waiting, arms poised to hold her again.

Unless, of course, Ethan had misread Angela. Understanding people and their intentions wasn't exactly his strong suit. Maybe instead of looking for Annie, Angela was looking for the captain.

Ethan opened his eyes, fixing them on the door. Any moment the captain could barge through, face blistered with rage, screaming like he did at those poor fishermen, set adrift as they helplessly watched their boat sink. Ethan had witnessed it all from behind a stack of Zodiacs on the rear deck, body shaking from the wind and from the realization that he himself could very well end up at the receiving end of that gun. He was not about to be set adrift in the South Atlantic Ocean, not after having come this far. And he was not going to leave this ship without Annie.

So he'd returned to the storage room and prepared for

an extended stay. He searched the boxes and found a few blankets, bottled water, a crate of organic potato chips. What a change from the *Emperor of the Seas*. From a hot tub to a cold floor, a king size bed to a cubbyhole hidden behind wooden crates. The constant dampness. The smell of brine. Moisture beading down the innards of the steel hull, patches of steel welded over patches of rust, a reminder of how tenuous these walls were and how near the ocean he lay. Yet it was all worth it. He was living an adventure now, just like Annie, and soon they'd be living it together.

During the late hours of the night, Ethan had ventured forth from his room to search for her. Careful to stay in the shadows, he avoided the lounge and the galley, the front deck and the bridge. He spent most of his time on the rear deck, hoping that she, too, was unable to sleep, that she might wander past. Needing fresh air, she would find him there in his CREW T-shirt, covered in the dry, salty sweat of sacrifice, and she would forget everything that drove them apart.

ROBERT

ROBERT WOKE ON THE STEEL FLOOR of his cabin, his forehead throbbing. He looked up to see Lynda standing over him. As she helped him back into bed, he let out a low moan.

"I brought you some ginger soup," she said. "They tell me it's good for the stomach."

"I'm not hungry."

"You should be."

"How long have I been down here?"

"About twelve hours. We're nearly across the Drake."

"Aeneas?"

"Not yet. But we've got his ship on the radar; we're getting close. I figured you'd want to join the party."

Robert sat up. Either the waves had relented, or he was finally getting used to them. A day ago, after they had entered the Drake, and the boat tossed Lynda across the bridge, Robert had teased her about getting seasick. *You boys in Washington think all we do is lie around on beaches*, she fired back.

If the shoe fits.

I spend half my days out on the water making drug busts, she said. *Worry about yourself. I'll be fine.*

Now, Lynda sat next to him on the bed as he fought through the fog in his head. He considered the soup, but his stomach still wasn't settled.

"Maybe Aeneas isn't so smart after all," Lynda said.

"What do you mean?"

"He was free of us. Had a clear shot to Antarctica. And then he goes and sinks that fishing boat. It doesn't add up."

"He'll attack any fishermen, not just the ones who hunt whales."

"So why'd he drain its tanks of oil before putting it down?"

"He didn't want the oil to pollute the ocean."

"Right. Aeneas is an *environmental* pirate. Maybe I'd know that already if I had someone to give me a proper briefing."

"I told you everything you need to know."

"Who's Noa?" Lynda asked.

"What?"

"You said her name. In your sleep."

Robert remembered his dream: Noa standing on the bridge, Jake behind her. They were somewhere in the North Atlantic; it didn't matter where. She leaned into him, and he put his arms around her waist. Neither of them spoke—it was a passing moment, and then she was called away. But the way she felt in his arms, the way he felt with her there—everything had aligned. In the dream, he had become Jake again, and he'd been exactly where he was supposed to be in life, and somehow he knew it, was certain of it.

"You know, Bobby, I can keep a secret," Lynda said. "Especially if it's my own partner's."

"Even if he violated policy? Lied to his superiors?"

"Especially if he violated policy and lied to his superiors. So what gives?"

Robert wanted to tell her. He was tired of carrying Noa's memory around all these years. But when he looked at Lynda, he caught the flicker of her eyes toward the door, and he knew he couldn't. Not now, anyway.

"Just a bad dream, I guess."

Lynda shook her head and opened the door. He felt a dry rush of cold air, sensing the change in atmosphere.

"Did I miss anything else up there?" he called after her.

She turned. "Captain Zamora made a pass at me."

"You sure *he's* not seasick?" Robert forced a smile.

"Ah, your sense of humor has returned, I see. I liked you better comatose."

She left Robert alone, and he cursed himself silently—for talking when he should've kept his mouth shut, for not talking when he'd had the chance. Yet a part of him worried that if he began talking about Noa, if the memories were spoken aloud, they might somehow not be his any longer—or worse, they might disappear entirely.

ANGELA

ANGELA SAVORED THE NIGHTS. Back when she was on land, her days were busy yet without a destination—no reason for ending, only solitary evenings in a leaky trailer. But out here, though her days were empty, she always had night to look forward to.

Like now—waiting for Aeneas under the threadbare white sheet of the bunk, listening to voices beyond the door in the map room. Earlier she'd left him with his crew to plan the next day's strategy and, knowing Aeneas, to have a drink or two afterward. She was beginning to think he'd be up most of the night, but then, just as she was about to fall asleep, she heard the creak of the cabin door opening, heard him stumble in. In the light from the hall she could see him smiling. He gazed at the outline of her body, and she waited. At times during the day, it seemed as if Aeneas barely recognized her, as if she hardly existed—but at night, alone in their cabin, his attention was singularly directed at her, as intensely as it was directed at whalers during the day.

Aeneas dropped a CD into a portable stereo, and the *Carmina Burana* blared. He kneeled next to her, put his hands under the sheet, moved them upward. When he kissed her, she tasted whiskey. She watched his face as he lifted the sheet and let it flutter down to the floor.

The next morning, Angela lay in bed, wishing the sun away. Soon Aeneas would leave her for the bridge. At least now her days were no longer aimless: She had a stowaway to feed, a purpose. She'd decided not to ask Aeneas about Annie last night. She should begin with a lower-ranking crew member; Aeneas had enough on his mind as it was. As he slept, his eyelids flickered, his lips twitched, and his arms and legs were in constant motion. Even in sleep, he never seemed to fully relax. He never spoke about the danger of his work, but she knew it weighed on him. Along with the volunteer who died. That there was a reason he kept a supply of alcohol on board.

She reached around to the back of her neck and unclasped the chain that held Diesel's stainless steel tag. She held it in her hand for a moment, then leaned over Aeneas, letting the tag rest on his bare chest as she hooked the clasp around his neck.

Aeneas awoke suddenly and tried to sit up. Then he winced and fell back into bed.

"Hangover?" she asked.

"Slightly." He turned his head toward her. "You slept well?" he asked.

She nodded, smiling. "I hope we weren't too loud last night."

"They don't call this latitude the roaring forties for nothing." He kissed her on the lips, then raised his head again as if contemplating another attempt at standing. She watched his hands find the chain around his neck.

"What's this?" he asked.

"My penguin tag."

"What's it doing around my neck?"

"I thought you could wear it for luck."

"I don't wear leashes."

"Penguins don't like them much either," she said, "but at least they don't complain."

"Angela—"

"It's too late. You're wearing it," she said, and stared at

him until he blinked.

"Very well. I will wear it on *loan*," he grumbled. "The minute this trip is over, I'm returning it."

"Fine." She noticed that the sheet had slipped when Aeneas reached out and cupped one of her breasts. She laughed and gave him a playful shove. "Don't you have a boat to drive?"

"What boat?" He chuckled. "They won't need me until we get into the icebergs. We still have plenty of latitude left." Then he slid his other hand down her thigh.

ANGELA ENTERED THE STORAGE ROOM carrying a sandwich and two chocolate chip cookies. Ethan sat on a wooden crate against the wall, below the lone porthole. He looked past her expectantly, as if hoping to see someone else. Angela felt bad for closing the door behind her.

When she'd brought him food that morning, he'd asked her about Annie within seconds of her entering the room. Now, she could tell by the look on his face that he was resisting the urge to do so again. She was relieved, because she had not yet found Annie.

It was a simple task, and she was embarrassed by her lack of success—but the truth was, she hadn't found the right person to ask. She still felt as though she were in the way on this ship—the crew members rushing around with their own jobs, turning down her offers to help as if they didn't trust her to do them. At least down here with Ethan, she could relax, and she knew he wasn't the type to judge.

Ethan stood and accepted the food. "Thank you," he said.

"I also brought you this." Angela reached into her jacket and held up a paperback copy of *Endurance*. "Something to pass the time."

He studied the back cover.

"It's about Ernest Shackleton," she said. "I found it in the lounge. Have you read it?"

Ethan shook his head and sat on the floor with the food. Angela took her position across from him, feeling the cold steel through her khakis. She'd done the same thing that morning, sitting with him as he ate, because it made her sad to think of him eating alone. But they sat in silence; talking did not come naturally to Ethan, as he'd confessed when he told her he was a computer programmer for an online matchmaking company. *I'm better at communicating with databases than with people,* he'd said.

He also avoided eye contact, and she assumed he was shy. Now she sensed there was something more, something beyond mere geekiness. An emptiness. An emotional vacuum that exerted an odd pull upon her. Or perhaps it was just that she could not resist the natural attraction between a scientist and an unsolved mystery.

THAT AFTERNOON, TO MAKE HERSELF USEFUL—and to maintain access to food for Ethan without drawing suspicion—Angela volunteered to help Garrett in the galley. He was short an assistant, and she was eager to be productive, to get her mind off the world she left behind.

Garrett's stream-of-consciousness meanderings were a welcome alternative to Aeneas's bouts of taciturnity, and she learned more from Garrett about the crew than she would have ever learned from Aeneas. Like D. J.'s pet gerbil, which lived in his cabin. Or Maggie's sexual orientation toward females, which was obvious to everyone except, apparently, Maggie. Or the time, two seasons ago, when Hedley married Garrett's assistant on the way down to Antarctica, only to get divorced on their way back—both sets of papers signed by Aeneas.

And then there were Aeneas's marriages, which Garrett documented in great detail. First was Jennifer, a scuba instructor from Miami, who joined the crew during the second season. She caught Aeneas cheating on her with his soon-to-be second wife, Deborah, the one from Los Angeles who divorced him in absentia when he failed to return home for two years. That was the only marriage Aeneas had told her about.

Though she did not show it, as Garrett continued, Angela could feel a part of herself shutting down, like a ship preparing for a storm. She found herself reverting back into the role of naturalist—a scientist, emotionally detached—and she began to think about Aeneas not as the man in her life but as another animal to be studied: its mating rituals, peculiarities, habits. Love and science occupied opposite ends of the continuum, but she knew that if she and Aeneas were to have a chance as a couple, she'd need to find a way to handle his personality, to take his past and his risks and everything else with the same dispassion she used in her work.

She wanted to make it work, to combine love and science, but Garrett was confirming that Aeneas was no different than the other men she had known in her life—lovely and passionate in brief doses, delegating attention long enough to make her fall for them but not long enough, never long enough, to make her stay. Nature was cruel, yet she'd grown accustomed to it. Love, too, was cruel, but when it came to love, she was still soft.

"So where's Annie been hiding herself?" she asked Garrett, forcing a change in subject. "I think she's the only crew member I haven't met yet."

"Annie?"

"Annie Miller."

Garrett's stopped chopping the carrots and gave her a quizzical look. "Have you asked Aeneas?"

"No. Why?"

"There is nobody named Annie on this ship," he said.

"Are you sure about that?"

"I think I should know." He put down the knife. "Time for a smoke."

She watched him leave and turned back to the carrots. The sudden silence in the galley was unnerving—not to mention Garrett's reaction to being asked about Annie Miller. Angela began to wonder about Ethan's story. He'd seemed so earnest, but perhaps he was mistaken; perhaps he'd jumped onto the wrong ship.

Or perhaps Ethan was the one she should be questioning. She'd been feeling so lost on the ship that she'd embraced him too quickly, without any evidence whatsoever that he was who he claimed to be. She suddenly wished she was back where she belonged, walking among the *quilembai* bushes, hearing her penguins calling to one another. That was where her world made sense.

Lauren poked her head in the galley. When she made eye contact with Angela, what little of a smile she was wearing disappeared. "Where's Garrett?"

"Up on deck," Angela said. "Lauren, I—"

But Lauren was already gone, the door swinging back and forth. Angela caught up with her in the hallway.

"You're clearly not happy that I'm on board," Angela said. "Why?"

"If I'm being short with you, it's because I've got other things on my mind, like making up for lost time."

"Due to me."

"Due to the FBI. Look, I'm here for the whales and the whales only. True, I don't have a great fondness for starry-eyed girlfriends who hop aboard thinking they're on the Love Boat—but it's nothing personal. Stay out of my way, and we'll get along just fine."

Lauren disappeared up the stairs, leaving Angela alone in the hallway. She didn't bother returning to the galley but instead made her way to the rear deck, where she would be shielded from the wind and from people. Once there, she saw that the albatross was still tracking the ship, gliding off the wind currents, hitching an effortless ride south to Antarctica. Wings outstretched, locked in place, the bird slowly circled the ship, as if suspended by wire on an equatorial mobile. She envied the bird its ability to stay so close and yet remain a few feet above it all, at perfect ease. If for only a minute she could exhibit such grace, such economy of motion, confidence, and calm, perhaps then she would not be standing alone.

Smoke from the diesel engine drifted into her hair and made her cough and turn toward the water. Below, a line of churned water fanned out into the distance. The wind at her back was a familiar feeling, bringing to mind days spent staring out at the sea from the hills of Punta Verde. But she could no longer hear the penguins, just the deep roar of an engine.

She felt an arm on her shoulder and looked up to see Aeneas. "There you are," he said. He kissed her forehead. "I thought for a moment you went overboard."

"Not yet," she said.

"Not yet?"

"Did I make the right decision?" she asked.

"How do you mean?"

"Joining you. Here."

"Of course you made the right decision."

"I feel as if I'm intruding."

"This is my ship. You are my guest. How could you ever intrude?"

"There are a few on this boat who may have a different opinion. Lauren, for one."

"She's got her hands full right now. Give her time."

Something caught his eyes, and he looked over Angela's

left shoulder. She followed his gaze but saw only waves. On land, she could spot a penguin under a bush from a quarter mile, while Aeneas couldn't see it until he was nearly on top of it. Out here, she was the blind one, the one in need of direction. She wasn't sure she'd ever adjust to this new arrangement, this loss of control. The confidence that she had back in Punta Verde had evaporated.

"You slept with her," she said suddenly, the thought occurring to her in that very moment.

"Who?"

"Lauren."

Aeneas paused, as if weighing his options. "Yes," he said. "Before I met you. Not since."

"You could've told me," she said. "At least I'd have been prepared."

"I didn't think you wanted a complete inventory of my love life. I certainly don't want one of yours."

"It would be a quick read," she mumbled.

He smiled and gently put an arm around her waist. "Angela, I am a sailor, not a monk. But that is all past tense now."

She pulled away. "Past tense for you, maybe. You told me you were only married once when we first met."

"I did?"

"Yes. You lied."

"I needed shelter. And, as you may recall, I was rather desperate."

"You're always desperate."

"Angela, I've spent a decade of my life defending whales, and occasionally I go too far. I bend the truth. I lie. One thing I've learned is that when you get too attached to something, whether a whale or a person, you do silly things, stupid things. I am a flawed man, and for that I apologize. But we are not all that different, you and I, which is why I wanted you here, which is why I'm glad you came."

She looked into his eyes for something she could hold on to, but he glanced past her again out into the ocean, wordless. She used to revel in his long bouts of silence. But now she wondered what else he was lying about by omission.

He pointed. "Look. Two o'clock. A sperm whale."

Angela turned around, and in the distance she made out what looked like an off-white, barnacled Volkswagen bus, parked between whitecaps. Almost motionless, the whale appeared to stand in place, watching them pass. She realized that Aeneas wasn't evading her but simply looking for whales on the horizon—always one eye on the horizon.

"How did you spot him?" she asked.

"It was he who spotted us. Then he chose to make himself known."

"You sound as if they speak to you."

"In their language, yes, they do speak to me," he said. "Don't your penguins speak to you?"

She pictured Diesel standing outside her office, tapping at the door with his beak, like a dog wanting to be let in. The first time she'd heard his knock, she'd opened the door, and he'd hobbled over to the bookcase, peering at the Patagonian field guides as if he had a book in mind. His breath was raspy, like a purr, which she had never noticed outdoors on the wind-deafening hills. Angela had stood by the door, holding it open; Emily sat at the desk. They remained motionless as Diesel toured the cramped room, investigating every eye-level oddity—the half-open file cabinet, mud-stained Wellingtons, a pile of knee pads, a fire extinguisher. She imagined him as an explorer among penguins, one given to researching humans. Off alone in the field, sacrificing his childbearing years, all for the greater good of knowledge. What notes would he take? *The humans are easily approached, yet spastic in nature and prone to outbursts. They seem oddly attracted to Punta Verde.*

Most visit for a few hours and are gone again. Perhaps the land is of spiritual significance. Tagging them will prove challenging.

Diesel had returned to the bookcase and looked up at Angela. He wasn't about to leave on his own, and if she could have gone back in time, to that room on that morning, she would have closed the door instead of ushering him back outside.

Aeneas put his arm around her again, and this time she did not resist. She turned to kiss him but a voice interrupted them. It was Lauren, standing just outside the door to the deck, speaking words they couldn't hear over the wind.

"What?" Aeneas pointed to his ear. Lauren walked closer, ignoring Angela.

"The radar," Lauren said. "We've got company."

Aeneas looked back at Angela, as if to apologize. She nodded and watched him follow Lauren back into the ship.

Robert

RADAR WAS USELESS NOW. Robert stared helplessly at a screen littered with shards of green static. The shards were icebergs, many as tall and wide as the Pentagon, and the *Arctic Tern* was a dot small enough to hide in their shadows. Just an hour ago, Robert was watching the dot racing toward what he thought at the time was an archipelago. Now he knew why the *Tern* was headed there in such a hurry: to hide itself among the icebergs.

Robert stepped outside to the wing deck and looked out over the floating white cathedrals. Above him, the clouds looked like galvanized steel. Captain Zamora was not nearly as reckless as Aeneas, and the *Roca* was now traveling in slow motion, tiptoeing around the white giants, careful not to disturb them, lest one of them awaken and roll over. Mother Nature was in charge now.

Lynda stood next to him. "Now I know why they painted their ship white," she said.

"We'll find them."

"Zamora wants to radio them."

"Tell him no."

"I told him. But he's going to call eventually."

"Aeneas won't respond."

"How can you be so sure?"

"Because I was with him when the Norwegian Coast Guard was on his tail. He never responded to them either. If you pretend your radio is broken, you can't be charged for not pulling over when ordered."

"That was a long time ago."

"Aeneas knows we're here, but he doesn't know if we're a tourist vessel, a fishing trawler, or what. He can't be sure until he sees us, or until Zamora gets on that radio and removes all doubt."

He could feel Lynda watching him, but he looked past her as he surveyed the horizon.

"Noa was Darwin, wasn't she?"

He raised his binoculars, as if he had seen something, but Lynda didn't take the bait.

"You heard me, so I'll just keep talking. Noa, the woman in that photo, the one you had your arm around, was Darwin, the suspect you had gone undercover to catch. And who, judging by the scant information you've provided, you *did* catch. Except, there's no record of it, nobody in prison—no body at all, in fact."

Robert looked at her finally. "What the hell are you getting at?"

"I'm trying to get at the truth. That's what I do, Bobby. And I don't appreciate being lied to, especially by my partner. That girl in the photo was Darwin. Right?"

Robert tried to convey a look of disinterest, but it was too late. She knew, and this little interplay was only to let him know that she knew.

"You still don't trust me, do you?" she said. "What sad little world do you live in?"

"This doesn't concern you."

"You think you're the first person in law enforcement history to boink a suspect?"

"I was a government agent."

"You were a man trapped on a boat with a woman. It's okay. I've seen her picture. She's hot, in a Woodstock sort of way. These things happen."

The satellite phone rang, and Lynda held it out to him. "It's for you," she said.

Robert looked at her. "Have you and Gordon been talking about this?"

"Jesus, Bobby, what would I have told him? I'm the last to know anything around here."

He took the phone and waited until she returned to the bridge.

"Where have you been?" Gordon asked.

"Under the weather."

"I thought you were immune to the ocean," Gordon said.

"I used to be."

"You have a visual yet?"

"No. We're within a mile. But I'm not sure if we should be chasing him through this ice field."

"What does your partner say?"

"She thinks we should wait him out, until the ships get back into open water."

"What do you think?"

"I don't think we're going to see much open water. And Aeneas would welcome the extra time. He would love to have a military vessel in tow when he meets up with the Japanese; it might give the whalers the impression that the Argentines are after them."

"I think you're right. And you should know that Greenpeace already has a ship shadowing the whalers right now, which means video cameras, blogs, you name it. If you're going to arrest him, best to take care of business now, before we become the stars of an anti-whaling documentary."

"Exactly how badly do you want us to catch Aeneas?"

"He says he's willing to martyr himself for the cause. If you happen to turn him into one, so be it."

After hanging up, Robert picked up his binoculars,

focusing again on the horizon. He was beginning to think that Aeneas had outsmarted him yet again, and then he saw it—movement between two icebergs. He looked again and noticed the faint blur of smoke rising from behind the ice. His heart jumped, and he returned to the bridge to find Lynda standing next to Zamora, who had the radio in his hand.

"What are you doing?" Robert asked. Zamora gave him a dismissive look.

"I warned him, Bobby, but it's his ship."

Robert felt the urge to grab the radio out of Zamora's hands. "What did he say?" he asked Lynda.

"He told Aeneas to silence his engines."

"Did Aeneas respond?"

"Nope."

"Figures."

"I bet he'd respond to you," Lynda said. She said something to Zamora, who held out the handset to Robert. After a lengthy pause, he accepted it.

"Aeneas, pick up the mic," Robert said into the speaker. No response. "Aeneas, I am offering you a chance to save your crew and your mission. If you surrender, they'll be free to continue on to find the Japanese. But if I have to come get you myself, I will take you all in with me, boat included."

The speaker crackled to life with a familiar voice, a sound that was as comforting as it was painful.

"Hello, Jake."

"It's Robert now."

"What brings you to these parts?"

"A warrant with your name on it."

"U.S. warrant?"

"That's right, and Argentina has one as well. They say you're a pirate."

"Pirate, eh?" Aeneas let out a mock laugh. "Well, shiver me timbers."

"You think this is funny?"

"No. I think it's shameful. You should be helping us, not chasing us. And you, Robert, of all people should know that."

"I have a job to do."

"So do I."

"You shouldn't have killed that girl," Robert said.

"A boatful of poachers killed that girl. Why don't you arrest them?"

"They're not on the warrant. You are. I'm sorry." And as he spoke the words, he realized that he really was sorry. Then he glanced over at Lynda, who wore a curious expression. He cleared his throat. "Silence your engines and prepare for boarding."

"I missed that last message, you're breaking up. We're losing you."

"Aeneas!" He turned to Lynda. "Tell Zamora to floor it."

ANGELA

ANGELA RETURNED TO THE STORAGE ROOM to find Ethan reclining against the wall beneath the porthole, reading *Endurance*.

He looked up when she entered the room. "Shackleton had a stowaway on his ship, too," he said.

"Who are you?" Angela asked him.

"Excuse me?"

"You heard me. Who are you?"

He looked startled. He closed the book and stood. "I told you. Ethan Downes."

"How come there's no one on this ship called Annie Miller?"

"I don't know."

"Somebody's lying to me. And I want to know who it is."

"It isn't me. I'm telling the truth. She was a volunteer with the CDA. She was planning to be on the crew of this ship. I swear."

"Prove it."

He paused before reaching into his pants pocket and removing a photograph. "I was wandering around the ship looking for her late last night, and I found this on a bulletin board." He handed it to her—a picture of a pretty young woman standing on a pier next to the *Tern*, facing the camera, smiling. And Aeneas, standing next to her, his arm around her shoulders.

"That's Annie," he said.

And then Angela understood why Garrett had reacted the way he did: He was covering for Aeneas, and poorly. Ethan's girlfriend must have been the victim of yet another love affair gone wrong—and, unlike Lauren, she hadn't stuck around to complete her tour of duty.

Ethan was watching her. "Do you believe me now?"

Angela nodded and handed the photograph back to him. "I'm sorry to tell you this, but Annie's not on this boat."

Suddenly, the boat heaved; the floor pushed her forward and into him, and he caught her in both arms. She winced as they slid to the floor, as boxes tumbled onto them, as he leaned over her to shield her. When they both managed to right themselves, she turned away from the look on his face: a sinking disappointment that she was certain mirrored her own.

She stood and brushed off her clothing. "I better go see what happened," she said.

When she emerged onto the open deck, the wind pushed her back against the ship. They were moving fast, dangerously so, and the icebergs appeared close enough to touch.

In the bridge, Lauren was behind the wheel. The tense, quiet faces of the others signaled something was wrong. Except for Aeneas, who was humming to himself, as if he were out for a Sunday drive.

"What's going on?" Angela asked.

Aeneas turned. "Where have you been hiding yourself?"

"I've just been downstairs."

"Come over here," Aeneas said. For the first time since she boarded, she hesitated to join him at his side. She sensed a coarseness in his manner, something she hadn't detected since Punta Verde, and she wondered again what she'd done, joining him here.

"You'll enjoy seeing this," he said, and she relented.

He kissed her on the forehead and handed her his binoculars. "Orcas. Eleven o'clock." He pointed, and Angela zoomed in on a pod of seven or eight whales. Yet her mind was not on them but on the man standing next to her, a man whose behaviors and mannerisms she was still cataloguing, still researching.

She'd learned that when he worked the bridge, he tugged at a lock of hair behind his left ear, leaving it sticking out oddly. That when he wasn't working, he drank his whiskey in large gulps, holding it in his mouth, like mouthwash, for several moments before finally releasing the liquid down his throat. She learned that he talked in private, even in the small cramped quarters of their shared cabin, in the same bellowing voice he used as commander of the ship. And then there was the steady stream of Blow Pops, one of which he held in his hand right now. Long after the candy was consumed, after the flavor had gone out of the gum, he gnawed on the white stick. Like an enormous toothpick, it remained in his mouth for hours, until he suddenly noticed it, flicked it into the trash, and reached into his pocket for another. She knew so much about his behavior but so little about his motives, the machinations occurring beneath that thick head of longish, uncombed hair. And she was beginning to doubt she would ever know.

She remembered the long diagonal scar on his back, which he told her during their first night together was from a ship's propeller. She'd believed him at the time—but times had changed. He was a man of heroic gestures, but he was also reckless: with the ship and, apparently, with the truth.

"What do you say, Lauren?" Aeneas said, looking over Angela's shoulder. "Should we pull over and say hi?"

"I'll drop you off, but I'm not slowing down," Lauren said.

Aeneas erupted in laughter. "D. J., what's the latest?"

"Less than two miles, and hauling ass."

Angela handed back his binoculars and started for the door, but he pulled her back to him and hugged her from behind. "Where are you going?" he asked.

"I'm going below." She tried to keep her voice down in the hopes that he would follow along. But Aeneas wasn't a man of subtlety.

Before she could head downstairs, the door on the other side of the bridge swung open. A man fell inside and onto the floor, followed by Hedley. At first, Angela thought someone had passed out drunk.

"Look what I found," Hedley said. "In the storage room."

Angela couldn't see behind the console, but she knew what was about to happen.

"Get on your feet," Hedley commanded.

And then Ethan pulled himself up, looking sheepish and awkwardly underdressed in his CREW T-shirt.

"Who the hell are you?" Aeneas bellowed.

"Ethan Downes." Ethan's voice trembled slightly, and Angela wondered if she was the only one who noticed. By now, she knew the rhythms of his voice and could tell by the way his eyes darted around the room that he was not as nervous as he may have appeared; he was simply looking for Annie.

Angela took Aeneas's hand, as if to hold him back, but he wrenched it away and circled the console until he was eye to eye with Ethan. They were the same height and build, but still Aeneas seemed to tower over him.

"I'm just a stowaway," Ethan sputtered.

"*Just a stowaway?*" Aeneas mimicked him. His anger made him cruel, Angela thought. "You expect me to believe that?"

"It's true," Angela said.

Aeneas turned to her. "You *know* him?"

"Yes. He's harmless. He's just looking for Annie Miller." Angela could tell by the way people responded—a mix of silence and slack jaws—that she had touched a nerve. But what nerve exactly, she didn't know.

Aeneas looked at Angela, then Ethan. "What do you want with Annie?"

"That's between me and her," Ethan said.

"You're lucky I don't throw you overboard right now."

"I know. I saw how you treated those fishermen."

"On second thought—" Aeneas stepped toward Ethan, and Angela stepped in between.

"Stop it!" She held out her arms and pushed them both backward a step. "Aeneas, Ethan is only looking for Annie. He doesn't mean any harm."

"Don't be so gullible, Angela," Aeneas said. "He's no stowaway. He's a spy."

"I'm not a spy. I'm looking for Annie. Truly."

"I'll be the judge of that. Where did you board our ship?"

"Puerto Madryn."

"What were you doing there?"

"I was on a cruise ship. *Emperor of the Seas.*"

"That floating ghetto docked next to us?"

"Yes. I swear."

Aeneas paused for a long moment, looking from Ethan to Angela and then back again. "Annie Miller is dead."

Ethan stared back at him. "No. She can't be."

"She's dead, son. That much I do know." He looked at Angela again, and she knew, with a sick feeling, that he was serious.

"How could she be dead?" Ethan asked.

"She was run over by a fishing trawler four weeks ago up in the North Atlantic. I'm sorry."

Angela felt her face go numb. Nobody said a word. Ethan stared at Aeneas, then looked out the window. "How?" he asked.

"How what?"

"How did she end up under a fishing trawler?"

"How do you think? She was a volunteer, like the rest of us. She placed her life on the line to protect sea life. She died with valor. She died doing exactly what she wanted to do."

D. J. spoke up. "Less than a mile."

Aeneas paused, and he seemed either confused or deep in thought. "Hedley, lock our stowaway here in the storage room."

"Lock him?" Angela asked.

"It's where he was hiding. What's the difference?"

Hedley pulled Ethan outside, and Angela felt the urge to follow, but she was too confused now, doubting her loyalties, doubting herself. The only thing she knew to be true was her sudden anger toward Aeneas, which she tried to suppress to a whisper.

"You're too hard on him," she said.

"He's a stowaway."

"You were a stowaway once," she reminded him. "And I took you in."

"It's different."

"How?"

"He's not the first. Five years ago we discovered an FBI agent working undercover. You remember the FBI, don't you? Paid you a visit at Punta Verde, right? Care to speculate who else is on that ship behind us besides Argentineans?" He paused, then jerked his head toward the door through which Hedley had led Ethan back out. "So what else did you tell him?"

"Nothing. We talked about Annie. That's it."

"You tell him where we're headed?"

"How could I? If you told *me* something once in a while, maybe I would be valuable to him. But, no, I didn't tell him anything. Ethan's not an undercover agent."

"You may be right. But I can't take that chance. I find it peculiar that we have a ship pursuing us at the same time we discover him. I hope there's no connection. But the last unwelcome visitor on my ship nearly killed me."

Right then, Angela was herself feeling unwelcome, and the ship, now churning wildly through the field of icebergs, was feeling more unstable by the minute. A bright orange immersion suit, thrust into her arms by a fast-moving crew member, confirmed that the situation was serious.

Aeneas looked at her and nodded. "Put it on," he said. "In case we go down."

"What about Ethan?"

"What about him?"

"If you want me to wear this, you'd better give him one. Even if he is a stowaway, he doesn't deserve to drown."

She let the silence build momentum, until he capitulated, called Hedley on the radio. He looked back at Angela and watched her step into the suit and zip it tight. She could tell by the engines, the high-pitched clanging of icebergs, that they had accelerated.

Angela moved to the left side of the bridge and looked out the side door. The other ship was now so close she could see the guns pointed at them, could read the worlds on the hull— ARA *Roca*. Looking ahead, she noticed penguins porpoising out of the water, out of the path of the fast-approaching vessel. She felt her body freeze at the sight of them panicking. To a penguin, the *Tern* was as much a predator as a leopard seal, and the penguins reverted to their instinctual evasive maneuvers— leaping out of the water, changing direction randomly.

"Angela."

She heard her name but did not look up, focused on the penguins perched on the ledges of icebergs. Adélies. Gentoos. Chinstraps.

"Angela!" She turned to see Aeneas staring at her impatiently. "You're going to want to hold on to something," he said.

Aeneas had taken the helm, and he began to swerve more

closely between the icebergs. The doors on both sides of the bridge were hinged open so that Lauren, on the starboard wing deck, and D. J., on the port deck, could see the outer edges of their ship.

"Does everybody have their survival gear on?" Aeneas said to nobody in particular. "Brace yourselves, people, here we go."

"Four hundred yards," D. J. said, looking back.

Ahead, they were approaching a narrow but towering iceberg, head-on. Angela watched Aeneas's hands as they began to steer the ship ever so slightly off the direct path.

"How am I?" he called out.

"Three feet more," shouted D. J.

"That's too close!" Angela said. The iceberg had a flared base, on which a half dozen penguins had assembled themselves. They were raising their heads, flapping their wings, trying to intimidate the oncoming beast as best they knew how. With twenty yards to go, penguins began to abort, sliding down on their bellies—yet some remained, frozen by panic. Angela, heart pounding, looked at Aeneas and said sharply, "Watch the birds."

He did not respond.

Angela cringed as the ship grazed the base of the iceberg, sending a loud thud echoing through the hull. So this is your plan, she thought, looking at Aeneas: Turn the Antarctic Peninsula into one big slalom course, cutting back and forth between the ten-story gates, hoping you don't sink along the way, hoping your pursuer is not as fortunate.

Once clear of the iceberg, the *Tern* dropped speed and banked hard to the right. From the starboard window, Angela saw the iceberg awaken, leaning left and then right. The Argentine ship appeared, staying as far from the ten-story pendulum as it could without getting too close to the iceberg on the other side. But the iceberg did not topple. And when their pursuer cleared the gantlet, Angela heard curses on the bridge.

When she faced forward again, she saw another, taller iceberg looming ahead—with at least a hundred penguins standing on the steep terraces of its base. This time, she spoke loudly enough for the entire crew to hear.

"Watch the penguins!"

"Angela, I don't have a choice," Aeneas said.

"You're going to crush them!"

"D. J., get me closer," Aeneas said, eyes focused ahead.

"Half a foot!" D. J. yelled. "But no more."

Penguins were clinging to the ice as the ship glanced hard against the glacier, sending Angela and the rest of the crew off their feet, a thunderous noise coming from below. Angela pulled herself up as they banked right again, glimpsing another unbalanced iceberg bobbing in the water, and the Argentine ship passed with ease. She felt the mood in the bridge turn grave.

But Aeneas did not seem to register the fear around him. He accelerated yet again, heading toward an iceberg shaped like the Matterhorn, rising more than six stories tall, with penguin residents along the waterline. This time, he lined up the ship to hit the iceberg on the port side, perhaps to give the starboard hull a much-needed break.

Angela had a direct view of the penguins, hopping up the edges of the ice instead of down, the poor creatures not understanding the intention of this mass of metal and noise. It would macerate them against the ice. She couldn't stand by and watch any longer. As the ship bore down on the iceberg, Angela's body swung into action almost before her mind registered what she was about to do. She grabbed the steering wheel, shoving Aeneas aside with a strength she didn't know she had.

"Angela, stop!" Aeneas tried to pry her hands away, and

she stood strong. But Aeneas was stronger, and with the boat's next lurch, she fell to the floor. She held her ears tight; she did not want to hear the cries of the penguins.

AFTER THE BOAT HAD SLOWED, Angela stepped outside the bridge and carefully began her descent down the stairs, now coated with glistening white dust and shards of ice. When she reached the rear deck, she witnessed a terrain of boulder-sized chunks of ice, as if a giant snowman had just exploded.

Then she saw the penguin.

A young Adélie, most likely a male, no more than three years of age. It looked especially small to Angela because she was so accustomed to Magellanics; this breed was three inches shorter, on average. Black body and head, brilliant white chest, white rings around its eyes. The bird flapped its wings and was limping badly as it moved about, directionless and frantic.

Angela got on her knees and shuffled slowly toward him. He tried to back away but didn't have anyplace to go. The penguin had no tag, which made him look somewhat naked in her eyes. She did not know where his colony was or when he was born. She knew nothing about him, only that he needed help. His feathers were coated with an oily substance that must have come from the deck. He had a dime-sized laceration above his right wing. There was no way he could survive in the water without being cleaned and mended.

She heard a noise and glanced up to see Lauren standing nearby. The look on Lauren's face told her that no matter how she may have felt about Angela, animals came first. "How can I help?" Lauren asked.

"Get me something to hold him in," Angela said. Lauren disappeared for a few moments, returning with a large plastic pail.

As Angela crept closer to the penguin, he turned and tried to run away, then fell over his bad left leg. Angela moved quickly and grabbed him firmly by its neck, his beak snapping wildly, and lifted him into the bucket.

She glanced over the rear deck at the immobilized Argentine ship, and for a moment she wished that it had succeeded in catching them, so there would be no more running, no more casualties. And so she could go home again.

She grabbed the pail by its metal handle and carried the frantically flapping penguin into the ship.

ETHAN

ETHAN HELD IN BOTH HANDS a full-body immersion suit, like the kind the surfers in San Diego wore during the winter months. A moment earlier, when the man they'd called Hedley opened the door and tossed the suit at him, Ethan assumed they would soon be tossing him overboard.

Put it on, Hedley had said. *In case we sink.* Then he shut the door again, and Ethan heard the lock click.

Ethan could tell by the rapidly increasing noise of the engines that they were accelerating. He tossed the suit aside—what good would it do if he couldn't escape from this room? Why bother at all? Annie was dead.

The ship lurched to the left, and Ethan found himself sprawled on the floor again, dodging the boxes that had scattered during the ship's wild swings. He crawled to the door and pulled himself up, clasping the door handle firmly. He pounded on the door, shouting as loudly as he could, but he doubted anyone could hear him over the sounds of steel scraping against ice. He kept an eye on the floor for signs of water seeping through.

At the next impact, Ethan let himself be thrown to the floor again; it was easier than trying to stay upright. Eventually, the noises subsided, the heaving slowed, and by the time the ship came to a stop, Ethan's mind was mired in a fog of memories and regret. Just as he'd believed, Annie had been on this ship—and he'd come so close to being with her. Now, he was trapped in this little room, having been downgraded from stowaway to prisoner. This was not what he imagined; for all his planning, for all the possible outcomes he'd run through in his head, this variable had never been among them. But he was not creative that way—he'd never been able to prepare himself for that which was not rational in life.

And maybe that had been the problem—or rather, one among many: that he was not creative the way Annie had been, that he was too predictable, too uncomfortable with any situation whose outcome he could not foresee within a certain degree of probability. He was the type to buy cruise tickets, to schedule airline flights, to draw up packing lists in Excel. She'd been the type to leave at a moment's notice, to forgo packing altogether, to throw herself under a boat to save a few fish.

What had he ever done in his life that could compare to that?

But that was what he'd loved about Annie—her sense of purpose. He'd wanted her to be as passionate about him as she was about all those animals, but that was impossible. Hers was a blind passion that could never be reciprocated, that wasn't meant to be reciprocated.

For so long, he'd been lost in a virtual world of if/else statements—*if he hadn't asked Adam that question; if he hadn't let Annie get away; if he hadn't left San Diego.* But now he began to wonder whether all those *if*s were not mistakes after all. Whether he was meant to be here, somehow.

He heard voices outside the door. When the door opened, he leapt up to see Angela in the hall, with another woman holding a set of keys. Angela thanked the woman, then stepped inside, carrying a bucket. "Help me," she said. "We need to create an enclosure out of these boxes."

Ethan peeked into the bucket. An anxious, fidgeting penguin looked up at him.

"It's important to keep him away from people," Angela

said, waving him away. "He needs to relax and not expend any more energy than necessary."

Ethan arranged the boxes, then stood back as Angela lifted the penguin from the bucket and placed him on the floor. The bird scurried into a corner, then turned and flapped his wings at them.

"Where did you find him?" Ethan asked.

"He fell off one of the icebergs we hit. Injured himself along the way. Do you mind assisting?"

"I'd love to."

Angela left to get supplies, and Ethan knelt on the floor, eye level with the penguin. "Now there are two stowaways," he said quietly. The bird only looked at him warily.

Angela returned with another bucket, this one filled with soapy water. "We have to clean the oil from his feathers; it destroys the insulation. We can't return him to the water until he's clean, or he'll freeze to death."

"Just plain old soap and water?" he asked, indicating the bucket.

"Dishwashing liquid," Angela said. "Specifically, Dawn."

Ethan followed her instructions, holding the bird as she massaged the viscous black oil out of the feathers, careful not to destroy the underlying structure. After half an hour, they switched roles. He could tell Angela was watching him carefully.

"Not bad," she said.

"You think?"

"You're doing great. Maybe when this trip is over, you'll visit me in Punta Verde. We could always use an extra pair of hands."

Ethan looked up to see if she was joking. But she smiled a genuine smile, and he felt his mood brighten, followed by an immediate, sharp pain. "Ouch!" He looked down to see the penguin's beak locked on his forefinger.

"Do not move," Angela said. "Hold completely still." She pulled open the beak until Ethan pulled away, blood dripping onto the boxes.

"I guess I'm better suited for working with computers," he said. He wrapped his hand in a T-shirt.

"You're not a true naturalist until you've got a few scars to prove it," Angela said.

He held the penguin as Angela finished the cleaning. Then she let it scurry off into its enclosure, and she disappeared again.

Ethan looked down at his throbbing finger, blood soaking through the shirt, and wondered again whether Angela was serious about him visiting her. Something about holding the penguin, about the unpredictability of the procedure, had been invigorating—in a way he'd never experienced before.

Angela returned with bandages for him and thin strips of extra-firm tofu for the bird. "I'm afraid he won't be eating fish," she said. "This will have to suffice."

She dropped the tofu into the enclosure and went to work cleaning and dressing Ethan's wound. He looked over at the enclosure, watching the bird snap at the tofu.

"We should give him a name," he said.

"No," Angela said. "No names."

"Why not?"

"The minute you give an animal a name, everything changes."

"Don't you name any of the penguins you study?"

"Not anymore," she said.

While keeping an eye on the penguin, Ethan had stretched out on a row of boxes and nodded off. When he opened his eyes, he saw Aeneas standing over the makeshift pen, studying the penguin solemnly. Aeneas had a faraway look and did not appear to notice Ethan sitting up.

"I'm not a spy," Ethan said.

Aeneas looked at him, then sat on a box. "I know that now. I reacted strongly, and I am sorry. Tensions have been running high since we lost Annie."

"If she really died, how come I didn't read about it?"

"She wouldn't have wanted anything to get in the way of our mission. She would have wanted us to move on, to continue the fight. And I couldn't have kept her out of that Zodiac if I tried."

"You could have kept her from falling out of the Zodiac."

"She didn't fall," Aeneas said. "She knew exactly what she was doing."

Ethan looked at him, not sure what to believe. He wondered what was going through Annie's mind as she faced the hull of the fishing trawler. Did she make a fatal mistake, or did she make a fatal decision? Once, he'd asked her how far she would go to protect animals. *It's not about how far you can go to protect them*, she said. *It's about how far humans will go to hurt them. I'll always go one step further.*

Aeneas stood. "When this boat touches land again, you'll be free to leave."

"What if I don't want to leave?"

"Excuse me?"

Ethan wasn't sure what he was saying, but he wasn't ready to go home—back to work, back to that empty apartment. "I could take Annie's place. If you still need volunteers."

Aeneas studied Ethan for a moment. "You ever driven a Zodiac before?"

ROBERT

THE *ROCA* HAD NEARLY CLEARED THE ICEBERG—nearly—and when the iceberg began to lean away from the ship, Robert thought they were safe. But he quickly realized that no matter what side you were on when an iceberg tipped, it was the wrong side.

The underside of the iceberg lifted the *Roca* diagonally out of the water, sending men sliding across decks, setting alarms blaring, and, by the sound of the screeching from the below, rendering the propellers useless.

As Robert watched the *Tern* pull away, he began thinking of the report he would file at the end of this trip, how similar it would sound to the report he last filed after pursuing Darwin. The reckless mistakes and the missed opportunities. Back then, Robert had offered to resign, but Gordon talked him out of it. *Ours is an ugly business,* he'd said. *Entrapment. Trickery. And we don't always get the bad guy.* Gordon had sent Robert on a forced vacation and cleared his slate. If only Robert could have done the same thing with his memories.

Now he was watching the *Arctic Tern* disappear behind an iceberg. He should have been more patient. He'd known Aeneas had wanted him to take the bait and chase him through this sharp-edged ice field—narrow passages favored small ships like the *Tern*. All the Exocet missiles in the world could not protect the *Roca* from an iceberg.

The ship's engines were silent, and in the bridge Zamora

tended to an array of frenzied lights and monitors. Men argued through the radio slung over his shoulder. And though everything was in another language, Robert understood perfectly what was going on. The ship was damaged, not fatally, but badly enough to require repair, not to mention reports and repercussions. Zamora looked nervous, as if he were sharing Robert's thoughts, wondering how he was going to explain this debacle to the higher-ups.

Robert watched as Lynda spoke to Zamora in her calm, matter-of-fact manner. She had a way of calming any man. She even got Zamora to crack a smile. What Spanish joke did she tell him? When Lynda turned and made eye contact with Robert, she was still smiling. In a matter of minutes, the end of the world had been put on hold.

"How long will it take to fix?" Robert asked.

"A few hours," Lynda said, and shrugged.

He left the bridge. On the rear deck, men in dry suits and scuba gear were lowering Zodiacs into the water. Robert found someone who spoke English and offered his services. He'd been pretty good at wet welding once, a skill acquired from his apprenticeship on the *Eminence*, stitching together old propeller blades and patching hulls. And so he spent the rest of the day with the engineers, diving into the ice water, holding on to a nine-foot steel blade as a blue torch made it pliable again.

The men took frequent smoking breaks, leaving Robert alone. He was just another grunt, seated on the deck, following orders—the life of a deckhand, a life he'd lived once. If only he had kept his mouth shut, he could still be living it. With Noa.

He watched the men mill about, a few in full uniform, machine guns strapped to their shoulders. There was a time he would have envied them—their swagger and camaraderie. As someone raised in a family that wasn't very much a family,

Robert had grown up with an unspoken urge for control in his life. A father off in a plane somewhere at 33,000 feet, a mother on a couch in the living room just as high on vodka and Vicodin. Everything would have been okay if his father had returned on occasion, paid the bills, and mowed the lawn. But one day during Robert's sixth grade, a weekend layover in London stretched into a month, then two, and all the teary phone calls from his mom couldn't bring him home again. His father had found someone else, began working a new route, and Robert's shrinking family was demoted from owning to renting, from private school to public school, from McDonald's to White Castle. In a matter of months, everything in his life churned in reverse: his mood, his attendance, his grades. By miracle or momentum, he made it into junior high, but fights dominated his school days, and it wasn't until the high school principal gave him a choice between the football team or the rest of his Saturdays in study hall that he found his salvation.

Coach Gibbs was a mean old man who laughed as he forced his young players to run hills on hundred-degree days. But Robert discovered something out there on those sweltering afternoons, when Gibbs would dole out only ice cubes during water breaks—he learned that on the playing field, all men were equal. It didn't matter that Nick's dad drove a BMW or that Rodney spent a summer in France. An open-field tackling drill was all Robert had needed to prove that he was as good as all the rest. There'd been nothing like laying out one of the richer kids to put a smile on his face, to make him feel as if his life wasn't the mess it was. Robert had been aware even then that this newfound happiness wasn't healthy, but it was something to get him through the days.

The coaches had given him rules, and the game, which he excelled at, had given him respect. Over the years, that sport kept him within bounds. His grades crept back up, the fighting stayed confined to the field, and he enjoyed having an excuse to stay away from the sad little apartment and a mother who would still get drunk and sometimes threaten suicide. Football got Robert a scholarship to a small college in Peoria, Illinois. Looking back, the FBI had been a fitting sequel— another fraternity of sorts, with rules of its own, the occasional bloodletting. He'd still needed rules and regulations to keep his life from getting away from him, and the Bureau gave him that, along with an I.D. and a handgun. And it should have been good enough. His colleagues, many of them also former football players, were content in their lives—but for Robert, since Noa, the pieces of his life never seemed to fit together they way he wished they would.

He was not one who usually suffered from moral ambiguity, but now he wondered if he should have set the bar higher. He used to think he was on the right side of the law. Now, in a part of the world where laws and borders were abstract concepts, he could not escape the nagging feeling that he was on the wrong side. The way the *Roca* had ended up on the wrong side of the iceberg. Perhaps it was nature's way. That's what Noa would have told him. He smiled as he remembered her in the bar in Los Angeles. *Mother Nature will fight back if man pushes her too far,* she'd said. *And that day is coming.*

A man in a mechanic's uniform handed him a beer, and Robert downed it quickly. He got up to get another and noticed the iceberg towering over the deck, only a few feet away, the iceberg that had nearly tipped a 500-ton ship on its side, now peaceful again, sleeping.

"You hiding from me?"

Robert turned to see Lynda. "Trying to."

"And drinking?"

"Brilliant deduction, Agent Madigan." Robert extended a can of Quilmes and was surprised when she accepted it. When he sat back down, she sat next to him. Yet she was mercifully quiet, and for once he didn't feel defensive as he usually did around her. Maybe it was that he was starting on his third beer, or maybe it was the realization that he was now past the point of caring what she knew, what anyone knew.

"You ever fallen for one of your suspects?" he asked.

"Fallen?"

"You know."

"Oh. Well, I was tempted once. I was working undercover as a dealer in this Boston club on Lansdowne Street. I'd never been so popular. I had male model types, even a few celebrities you'd know, hanging all over me. But it was a fantasy life, you know? They didn't want me; they just wanted to get high. Around that time, I went on a blind date with this guy from my old neighborhood, and I was all full of myself, an ego the size of the Green Monster. I'd gotten used to being around all this money, and I suggested we go to this fancy seafood place. I could tell he was uncomfortable there—wrong clothes, nervous as hell. And then when I made fun of him for ordering a beer instead of something off the wine list, he called me an asshole and walked out."

"So what'd you do?" Robert asked.

"I married him." Lynda smiled. "So when were you planning on telling me about Noa?" she asked.

"I wasn't. She's dead, so there's nothing to talk about."

"Humor me. We've got time."

Robert paused and looked around the ship, at the men who spoke no English, at the mesas made of ice that surrounded them. If he were going to pick a place to spill his secrets, this was the place to do it. So he told Lynda everything, from the first time he'd met Noa all the way through to the ice fields. As he spoke, he finished his beer, feeling his shoulders loosening, the pressure within easing.

The deck began to shudder, like a car with wheels out of balance. Then Robert noticed movement. As the ship accelerated, the shuddering eased, though not fully.

"Sounds like those propellers are going to fall off," Lynda said.

"They just might."

"Looks like the chase is on again."

Robert stood and helped Lynda to her feet. "This is just between us," he said.

"Yes, Bobby, of course. But let me ask you this. How can you be so sure Noa is dead?"

"I'm sure."

"Are you telling me you never once considered the possibility that Aeneas rescued her?"

"I had her name on a watch list for years. If she survived, she sure as hell did a good job of playing dead."

"I'm just saying."

"You're not going to let go of this, are you?"

"Suppose, for argument's sake, that she got off that ice," Lynda said. "Where would she go?"

"I don't know. Off the grid."

"Exactly. She's not stupid, and Aeneas isn't either. He wouldn't keep her around. She's a liability."

"Aeneas is the liability."

"True. But he's smart. He knew that if you assumed she was dead and he confirmed it by radio silence, then he'd be free to live another day, which is exactly what happened. How many times has he slipped away from us? Aeneas is a survivor. I don't think it's a stretch to assume the same of Noa, do you?"

As much as he wanted to believe it, at the same time Robert did not want to exhume the past any further. In a sad, strange way, it had helped to assume Noa was dead because his life with her, however fraudulent and fleeting, had also died back there on the ice. When he left her behind, he'd left Jake behind as well—and he'd thought for a long time that Jake had been the better part of himself, the part he wished he could be in his real life.

And now Lynda was putting ideas in his head. Now he was imagining Noa's face again. She would be nearly forty now, four years his senior. Would there be lines around her lips, her forehead? Would her hair still be in dreadlocks? Would she still be wearing madras skirts and tank tops? The tattoos would still be there. Infinity on her wrist, perhaps faded by the sun and the years. And where would she be now, if she wasn't chasing whalers? She was passionate about so many species—the endangered Kudu of southern Africa, the dolphins slaughtered annually off the coast of northern Japan, the Cape fur seals of Namibia. Only Aeneas would know these things.

"Bobby, you're getting all quiet on me again. What are you thinking?"

"That she wouldn't take me back anyway."

"Perhaps. But how much of Jake was acting, and how much of him was you?"

"What do you mean?"

"I mean, who do you think Noa was really in love with? Jake? Or you?"

Robert watched her return to the bridge. He thought back to his last night with Noa, in her bed. He had closed his eyes and leaned into her. She'd covered his head in her arms and pulled him close. Sleep came easily, without sex or alcohol, the gentle embrace under covers, the warmth of her breath on his neck. He felt wanted, such a simple feeling, but a feeling he hadn't encountered often in his life, and now he wondered if he would ever get that feeling back.

ANGELA

ANGELA STOOD ON THE FORE DECK and braced herself against
a biting headwind. The sting of the cold air on her face
reminded her of where she was, whipping her skin as harshly
as a slap, as if to wake her up—to rouse her from the dream
world she'd succumbed to when she first decided to follow
Aeneas onto his ship.

Their relationship was nothing more than an illusion, she
realized: When Aeneas had landed on her shore, drenched and
helpless, she'd projected onto him the vision of the man she
wanted, someone dependable and safe. He was none of these
things, yet she'd told herself that maybe he could be—that
maybe her gentle voice would help him sleep, instead of the
liquor he turned to every night. That her body would make
him forget about all other bodies—past, present, and future.
That her dreams would become his dreams. It was all selfish,
of course, and naive. Illusions always were.

Now the illusion was gone, and she faced an interminable
trip with a man she recognized less and less with each passing
day. She loved him, and probably always would—but she used
to hope that once the whales were safe, once the Japanese and
the Norwegians and the Inuit turned their boats around and
returned home, Aeneas would turn his boundless energy
toward her. But now she knew he would simply move on. To
albatross in the Falklands. To sharks off the coast of Ecuador.
He wanted to wage war with every fishing vessel in every

ocean, and if he had enough time and money, he would. If Angela wanted to be with him, she would have to sail with him through all of these oceans. Ports of call would offer moments of stability, but only moments. And the only penguins she would count would be those that porpoised alongside his ship.

She made her way down to the storage room. Ethan was not there, and she wondered fleetingly where he was before turning her attention to the penguin. Still in his enclosure, he watched her approach. His wings were nearly clean of oil, but frayed from all the scrubbing. The laceration above his wing was no longer bleeding, yet he still walked with a pronounced limp and seemed to favor resting on his belly rather than standing. If he appeared injured, the females would avoid him, thinking him unreliable as a mate and provider for their chicks. Angela believed in natural selection—to disagree with the premise was to implicitly embrace some God holding all the strings—but at times like these, she took issue with the lack of flexibility of such a theory. She wanted to believe that even an injured bird could find a mate.

The penguin allowed Angela to apply a damp towel to his feathers, working out a few remaining spots of oil that had risen to the surface. Her mind wandered toward her camp at Punta Verde. She thought of the penguins she'd tried to rescue last season, the two dozen birds caught in an oil spill who tried to continue raising their chicks despite being covered in muck. They had such a tragic air to them. They did everything right. They filled their bellies with food; they made it back to their nests despite the oil sheathing that weighed on them like suits of armor. They'd survived so much, only to watch their children die, not realizing that the food they were giving their children bore the poison that killed them. The parents looked so confused, so helpless. Nudging the carcasses with their beaks. Trying to force open the chicks' beaks to ask for more food. Like their human counterparts, they wanted to be needed.

She heard a noise and turned, expecting to see Ethan at the door. It was Aeneas.

"I thought I might find you here," he said. She turned away and continued to bathe the penguin. He approached and took a seat where he could watch. "I think this is one breed of penguin that hasn't bitten me yet," he said.

"Better keep your distance, then."

He chuckled.

"Where's Ethan?" she asked. "You haven't tossed him over, have you?"

"I put him to work."

"You what?"

"He volunteered. He's a deckhand now. Seems to have taken to it."

"He didn't have much of a choice."

"Angela, he approached me. What more can I do besides say I'm sorry?"

"I don't know."

"Now I have to figure out a way to get *you* out of this room." He reached for her shoulder, but she pulled back. "What's the matter now?" he asked.

"You have no plans to return to Argentina, do you?"

"What?"

"That line you fed me, about creating some sort of penguin protection sanctuary? When would that have happened? Before or after you went to prison in Buenos Aires?"

"This is not the best time to talk about this."

Angela let the penguin go and climbed out of his enclosure. "I'm getting the feeling that there will never be a good time to talk about this."

"I meant every word. But it's not very practical for me to return to those waters now, given my reputation there."

"I don't expect you to return now, or ever. But it might have been nice for you to tell me that before I sacrificed everything to join you."

"I didn't force you to come along."

"Is that what you told Annie before she died?"

Aeneas didn't answer, but Angela could tell by his pained expression that she'd struck a nerve, and she regretted it. She could have let it go right then. Spared him any more anguish. But she wanted him to hurt, especially now.

"You're the captain of this ship. She was a young, idealistic girl. You could have prevented it. You could have stopped her."

"I let her on that Zodiac because that's where she wanted to be. Everyone on this vessel is here by choice, including you. The risks, though acute, are accepted. She may have been young, yes, even idealistic. But she knew very well what she was doing."

Angela didn't respond. She suddenly pictured Diesel, standing outside her office door waiting to be let in. She remembered how Aeneas once said that penguins were clumsy creatures. *They're just out of their element,* she responded. Now, on this boat, Angela was out of her element; she was the clumsy one. Aeneas was pelagic by nature, having grown up on the sea. But she was not. She grew up in upstate New York, along the Hudson. She spent her life watching boats glide past. People on the coasts are used to people coming to them, but people on river towns get used to watching other people pass them by.

She knew Aeneas couldn't take all the blame for her misgivings. They were two different species, neither more important than the other. She'd heard what she wanted to hear. She had been running from something—herself, most likely—and it had taken her this long to realize that she could not escape.

"Angela, what do you want from me?" Aeneas asked. "My life is this boat. This mission. Everything else is secondary. I thought you knew that."

"I did. And I understand it. Penguins come first with me. Or at least they did once."

"You'll get back to them. I promise."

"I hear we're going to be passing Palmer soon."

"Yes."

She looked down at the bird in front of her. "I'm going to take him there so I can release him."

"And how do you expect to do that?"

"You're going to drop me off."

"I can't afford to slow down, let alone stop."

"You will slow down. You'll stop. And you'll let me take him off the ship."

"Only the bird, right?"

Angela said nothing. She wanted to punish him with her silence, let him feel some of the uncertainty she had been feeling.

Aeneas waited a few moments, then got up and left, closing the door behind him.

ANGELA RETURNED TO THE CABIN and unzipped her backpack. She removed her log book, caliper, handheld scale, and nylon strap and placed them on her bed. Relics of a previous life, they seemed foreign to her now. At the bottom of the backpack she found the satellite transmitter. Brand-new, it had not yet been activated. She was supposed to have attached it to a penguin in the south end of the colony the morning that Aeneas returned to her, the morning she ran away. And now it served only to remind her of her dereliction of duties, of those she left behind.

She could feel tears welling, but she resisted them. She could feel the boat's engine begin to slow. She looked out the window and saw Palmer Station in the distance. For anyone who wasn't a scientist, there was nothing attractive about Palmer Station; it looked like an industrial park, with corrugated metal structures scattered about, containing dorms and labs, mostly painted blue. But to her it looked like the closest thing to home.

Angela returned everything to her backpack. She had nothing new to add to it but her white CREW T-shirt. She located her passport, something she might need as she began to reenter civilization.

She paused and removed the satellite transmitter once again and looked over at the bed, where Aeneas's yellow jacket lay. Then she activated the device.

THERE WAS NO BERTH FOR LARGE SHIPS at Palmer Station, so the *Tern* docked offshore, and a Zodiac was lowered. Angela found Ethan on the rear deck, learning how to operate the crane. He was intent and focused, and he smiled at her when she waved him over.

"You can leave with me if you'd like," she told him.

"Thanks," he said. "But I think I'll stay."

Angela leaned over and kissed him on the cheek, and he grabbed her in a tight hug. She noticed Aeneas standing off to the side, looking irritated. "Any day now," he said.

Angela slung the backpack over her shoulder and picked up the penguin in a carrier Hedley had fashioned from a wooden crate.

"What's with the backpack?" Aeneas asked.

"I'm sorry," she said.

"Are you leaving for good?"

"I'm going home."

Aeneas studied her face. "And I can't change your mind?" he asked.

"Not this time."

He sighed. "Very well, then."

Aeneas piloted the Zodiac with Angela and her penguin seated at the front. She looked up at him, but his eyes were fixed above her head. When the Zodiac reached the pier, Angela lifted herself up. Aeneas handed her the carrier. "Are you sure?" he asked.

"No," she said.

"I guess we were only meant to sail together for a short while."

"I guess." She turned away.

"You forgot this," he said. When she turned back, he tossed her a necklace, and she caught it. It was her penguin tag, the sharp indentations of the punched numbers catching the sun. Zero four two two nine. She had come to believe that it had brought Aeneas luck as he sideswiped the icebergs, and she could not imagine him not wearing it as he did the same while chasing the Japanese.

She tossed the necklace back. "Return it to me when you're finished."

"It might be a while. It might be a very long time."

"I'll wait. You'll know where to find me."

"In absentia?" he asked, his eyes coming alive again.

"Right. In absentia."

Angela wanted to return to him suddenly and hold him, prevent him from leaving. Why couldn't she take him back home with her? Why did they both have to be so stubborn, so independent? She didn't want to regret this moment, and yet she knew she would. She already did.

Aeneas put the boat in reverse, backed out a few feet, then spun around. Within minutes he was back at the vessel, and thick wires drew the Zodiac up out of the water and onto the deck.

ROBERT

THROUGH THE GERLACHE STRAIT, past Palmer Station. Past Adelaide Island, through an ice-choked, slow-going passage known as the Gauntlet. Finally into the Amundsen Sea. Twenty-one hours to reach Aeneas.

When the Argentine cutter finally came within sight of the *Tern*, they were, as Robert predicted, too late. The battle was well under way, the *Tern* in close pursuit of a Japanese whaling ship, and, following well behind, a Greenpeace ship.

Robert, in the bridge with Lynda, was reminded of the days of being Jake. He now found it hard to play the role of bystander; he wanted to be a participant. But this was not his battle. He could only watch and wait it out. Wait for his opportunity to board the *Tern* and arrest Aeneas.

The Japanese whaler, the *Takanami Maru*, was a large-hulled ship painted blue and black. It was nearly twice as long as the *Tern*, its deck a good fifteen feet higher. Seeing the *Tern* chasing after the *Maru* reminded Robert of a Chihuahua making a run at a mastiff; it would have been comical if it weren't so tragic.

Over the radio they could hear Aeneas: "This is the captain of *Arctic Tern*. Acting under full authority of the Antarctic Treaty, we demand that you cease your whale slaughter immediately and leave these waters. Failure to do so will result in a direct action. This is not a protest action. Repeat: This is not a protest action."

The *Maru* was silent, seemingly indifferent. Instead of running in a straight line, the *Maru* was moving diagonally, tacking ever so slightly, as if the *Tern* did not even exist. When Robert raised his binoculars, he realized the reason for the ship's trajectory—it, too, was in pursuit of something.

A whale.

A misty cough erupted from the water just ahead of the *Maru*, then the gray bulge of a humpback. Robert panned back to the helm of *Maru*, where a man stood at attention behind a harpoon mounted in what looked like a rocket launcher. Robert remembered what Aeneas told him once: *If a harpoon hits you, pray that it goes straight through you.* The tip of a harpoon contained twenty grams of penthrite, one of the world's nastiest explosives, designed to detonate a foot or two within the body of the whale. Yet despite the explosive, the harpoon rarely killed them.

A cloud of smoke suddenly enveloped the man at the harpoon. By the time Robert heard the explosion, the damage was done. He didn't see the harpoon in the air, but he saw the impact, the explosion of blood, a sudden curvature of a black body in the water. A wire drawn taut began to pull in its prey. Blood gushed as if from a fire hose.

Through his binoculars, Robert watched the whale, helpless, bleeding from all orifices. And then he noticed a smaller whale, a baby, following close behind. He glanced at Lynda, who was watching wide-eyed and silent. "The pup always stays close to its mother," he explained. "So they kill the mother first. They take their time with the second."

The injured whale was still moving, its tail slapping against a pool of its own blood. But the whale could not keep itself from being dragged to the side of the ship, where men in bright blue uniforms reached out of an opening in the hull with metal prongs. They began sending large doses of electricity through the whale. The body convulsed for a few seconds, then went limp.

"Jesus Christ," Lynda said.

Aeneas accelerated the *Tern,* and it became clear that the two ships were on a collision course, with the Japanese cutting across the *Tern's* path.

Finally, the radio sputtered to life, and Robert heard a man's voice speak in halting English. "Leave us alone. You are in our path."

"We will not leave you alone, sir," Aeneas responded. "Only when you stop killing whales in blatant violation of international law will we leave you alone."

"You are terrorist."

"That's your opinion. Would you care to ask the whales what they think of me?"

Robert watched the crew of the *Tern* ready themselves on the deck to hurl a grab-bag collection of stink and smoke bombs. At the front of the *Tern,* a crew member manned the fire hose and began spewing out a steady stream of ocean water. The whaler's horns began to blare, and the *Tern* fired its horn back, creating a cacophony of noise as the two ships headed for a collision.

From Robert's point of view, the impact appeared to be nothing more than a glancing blow, the Japanese hull passing by like the side of a bus. But the *Tern's* crew told a different story—crew members upended, neatly stacked and strapped Zodiacs strewn about. It was if an earthquake had struck, and Robert half expected to see the fragile *Tern* split in half.

Instead, ever so slightly, the *Tern* began to veer away from the *Maru* and then stabilize. Robert could hear shouts from the crew, could see objects and smoke bombs being thrown. The fact that the *Tern* could have gone down in an instant, bodies drowned, did not appear to mean anything. Even the weather, which had turned ominous—an overcast sky spraying mist, the wind gathering strength—did not slow anyone down. More Zodiacs were dropped into the water, and they pursued the Japanese ship like flies. But like the boats before, they were just as ineffectual. Above, the clouds darkened, and rain began to spit.

Robert turned to check on Lynda. Her face was red, her eyes still glued to the bleeding, convulsing whale hanging from the Japanese ship's hull.

"It's tough to watch, I know," he said.

"My husband wanted to become a sport fisherman when we moved to Florida," she said. "I didn't think anything of it until he took me out one day to catch marlin. That poor fish was dragged kicking and screaming for miles—I'd never seen such a display of courage. And for what? To be strung up and photographed. I told the hubby if he wanted to stay in Florida, that would be the last fish he caught."

"Was it?"

She forced a smile. "He was never any good at it anyway. I think he was relieved. I wonder if the whalers would feel the same way, if we sent a warning shot or two."

"I wonder," was all Robert could muster in response. He was ready to give the command, to blow that Japanese ship out of the water, if she were willing to translate. But he knew that Lynda was speaking from anger, from empathy, and that there was no sense in taking any more lives than necessary. This was not their war. Not yet.

He followed Lynda's eyes back to the ships. They were approaching a wall of fog, and soon everyone would be enveloped in suspended moisture. Maybe this would be enough to give the whalers pause.

"Let's get this over with and go home, okay?" Robert said. "Okay."

ETHAN

ANNIE USED TO SAY: *Life can only be understood backward, but it must be lived forward.* This was the dilemma that Ethan faced. He didn't fully understand what he was about to do; he only knew that, unlike a computer keystroke, it could not be undone.

He boarded the Zodiac and lowered himself to the water. Nobody noticed him, which formerly had annoyed him but which served him well now. He started the engine and left the *Arctic Tern* behind, standing alone at the stern, tiller handle firmly in hand, his eyebrows dripping icy salt water. The boat hopped across the waves toward its target, the *Takanami Maru*.

Moments before, Ethan had been just another crew member, futilely hurling stink and smoke bombs at the Japanese whalers. Off starboard, Ethan had watched the hull of dark blue steel approaching. Fifty feet to go, then twenty, then ten, then the sound of steel grinding against steel. The *Tern* shuddered, and Ethan grabbed the opposite railing.

He felt his lungs convulse and lunged across the deck to the crate of ammunition. He tried to grab a rescue flare, but the *Tern* arched up and heaved to the left, tossing him down to the deck. Finally, the *Tern* began to veer away from the *Maru* and then stabilize. While the ship idled, Ethan had descended to the water.

He didn't notice the fog rolling in until the *Maru* faded into it. When he looked back, he saw only fog behind him.

He slowed the engine. Seeing a white patch amidst the sea of gray, he headed for it until he realized at the last moment that it was not the *Tern*, that he was about to run straight into an iceberg. He killed the engine and listened for a ship, any ship. He hadn't brought a radio.

He rummaged through a supply box and found an emergency flare, but he hesitated to use it. He could imagine Aeneas right now, kicking himself for letting Ethan get away in a Zodiac. Yet this only made Ethan more determined.

He heard a loud exhale and looked down to see a whale piercing the surface of the water, barely, just enough to be noticed. He wished he could identify the breed, to know what Aeneas knew, what Annie might have known, as he watched the whale descend below the surface, a shadow merging into the indigo water.

He took a seat on the floor of the boat and rested his eyes. Seeing the whale had put him at peace, as if he were alone but not truly alone. Although he knew little about where he was or why he was here, he felt that everything was working according to plan. Not his plan, despite his best efforts. But a plan. He was a player in a larger script, God's algorithm, a purpose not yet clear to him but unfolding without bugs or buffer overflows, a seamless string of code.

ROBERT

BY THE TIME AENEAS made the distress call, Robert figured it was too late to find the *Tern*'s missing Zodiac, let alone rescue its passenger. Yet when he heard Aeneas's voice on the radio, asking for help, Robert wanted to help, and he hoped he could. He also knew that if he could locate that Zodiac before Aeneas did, he might have the leverage he needed to bring this chase to an end.

Robert stood in the bridge staring into the fog. Zamora guided the *Roca* slowly, mindful of the dozens of icebergs surrounding them. The radar screen would be of no help for locating the Zodiac, and the thick fog rendered binoculars useless. The best they could do was assemble as many pairs of eyes around the ship as possible.

After a while, Robert left to find Lynda, who was on the lower front deck.

"Anything?" he asked.

"*Nada*," she said. "I'm just curious here, but what's your grand plan for when we do get to the *Tern*? You think Aeneas is just gonna pull over so we can board?"

"If we find this Zodiac first, Aeneas will have no choice," he said.

"And if we don't?"

Robert said nothing. He had no backup plan. He only knew he didn't want another slalom race. And if the *Roca* did get close enough to deploy its own Zodiacs, he also knew

217

Aeneas would be waiting with water jets, smoke bombs, and railings lined with barbed wire.

"You know what we need to get on that ship?" Lynda said.

"What's that?"

"A Trojan horse."

"One that floats."

"Okay, then. A Trojan *seahorse*," she said, then laughed at her joke. Robert looked at her thoughtfully. Her smiled faded. "What is it?" she asked.

"You just gave us our plan," Robert said.

"I'm *joking*, Bobby."

"I'm not," Robert said.

THE PLAN WAS SIMPLE: If Robert could not locate the missing crewman, he would impersonate him. Suddenly, those days spent spying on the *Tern* back in Argentina were paying off. Robert knew the color of the immersion suits the *Tern* kept on hand, which would help him craft a disguise that would get him rescued by the *Tern*—lifted, Zodiac and all, onto the deck, arrest warrant in hand, before the *Tern's* crew discovered he wasn't one of their own. It was a plan that even Aeneas might appreciate, had he not been the target of it.

There was still the chance that Aeneas had already located the errant Zodiac. But the fact that the *Tern* was still hovering a few miles away in the fog instead of pursuing whalers was a sign that they were still searching. Either way, it was worth the risk.

Robert and Lynda were lowered to the water in a Zodiac. Lynda had instructed the captain to head in the opposite direction so as not to draw attention to the *Roca*. They needed to be truly alone if they were to trick Aeneas.

Robert pulled on the reflective orange survival suit and donned an oversized black hooded sweatshirt.

"I'll pull the hood up when we get within view," he explained. "And when I give the word, you'll hide under this tarp."

"Yeah, yeah."

"And there's one more thing." Robert pulled out his handgun. "Stand over here," he said, motioning her to his side.

"What?"

Just as Lynda moved over, Robert quickly fired a shot into the rubberized wall of the boat. The gunshot was echoed by the sound of air escaping.

"What the hell!" Lynda said.

Robert watched the wall implode slowly, lowering what little barrier there was between them and the choppy water. The Zodiac began to list, and Lynda's face turned crimson with anger.

"Bobby, what the hell are you doing?"

"I had to do it."

"Why?"

"Because if they look close enough they'll know I'm not one of them. This way, they'll see a boat in distress and they won't hesitate to pull us up. We have to appear close to sinking."

"We *are* close to sinking."

"We'll be fine. Besides, did you notice the Argentine flag on the outer wall of this Zodiac? That's what I pull a bullet through."

"Oh." Lynda quieted down as the logic sunk in. Holding his gun, smelling the exhaust of the spent cartridge, made Robert feel like an agent again. He realized he'd needed the push to get back into character. Then he wondered why he needed to get into character at all. Had he only been playing an agent all these years? Had he truly been more like Jake all along? He forced the thoughts out of his head.

Robert could see, through the fog, the white shadow of

the *Tern* becoming sharp around the edges. He heard voices, people shouting. Perhaps they were calling out to Robert, thinking he was the missing crewman. He pulled the hood of his sweatshirt up over his head and motioned toward the tarp. Lynda lay down on the deck and pulled the plastic over her.

"Figures it would be a guy driving that missing boat," Lynda said, her voice muffled from under the tarp. "You men always have to be the ones at the wheel. And no wonder he got lost. Men *never* ask for directions."

"Quiet. We're getting close." The *Tern* was less than fifty yards away. Robert kept his head angled toward the water to prevent anyone from getting a good look at him. He waved at the ship and he heard more voices, the volume increasing. He glanced up quickly and saw the white hull overshadowing him, until he was alongside the ship. He heard a mechanical sound and looked up to see a crane swinging into position.

A wire was lowered. Robert grabbed it and attached it to his Zodiac. The crane emitted a whine and the floor began to wobble as it left behind the water. Robert grabbed onto the wire and reached inside his jacket for his gun.

"You ready?" Robert mumbled to Lynda, face held down.

"Just give the word."

They were hovering above the deck now. The crew were silent. Robert held his breath until he felt the bottom of their boat becoming one with the deck of the ship.

"One, two..." he said.

Robert stood, pulled the hood back, and revealed the gun. The dozen or so crew members who surrounded them stood motionless. Even Aeneas, who hadn't aged a day since Robert last saw him, appeared surprised. Robert cautiously stepped out of the Zodiac and took a step toward Aeneas, who looked back at the crew members behind him.

"Look what the cat dragged in," Aeneas said.

ANGELA

ANGELA SAT IN THE WOOD-PANELED LOUNGE of the *Narwhal* as waiters in red vests took drink orders. Marcus, the expedition leader, stood at the front of the room, next to the bar, and foreshadowed the next day's events. A tour of grounded icebergs. A lecture on the leopard seal. A landing at the Aitcho Islands to view gentoo and chinstrap penguins.

Angela stared out the window, her mind elsewhere. Earlier that day, she'd stood on the rocky shore near Palmer Station and opened the makeshift penguin carrier. The bird had stepped out gingerly, unsure of his surroundings. He was thoroughly cleaned and ready for reentry, but though the water was only ten feet away, he approached it cautiously. Angela told herself that he would quickly find his way back to his colony, though researchers still had little clue as to how penguins navigated the oceans and returned to their homes year after year. Some speculated that they used the moon and the stars, floating on the surface in the darkness. But what about the Southern Ocean, where the night skies were elusive? These were the questions that Angela asked herself, and even asked the penguins when no one was looking.

She'd wanted to tag this one but did not. This penguin would return to the water as anonymously as it left. No numbers. No names. For so many years she'd managed to keep her emotional distance—and then Diesel had come along, that persistent little bird. Last night, Angela dreamed about him. She'd been swimming underwater, without need for air, and she could see him ahead amid a half dozen other penguins. She recognized the markings on his belly, a pattern she had memorized long ago. She followed the smudges, the Southern Cross, until they blurred together and she was floating, lifeless, surrounded by nets, waiting to be pulled in.

Now, the nameless penguin took a few more tentative steps toward the water's edge. He looked back at Angela for a moment, like a child waiting for an adult's approval, then he turned and flopped into the water and was gone.

Angela looked across the water, hoping to get one more glimpse of him, when she saw the *Narwhal* pulling into harbor, a large hundred-passenger cruise ship, and an old acquaintance. It was then she knew that she would be returning home soon as well.

GOING FROM THE *TERN* TO THE *NARWHAL* was like being upgraded to first class. The moment Angela boarded the ship, she became acutely aware of how dirty and ragged her clothes had become; she walked past passengers in neon-colored fleece jackets, cameras dangling from their necks.

The expedition leader, Marcus, remembered Angela from a cruise she'd worked on years before, and he agreed to return her to Ushuaia in exchange for assisting with landings and nature walks. Making small talk with tourists would be a small price to pay for a trip home. And yet, seated in this room between men in sport jackets and women in silk blouses, so far removed from the battles looming in another part of Antarctica, she felt shortchanged. Mostly, she felt guilty for leaving Aeneas, for slowing his ship's progress, for choosing one cause over another.

In the morning, instead of a vegan breakfast, Angela

found a buffet of eggs, bacon, sausages, and seafood. She could hear Aeneas's voice in her head: *Animals take only what they need to live, and sometimes less. Humans have buffet lines.* She ate only fruit and toast.

The *Narwhal* dropped anchor just off the Lemaire Channel. Normally, tourists couldn't get close to an iceberg, but this shallow stretch of water grounded the bergs, providing an opportunity for Zodiac tours. Angela piloted a group of tourists through the labyrinth of ten-story ice sculptures. Two tourists urged her to zoom through a tunnel that cut through the base of one berg, and for a brief moment she actually considered it. She could feel herself back on the *Tern*, slipping in and out of the icebergs, the friction of ice against steel, the coating of snow on the rear deck. She felt the urge to open up the fuel line, let the engine propel them straight through the tunnel, then another, until the ship was out of sight and they were alone among the sentinels, like a child playing under the table, the joy of being invisible. The voices of the tourists grew louder, urging her to go for it, perhaps anticipating her thoughts.

She shook her head. "This is as close as we can get, safely," she said.

Later, at Barrientos Island, Angela was stationed in the gangway, where the passengers queued with their parkas zipped and life vests buckled. One by one, they stepped into buckets of disinfectant, sterilizing their boots before walking down a short metal stairway to the outstretched arms of the naturalist manning the inflatable.

On land, Angela led a group of six adults and two teenagers up to a chinstrap colony half a mile up a steep slope. The smell of guano was a welcome reminder of her past visits, and she watched the tourists wrinkle their noses. The penguins in Argentina, by virtue of being widely dispersed and living in burrows with absorbent soil, did not give off the same level of odor—but Angela loved the smell of Antarctic penguins. After one trip, she'd held off washing a pair of cargo pants just so she could remember her time there. When she'd confessed this to Shelly, Shelly had suggested that this was one reason Angela had difficulty meeting men.

There were no burrows here in Antarctica, only piles of rocks stained red and white by decades of guano. Angela looked around, losing herself for a moment before remembering that she had a job to do. "Why do you think they established their colony way up here?" she asked the group as they stood among the jagged rocks at the top of the hill.

"To avoid the gentoos?" an older man asked.

"Perhaps," Angela said. "The colonies don't interact much with one another. But there's a more practical reason why these penguins chose this particular slice of hill. And if it were sunny out, it would become more obvious."

"No snow," said one of the teenagers.

"Exactly. When there is snow on the ground, the penguins cannot incubate their eggs. This piece of land is more exposed to the sun and tends to dry out more quickly than the areas down below."

As Angela watched a trio of penguins lean their way up the hill, she realized how much their movements mirrored her own life—a constant, methodical gait, always ending up back where she started. The penguins, of course, knew no better: All they knew was how to eat and reproduce and stay alive. Angela began to wish her own life could be as simple.

On the Zodiac back to the ship, a penguin porpoised next the boat—a Magellanic. Was he headed home? she wondered. Or was he lost? Even penguins sometimes got lost. A Magellanic was found in a Humboldt colony in Chile one day last year, a thousand miles away from any Magellanic colony, standing alone on the beach, turning its head from side to side. Eventually, Shelly sent a researcher to retrieve it.

At dinner, Angela sat at a table of passengers, making herself available for questions. But her dining companions talked only of the animals they had not yet seen, pictures not yet taken, to-do lists not yet completed. An overfed man in his sixties who carried a satellite phone on his hip made a stupid joke about the length of the walrus penis.

"Twenty-eight inches," he said.

Twenty-seven inches longer than yours, Angela wanted to say.

"You're not eating the toothfish?" a female passenger asked.

"I don't eat fish," Angela said.

"You're missing out," said the woman's husband. "You don't get fresh Patagonian toothfish any day. Plus, they use a sustainable fishery."

"Guilt-free," the woman said, smiling.

Angela felt her shoulders tighten. "They can say it's sustainable, but they don't know for sure."

"What do you mean?"

"The toothfish live two thousand feet below the surface," Angela said. "It takes them seven years to reproduce, and there has never once been a census of any kind conducted. It's easy to say that these fish are sustainable if nobody can verify that they're not."

"Then why would they tell us that it's sustainable?" The woman seemed irritated.

"Because they use a fishery that adheres to certain quotas. But that doesn't take into account the poachers, the pirates, the ships who frequent the same fishing areas and take whatever they can, longlines and all."

"What are you saying?" the woman asked. "We can't eat toothfish anymore?"

"Excuse me." Angela stood and made her way to the observation deck. She could picture the woman complaining to Marcus, another door of her career closing behind her. But she didn't care.

With everyone inside at dinner, she was alone on the deck, a familiar feeling. And her mind was vacillating in a familiar way as well—a part of her wondering why she'd left Aeneas, another part realizing why. From the moment she'd boarded his ship, she'd been looking for reasons to leave, to go back home. It was safer that way. She couldn't stand to have another Diesel in her life.

It was late, and the lounge was deserted. The only people awake were in the engine room and on the bridge. As the boat churned its way into the Drake, Angela made her way to the computer room and found it empty. Usually there were lines of people waiting to check e-mail or send off photos. But the late hour and the high waves had given her a moment of peace.

She input the URL, an address she had memorized long ago for a website hosted by a satellite company, the company from which her research group rented time. She entered her user I.D., a password, and then watched the map assemble itself in pieces. It was a map of the South Atlantic Ocean with scattered red dots blinking against a blue background—each dot representing a penguin wearing a transmitter.

She entered a new number, the number of the transmitter that she carried with her from Punta Verde, the transmitter that she'd activated before tucking it away in the upper back pocket of Aeneas's yellow jacket—a jacket so bogged down with Blow Pops and maps and other gear that he would never notice the extra few ounces, or the small antenna peeking out of the zipper.

The map redrew itself, filling out the Southern Ocean in

blue, outlining the jagged edges of Antarctica. And then it appeared—a pulsing red dot in the Amundsen Sea. Nearly a thousand miles away from her now, with the distance steadily increasing.

She felt her body relax. She was with him again, and he was still above water. She pictured him with the Blow Pop in his hand, barking out commands as the *Tern* approached a whaling ship. For six weeks—eight possibly, until the battery died—she would be with him. She wouldn't have to let go of him, not yet.

ROBERT

DESPITE THE THRILL of catching one of the FBI's more elusive suspects, now that Robert had applied the handcuffs and read Aeneas his rights, he found himself plagued with second thoughts. Once the angst had been released from his body, the feelings buried much deeper began working their way to the top. For a brief moment, after pointing his gun at him, Robert wanted to fall to his knees and beg forgiveness. For so many years he'd craved the opportunity, hoping that the very act of asking for it would ease the pain.

The crew assembled around the deck. Aeneas looked at his troops and nodded agreeably as he scanned their faces. "Remember, you still have a job to do. You are here for the whales. I do not need rescuing. Forget about me. But don't forget about them."

With his own Zodiac damaged beyond repair, Robert pointed Aeneas into one of the *Tern's* Zodiacs, and they were lowered into the water. The boat had been prepped for battle, with a mass of barbed wire in the bow. Aeneas sat to one side; Robert stood holding the engine tiller. Above them on the main deck, the crew members watched silently, as well as Lynda. She would stay with the *Tern* as Robert transferred Aeneas to the *Roca*. From there, they could transport him by helicopter to the research base at McMurdo.

As they bounced across the waves, Aeneas gestured toward the *Takanami Maru* in the distance. "What is wrong with this picture?" he asked.

"What do you mean?"

"Tell me why they haven't run? The goddamned Argentine navy is here, and they're still hanging around, business as usual."

Robert could imagine what was going through Aeneas's mind, but he didn't want to get lured into looking at the world through his eyes. Empathy was a risk at times like these. It made you indecisive, compassionate, weak. And in those weak moments, you were most vulnerable to your enemy.

"Let's go after it," Aeneas said, with a grin on his face. "You drive, and I'll toss the prop fouler. Like old times. You can't tell me you don't miss this, at least a little bit."

Robert resisted the bait and kept his eyes straight ahead.

"Fair enough," Aeneas said. A moment later, he added, "But you can't tell me you don't miss Noa. For what it's worth, she misses you too."

"Noa's dead."

"Denial isn't healthy, Jake. But if it's closure you seek, that is certainly one way to go about it."

Robert ignored him, ignored the old name, telling himself that he was being baited, tricked. Aeneas always knew his opponents' weaknesses, and he knew Robert's well.

"You don't believe me? Then how about this," Acneas said. "I tell you where she is, and you let me have one last shot at the Japanese."

Robert eased up on the engine. "Give me one good reason why I should believe you."

"She's still single."

"I'm serious."

"So am I," Aeneas said. "I found Noa on the ice that day. It was a miracle that we both didn't fall through. Turned out she had a radio on her after all. So we survived. As did you."

Robert stared at him, wanting to believe him but at the

same time knowing he shouldn't.

"Perhaps you still feel regret," Aeneas continued. "Perhaps you're looking for redemption. The least you could do is find a cause worth defending, something more important than a flag."

"By this you mean a whale?"

"Nature tolerates us like one tolerates a headache. But it will not miss us when we're gone. Didn't you learn anything on my ship?"

"I learned how to fight a losing battle."

"Who said anything about losing? Nature is on *our* side, and she's patient."

Robert sighed. "Don't make me regret this," he said.

Aeneas looked back at the Japanese ship, now diminishing on the horizon, then held up his handcuffed wrists, awaiting the key.

Robert shook his head. "First you tell me where she is."

"There is plenty of time for talk. They're getting away."

Robert unlocked the handcuffs, then cut off a length of thick plastic line from the prop fouler and tossed it at Aeneas's feet.

"What's this for?"

"Tie one end to your right ankle and the other end to that hook on the floor."

"Do you honestly think I'm going to try to swim away?"

"Just a little insurance. To make sure you don't get too carried away out there."

Aeneas sat on the edge of the boat and fastened one end to his ankle.

"You can do better than that," Robert said.

Aeneas glanced up, then cinched the rope tight. He leaned over and fastened the other end to the floor. A shiny metal necklace dangled below his collarbone.

"What's that?" Robert asked.

"It's a penguin tag. Supposed to bring me luck."

"Doesn't seem to be working all that well."

"Better to be an optimist who fails than a pessimist who succeeds," Aeneas said, then grabbed a length of wire. "Into the breach."

Robert opened the throttle, and they leapt over the waves toward the Japanese ship. Robert felt a vague rush of adrenaline as they chased the five-story monster, remembering piloting the boat with Noa, watching her hair fly as she held the prop fouler, determined and patient.

Everything was in motion: the waves, the factory ship in the distance, the clouds above, the icebergs they navigated. Aeneas was right about the Japanese vessel—it demonstrated no fear of confrontation. As they got closer, Robert glimpsed men looking down at them over a railing.

As they drew alongside and began to approach the bow, sharp blasts of water sprayed down from above, the fire hoses at work. Then a popping noise.

"They're firing on us," Aeneas said.

Robert followed the noise to a man with a rifle, leaning over the railing. Robert pulled his gun and quickly released three rounds. The map slumped backwards, and Robert could not tell whether it was by fear or by force.

They were now drawing even with the bow of the ship. Aeneas held the prop fouler in both hands, waiting for Robert to cut across. Robert knew they had to be close enough to the ship so that the line would be consumed by the ship's natural currents, sliding under the hull and into the propellers. If they deployed too far ahead of the ship, the line could get pushed aside or too far below. Robert pulled ahead, eyes on the ship, preparing to veer across the bow. "You ready?" he asked.

But as he glanced at Aeneas, he saw that Aeneas was looking at something else, and Robert followed his eyes to see a Zodiac appearing out of nowhere, bearing down on them. Robert pulled on the tiller, but not in time. The deck beneath him heaved up, and he was in the air, then in the water, freezing water seeping through the cracks of his poorly sealed immersion suit.

The sky went black, or maybe it was the water and the fact that the hull of the *Maru* was passing by, blocking the sun. Robert couldn't think, he could only kick and paddle and pull his body back to the surface. He began to fear blacking out from the shock of the cold and the lack of air.

The sun returned, and he could see the sky through the water. He struggled for it, broke the surface, and heard himself panting, sucking in the air, then coughing up the water he ingested along the way. The ship? He looked to his left and could see the *Maru* moving away. Aeneas? He didn't see anyone else in the water, but he saw the rubbery outline of a Zodiac bobbing in and out of his line of vision, about a dozen yards away. He began swimming toward it, remembering how he'd leashed Aeneas to the boat, hoping now that he wasn't trapped beneath it.

But as he neared the Zodiac, he saw that it was upright and empty. He grabbed the outer handle and hung on for a few moments, gathering strength before pulling himself inside. He knelt on his knees and scanned the iceberg-strewn horizon, squinting into the patches of fog that had just begun to pockmark the landscape. He watched the *Maru*, pursuing another whale, nearly disappear into the mist. Robert could not see the all-white *Tern* at all. And Aeneas? The other Zodiac? He looked at the water for signs of shredded rubber floating, but amid the high waves and clouds of fog, he detected nothing.

Then the *Maru* emerged from the fog, having turned and headed back in Robert's direction, still in pursuit of its prey. Robert was tempted to fire off a couple more shots—perhaps he could save the whale, if nothing else about this mission—

but when he reached for his gun, he realized it was gone, sunk to the bottom of the ocean.

Then the high-pitched sound of a small engine filled his ears, and a Zodiac emerged from behind an iceberg, moving full speed. And there was Aeneas, alone at the controls in his bright yellow jacket, his hood down tight against the wind and sea spray. Robert fumbled to start up the engine of his Zodiac to give chase, to catch Aeneas before he boarded the *Tern*. But just as the engine came to life and Robert began to gain momentum, he realized that Aeneas was not headed for the *Tern*.

His destination was the *Maru,* and he went at it headfirst. He did not stop, did not turn. He picked up the prop fouler and held it up, and as Robert watched, in one horrifying and sickening moment, both man and boat were consumed under the bow of the *Maru*.

The *Maru* lurched to a halt as if it had struck an iceberg. Alarms sounded on the top deck. Robert frantically began searching for any sign of life, but he already knew the outcome: Like Noa, Aeneas would rather die than go to prison.

And, once again, Aeneas had taken Noa with him.

ANGELA

EVEN AFTER DISEMBARKING at Ushuaia, Angela could still feel the waves under her feet, the phantom ocean not yet releasing its grip on her body. Along with most of the *Narwhal's* passengers, she boarded a plane to Buenos Aires. From there, she headed south again, catching a flight to Trelew. While those around her chatted and read books and magazines, she kept her eyes out the window.

In Trelew, she stopped in to an Internet café and prepaid an hour. It had been ten hours since she'd last tracked Aeneas, and she felt nervous as she logged into the satellite portal and entered the transmitter number. The blue pixels assembled themselves, and she waited for the red dot to appear. It never did.

Angela stared at the screen, thinking that maybe her eyes were tired, the screen failing. She reentered the number. She refreshed the browser window. She switched from map view to chart view, scanning a long list of coordinates and dates and times.

According to the log, Aeneas's transmitter was last heard from eight hours and twenty minutes ago. Angela forced a deep breath and began to talk herself away from the precipice of fatal thoughts. The satellite simply hadn't detected the signal. Perhaps Aeneas was working down below in the engine room. Or maybe he'd finally put his yellow jacket into a washing machine; it would be just like him to leave everything in the pockets.

Angela felt her heart pounding. She stood and paced the room, then refreshed the map one more time, still hoping. But the red dot was gone, yet another in a long string of red dots gone missing from her life. Her computer time expired, and she stood and exited the café. She started toward the bus station but then reversed herself.

Back in the café, she purchased another hour.

She brought up the CDA website and was redirected to a black screen with nothing but a photo of Aeneas in the middle. Under it were the words *Rest in Peace.*

"Oh no," she heard herself saying. "Please, no."

She could feel her insides crumbling, her lungs seizing. She braced herself at the table, then she tried a search engine. She refused to believe it. He had died before, he used to tell her. And he'd always risen from the dead. In the search window, she entered *Aeneas* and was handed back more than a million results. She switched to news entries only and added the word *whale,* and she found an article in *The New York Times,* dated the day before. The headline was *Whale Warrior,* and the article included a quote from Aeneas: "We're doing what the rest of the world apparently does not have the stomach for—protecting its wildlife."

Another article, with the headline *Japanese Whalers Meet Resistance,* also featuring an Aeneas quote. Angela began to feel her mood rising. The CDA site was just a ruse, another device to throw off the authorities and nothing more.

Then she found a Reuters headline: *Tragedy in Antarctica.* She followed a link to a video clip credited to Greenpeace. She waited for the video to load, seconds that felt like forever, and then it was playing, the video screen shaky and blurred with mist. The scene was a familiar one—icebergs and low-lying clouds and Zodiacs skipping across the waves. Then, in the distance, an aging blue whaling vessel, a Zodiac headed for its bow. A man, alone, in a yellow jacket. She tried to make out the face, but the screen was too small, the video blurred.

She went to the Greenpeace website, then to other news sites, other search engines. She played the clip again. She tried full screen. A man in a yellow jacket. A man in a yellow jacket heading for the bow of a whaling ship, then falling under.

The video was too blurry to be believed, or maybe it was her eyes. But she would not accept it. There was simply not enough data. She arrived at the home page of *The Sydney Morning Herald.* Angela saw only headlines about taxes, fires, cricket. She began to exhale, until she scrolled down the page and saw: *Anti-whaling Leader Confirmed Dead.*

In the article, Lauren Davis of the CDA confirmed his death. Aeneas had been sucked underneath the Japanese whaling vessel *Takanami Maru*, she said. She credited Aeneas for saving the lives of three hundred whales by disabling the vessel. "The battle continues," she was quoted as saying. "We have only just begun to fight." Greenpeace reported hauling in the remnants of a Zodiac along with a shredded, bloodstained yellow jacket.

Angela closed her eyes. He was gone, truly gone—and this was how she had to learn about it: satellites and computer screens. A century ago, months would have passed before she learned the news, months spent going to sleep hopeful. Now the facts arrived too quickly. How she hated technology.

She opened her eyes and read his obituary, which, given the risks he liked to take, had probably been ready to go for years. He had tempted death long enough for every newspaper to have an obituary on hand.

Yet even in death, Aeneas managed to surprise her. Neil Patrick Cameron had been born in Port Townsend, Washington, inherited a fishing boat, spent a year in college before dropping out, was married and divorced twice—this she now knew. What she did not know was that Aeneas was survived by a son, Neil Jr., age 28. A son from his first marriage.

Her Internet time expired. She stared at the blank screen, until someone tapped her on the shoulder. A young tourist waiting in line.

ANGELA CAUGHT THE LAST TOUR BUS to Punta Verde, arriving in the evening. The research office was empty, her former colleagues most likely at dinner. She started toward the dining hall, then stopped. Her mind had gone blank. What story would she tell them? The narrative no longer made sense. She ran away with a man, like a schoolgirl, had her heart broken, and then ran away again. And now she was home, no more secure than when she'd left, haunted by indecision and not fully whole, a part of her still down there eluding ships, hiding behind icebergs.

She made her way to her trailer and stopped at a small wooden cross placed where Diesel used to live. On it was inscribed:

Diesel
Rest in Peace

Angela heard a noise and turned to see Shelly standing behind her. Her hair was streaked with emerging sparks of gray, a reminder of how long Angela had been away. The molt was well under way. Angela wasn't sure what to say, so she let Shelly speak first.

"Doug suggested *Molt in Peace*," Shelly said. "I overruled him."

"Thank you."

"How was your leave of absence?"

Angela avoided Shelly's eyes and stared at the cross. "I'm sorry I lost the transmitter."

"At least *you* returned."

"You don't mind if I stay?"

"Mind? Of course not. I need you to take Doug off my hands. He's rather clingy."

THE NEXT DAY, ANGELA TOOK DOUG to the Back Bay, a flat stretch of land near the water. She watched him remove a juvenile from its burrow with one fast-moving hand. He weighed and measured the bird before returning it to its agitated mother.

"Nicely done," Angela said.

"I had a good teacher," he said. "Listen, I'm sorry I pressured you about Aeneas."

"That's okay," she said. "It's natural to feel protective of this place."

"Had I known who he was, I would have helped. We all would have. I should have just kept my mouth shut. Next time, I will."

"Don't worry. There won't be a next time."

They found a red-dot bird, and this time Angela let Doug do everything on his own.

"How old is this one?" he asked.

Angela did the math in her head. "Twenty-nine."

Doug laughed. "Wow. He's older than I am." He looked up at Angela and caught himself.

"No offense taken," she said. She wanted to laugh along with him. She wanted to rejoice in the accomplishment of this small animal, surviving so long under such conditions, so many predators and risks. There was a time she would have. But not today.

ROBERT

WHEN ROBERT ENTERED the windowless conference room at FBI headquarters, Gordon and Lynda were already seated around a table with three others.

"Sorry I'm late," Robert said.

"I thought you were on vacation," Gordon said.

"Not yet."

Robert took a seat next to a rotund man that he recognized from the Pentagon. Across from him was a woman who had the look of some sort of analyst, bookish and cold. The overhead lights were dimmed, and a video was projected onto the wall.

"Is this the Greenpeace footage?" the woman asked.

"Yes," Gordon said. "They were the only ones filming. You're going to see several versions of the clip. The first is original footage, followed by a close-up, and then another close-up in which we ran a sharpening filter."

Robert looked up at the screen, watching a man in a yellow jacket standing alone in a Zodiac approaching the bow of the Japanese ship. The man, with his back to the camera, held aloft the prop fouler with one hand, the steering bar of the Zodiac with the other. It was rather cinematic, Robert had to admit, and it was just like Aeneas, as if he'd known a camera was on him the whole time. The camera began to shudder, and wisps of fog blurred the scene. The yellow jacket disappeared into the water, and the bow consumed the Zodiac without pause.

"No body was recovered," Gordon said. As the scene iterated again and again, the ending remained the same.

"Probably wrapped around the propeller along with the barbed wire," the large man said.

"I'd expect them to find nothing, given the circumstances," someone added.

"Body or no body, we're confident this was Aeneas," Gordon said. "We had documented every crew member of the *Tern* in Puerto Madryn, and we did so again after this incident. Everyone was accounted for. Only Aeneas was missing."

"Looks more like he jumped in than fell," the large man said.

"What's the difference?" Lynda said. "The result's the same."

"An interesting case study," the woman said. "He had come to view the human race as some sort of invasive species, like weeds."

"That just goes to show that we can't overlook the potential of the homegrown ecoterror movement in this country," the large man said. "This is no different than a suicide bombing."

The meeting droned on, and Robert tuned them out until lights came up and the room emptied. Robert felt Gordon looking at him as Gordon walked past on his way out, but Robert didn't acknowledge him. Although the wall at the front of the room was blank again, Robert continued to stare at it, then noticed Lynda standing over him.

"You know, you're not getting any overtime for being here," she said.

"Do you really think Aeneas jumped?"

"Somebody jumped," she said. "Aeneas is the only one missing. So, yeah, I think he jumped."

"He would never have done that."

"Then who did, Sherlock?"

Robert wanted to suggest someone else, anyone else, but who else was there? So he kept his silence. If he were to start asking questions, he would only disrupt her life along with his.

"How's your husband?" Robert asked. "Glad to have you back?"

"You have no idea," she said. "He was so bored and lonely he actually fixed the leak in the bathroom. Another week and he might have actually painted the garage."

Lynda reached into her purse and removed a manila envelope.

"Here. Since you didn't bring a camera, I made extra copies. Something to remember me by."

After she left, Robert opened the envelope. Inside was a photo of him staring over the railing of the *Roca*, looking terse, before everything fell apart. A photo of a whale—a small dot on the horizon—and photos of penguins in Punta Verde, icebergs, the Japanese ships. A photo from the *Tern* when they first boarded her, with Lauren standing defiantly in the background. A picture of the crew, taken after Aeneas had disappeared, faces vacant, shoulders slumped.

"Case closed."

Robert turned. It was Gordon. He stood and looked his boss in the eyes. "It doesn't feel closed."

"It never really is." Gordon leaned against the table and folded his arms. "There is something we picked up on the wire taps that I didn't share with the group. Care to speculate who the new leader of the CDA is?"

"Lauren Davis."

"How'd you know?"

"Lucky guess."

"It's just a matter of time before you'll be arresting her."

"What makes you think I'll have to?"

"Aeneas's death has been a boon for fundraising and

volunteers. They're going to purchase a second ship."

LATER, ROBERT LEFT HIS MUSTY APARTMENT and went for a jog. The air was warmer than usual, and he found himself running for more than an hour, his mind circling the events of the past two weeks.

Back home, after a shower and a meal, he eyed his luggage, still sitting in the corner, packed. Oddly, there was a part of him that didn't want the trip to end. As if he could go back and change things.

He emptied his bags onto the bed. Clothing and toiletries, passport and files. He noticed a photo that had slipped out of one of the files and picked it up.

It was a picture of Ethan Downes, from the *Emperor of the Seas*. The cruise ship passenger gone missing. Robert sat on the bed, his heart suddenly pounding, and studied the photo. He had seen this face before, but where? He closed his eyes, picturing Ethan's face, searching for a match, for context.

His eyes flew open as he realized he'd seen the same face aboard the *Tern*. He was sure of it. Through his binoculars, watching the crew members throw bombs at the *Maru*, he'd seen Ethan Downes, somehow, among the deckhands. But it didn't make sense.

He opened the packet of photos from Lynda, removed the group picture of the *Tern*, taken after Aeneas had died, and focused on each and every person. Ethan was not among them.

But Robert knew he was right. At some point in time, Ethan had been on that boat.

ANGELA

DAYS PASSED, THEN WEEKS. She tried to forget him, but Aeneas was like Diesel: Every day in the field triggered a memory. The way Aeneas would yank on his end of the rope, pulling her toward him so he could kiss her. The spontaneous whistling behind her as she hiked through the brush. The sound of his breathing, heavy as they climbed up the dried riverbeds. Now there was just the sound of wind.

On a drizzly morning, Angela set out to visit a crèche near the tourist trail. When penguin chicks reached a certain age, they congregated together in large flocks, still dependent upon their parents to emerge from the water and feed them, but only a few weeks removed from entering the water themselves.

When Angela arrived, two caracaras were fighting over the carcass of a chick, and she waved them off. The safest part of the crèche was the middle, protected from predators, the weather, and the occasional aggressive adult. The chicks on the outer edges were the weaker birds, or the sick, or maybe just different.

It occurred to Angela, standing there watching them, that she, too, had been on the outer edge of the crèche when Aeneas washed ashore. Voluntarily, she had isolated herself from the group, living in a trailer instead of the *cueva*, eating alone, walking alone so many nights. By the time Aeneas had arrived, she was vulnerable, and perhaps she left too soon, without knowing fully how to swim.

Up over the hill, she heard the honking of horns. The gate had been lifted, the tourist trail opened. Dust and smoke clouds billowed. She turned and walked in the opposite direction. She decided that it was time she completed a few other circles that she and Aeneas had left unfinished.

She headed north. She passed guanacos on the hill, standing between her and the ocean, watching her with one eye as they nibbled on scrub grass. She angled toward the water, toward the place she'd first found Aeneas, the shells crunching underfoot. She stopped and looked out over the water, hoping for a vessel of any kind.

"What happened to you?" she asked aloud. She could still see Aeneas standing on the bridge, nose to the front window, hair falling over his ears, eyes focused on the icebergs ahead.

She finished the circles, then sat on a hill and nibbled on a peanut butter sandwich. This would be the last time she traveled this far north this season. The penguins would be gone soon, headed north themselves, following the food. She would worry about them but remind herself that they were exactly where they belonged, in their comfort zone. The land was always a temporary diversion for them, as the sea had been for her.

A glint caught her eye and she poked her head into a burrow in search of a band. Could this be a red dot? she wondered. She opened her notebook.

"Hello, *pingüina*."

She turned and looked up, squinting against the light. Aeneas. She stood and took him in, blinking, unsure whether he was real.

He wore a faded camouflage jacket, torn in a few places. His beard had filled in and was grayer than she'd imagined it would be. He'd lost a few pounds. His face was weary.

"What are you doing here?" she asked.

He reached into his pocket and pulled out the necklace she had given him. Her penguin tag.

"I told you I would return it to you," he said. He came closer and opened the clasp, then reached around her neck. Angela stood still as he attached the chain. She felt herself wanting to hug him, to wrap her arms around his shoulders and band herself to him forever. But she remembered the news articles. The video. If he didn't go under that ship, who did?

"Where's your jacket?" she asked.

Aeneas looked down as if to confirm that it was indeed missing, then looked evasively at the horizon, then, finally, returned his eyes to her.

ETHAN

WHEN HE'D OPENED HIS EYES he'd seen blue sky, a window in the clouds above him. He sat up, realizing that he had slept. The clouds still hung low, some scraping the water.

He heard an engine, a low throttled sound that he felt more than heard—a large ship, but that was all he knew. He started the Zodiac and headed toward the noise. The wind had begun to blow again and, with it, the clouds. Soon Ethan could make out icebergs all around him, then he saw the source of the noise: the *Maru*, only a half mile ahead.

His heartbeat quickened—it was time. Time to do what he'd planned to do before losing his way in the fog. Maybe it was meant to happen this way, he thought. Maybe he'd had to lose his way in order to find his way all along.

He accelerated, squinting into the wind, feeling the cold penetrate his jacket, yet not actually feeling cold. Instead he felt powerful, invincible, like a bullet fired true with nothing but gravity and inertia to stop it from reaching its target. He was that bullet as he neared the bow of the *Maru*. Water rained down on him from above. He squinted more, was now ahead of the bow, then he cut across and reached down for the prop fouler.

When he looked up, he barely saw the other Zodiac, and then it was on top of him. He was in the air, then down again, caught in the wire. The sky darkened as the *Maru*'s hull passed by. But his Zodiac had, somehow, remained upright, and when he pulled himself to his knees, he saw Aeneas in the water next to the other Zodiac, now empty. He thought he glimpsed the flash of someone else in the water as he hurried to Aeneas, who was waving him over.

Ethan pulled him in and, using a knife from the supply box, cut off the rope around his ankle. Aeneas, shivering, muttered, "FBI," and motioned for Ethan to head back to the *Tern*, still off in the distance, mostly shrouded in fog. Ethan looked back and saw a man in the water, paddling his way to the empty Zodiac.

And as Ethan headed toward the *Tern*, he realized there would be others with the FBI, perhaps already on board, who would capture Aeneas all over again. If they returned to the ship now, Ethan would be delivering Aeneas straight to them.

He turned the Zodiac around and headed behind a group of icebergs. Aeneas said nothing; his eyes were glazed and he looked frozen nearly all the way through. Behind a towering berg, Ethan found a slab of pack ice, thick enough to walk on. He pulled alongside and helped Aeneas onto the ice.

"What?" Aeneas asked.

"Here, take my jacket. It's dry."

Ethan removed his jacket and waited for Aeneas to remove his. He was surprised when Aeneas did as instructed. As he pulled on Ethan's jacket, Ethan boarded the Zodiac again, donning Aeneas' dripping yellow jacket.

Then he tossed Aeneas the emergency flare. Aeneas would know when to use it. As Ethan pulled away, he heard Aeneas call his name, but he did not turn back.

The wind had strengthened, and the waves were so high that the Japanese ship briefly disappeared from view. One wave—a dark gray, white-tipped mountain—bore down on him, threatening failure, but then he pushed up and over the mountain and saw his target once again.

He kept the jacket's hood drawn tight. As he passed the *Tern*, he turned his face away. He felt sorry for what they were about to witness.

Ethan looked ahead at the bow of the *Maru*, searching for men with guns aimed at him. He saw only one man stationed at the harpoon, which was aimed directly at him.

The bow of the ship was nearly above him now. He grabbed the prop fouler and held it up. Strangely, he wasn't afraid, even knowing what was about to happen. That his boat would be cut in half. That he would be pulled under the bow and into the propeller. That his body, along with the nest of plastic, hemp, and barbed wire, would stop the propellers.

Before, he'd lived his life with the comfort of a nearby *undo* button. Now, there would be no more *undo*s. As the ship began blaring its horns, wind narrowing his eyes, a mountain of black steel rising up, there was nothing more to regret.

He remembered the lady walking into the river in St. Louis. Back then, and for most of his life, Ethan had been someone who'd stopped at the water's edge, while others kept going. His father. Annie.

He could see the churning. Coming fast. The bow of the ship obstructed the sky, the water darkening. He held up his arm, prop fouler tight and ready.

It all made sense now. Finding Annie. Losing Annie. Finding Aeneas. Annie had been his perfect match. Aeneas's jacket was a perfect fit.

He could feel motion under him, the ocean taking control. And he kept going.

ROBERT

Tourism, Gordon liked to say, was the true opiate of the masses; it fostered the illusion that people could escape. You might leave your home, your country, your continent. You might even end up in Antarctica. But you could never escape yourself. And perhaps that was why Gordon didn't question Robert when he said he was taking a leave of absence and didn't know when or if he would return.

"I need closure," Robert said. And Gordon extended a hand.

The Ethan Downes case was still open, but the two junior agents assigned to the case were already back in Washington. There was no sense of urgency or optimism. Once the media and the cameramen had begun packing, so, too, had they.

Robert had carefully chosen the itinerary for his so-called vacation, and it was in part because he could not stop wondering about Ethan. He could connect the dots in his head; he could logistically place Ethan on the Zodiac that knocked him into the water, but he could not, for the life of him, understand *why*. Why would a tourist martyr himself for such a cause? Or maybe all Robert's questions and theories were nothing more than a sad attempt to keep Aeneas alive, and, by extension, to keep Noa alive.

All these theories were leading him south again. Another layover in Miami, another long flight to Buenos Aires. He had Lynda's voice in his head now—*Are you sure, Bobby?* This time, he would be sure.

THE TOUR BUS TO PUNTA VERDE swayed as the currents of
the Andes tried to push it off the road. At the tourist trail,
Robert followed the hordes for a few hundred yards, then
veered down a path devoid of penguins and, not surprisingly,
devoid of tourists. He hopped the rope and headed into the
brush. He walked quickly, slightly crouched, to avoid the eyes
of a park guard or any naturalists. He headed for the last hill
overlooking the water, knowing that once he crested it, he
would be hidden from the public. Surprised penguins darted
about as he passed, some snapping at his legs.

Robert headed north for a mile and then angled back
inland for the tallest hill in the area. He raised his binoculars
and scanned the horizon. At first, he saw nothing. He thought
about continuing on but decided to wait. He sat and watched
the penguins stare at him from beneath their bushes. A large
chick inched toward him, its parents braying at it from their
burrow. Robert remained still as the penguin pecked at his
hiking shoe, then turned and scurried home. He felt guilty
for having left the tourist trail, for trampling over ground
reserved for smaller feet and the few who study them.

He stood and scanned the area once more.

In the valley, to his north, he noticed movement, then
zoomed in, and saw two people dressed in khaki-colored
clothing. They were on either end of a length of rope. On
one end, he recognized the researcher he'd met the first time
he'd come—Angela. On the other end of the rope was a man,
crouched, his head inside a penguin burrow. When the man
stood up, Robert saw his face.

Aeneas.

Robert stared through the binoculars for a few more
minutes, then lowered them. He didn't know what surprised
him more, seeing Aeneas—a living, breathing Aeneas—or

knowing that his instincts, for once, had been spot-on.

With one call, Robert could close two cases, once and for all. The missing cruise ship passenger. The supposedly dead ecoterrorist. He would receive a promotion, a raise. Maybe he would buy a house, finally settle down. Live the life he should have been living all along. With one call.

He raised the binoculars once again. The two looked like an old married couple, a harmony between them, she standing in the middle, scribbling in her notebook, while he orbited. He could leave them alone, and probably should. At the same time, he and Aeneas still had unfinished business. And, as he had for so many years, Robert wanted to finish it.

He pocketed his binoculars and made his way, carefully, down to where they worked.

ROBERT AWOKE TO THE GLOW of the flight tracker's bluish screen. He'd fallen asleep and, thankfully, had given nobody a reason to awaken him. No nightmares, no shouting.

He sat up in the dark and blinked at the screen. The little white plane was suspended over blue water, its nose nearly touching the eastern coast of South Africa. Another two hours and he would be in Cape Town, waiting for a connection to Windhoek. The resignation letter would arrive on Gordon's desk at about the same time Robert arrived in Namibia.

The screen refreshed, the nose of the plane now suspended over Africa. He returned the flight tracker to his armrest. Robert looked out the window to find only clouds, but he knew where he was headed. Aeneas, fulfilling his end of the bargain, had told him everything at Punta Verde. And Robert, fulfilling his end of the bargain, left them alone together, without a word to Gordon or anyone else.

It was the time of the culling. Soon the Cape fur seals

would be giving birth to pups. Noa would be there, defending them. And, if not, it was a good enough place to begin.

ANGELA

ONE NIGHT, ALONE IN HER TRAILER, Angela heard a noise. She pulled on her jacket and stepped outside. It was a windy night. Geraldo, standing next to the trailer, scurried off toward the water, into the darkness.

It was the end of the season, time for the penguins to return to sea, time for good-byes. Aeneas's ship had returned two weeks ago, and he left with it. She knew she couldn't keep him forever, and she didn't need forever. There were battles still to be fought, whales to be saved, penguins to be counted.

As the penguins left, so, too, would the humans. First the tourist trail would go empty. Then the naturalists, with nothing left to study, would pack up and leave. Angela would be needed in Boston, to finish her Ph.D., grade papers, administer exams—but lately, she'd been thinking of wintering here instead. Extra time alone would not be such a bad thing, or so she told herself. The true reason would be to keep an eye out for him, a man washed upon the rocks in need of a sheltering shore.

Angela crested the hill and sat in her usual place. She reached up to touch the penguin tag around her neck. A penguin approached, a young male, by the looks of him. Probably curious to see such a large creature as herself, and apparently glad to find her unattached. He circled her, brushed her with his flapping wings. The old familiar circle dance. He danced to win her, to draw her to his nest, such a sad, fruitless, beautiful gesture.

Angela sat still as the bird circled her, continuing his ancient ritual, as she watched a light on the horizon, moving slowly across the water.

ACKNOWLEDGMENTS

This novel is dedicated to the many researchers and activists who have dedicated their lives to protecting animals, a handful of which are listed below:

Animal Legal Defense Fund
www.aldf.org

Center for Ecosystem Sentinels
www.ecosystemsentinels.org

Farm Animal Rights Movement (FARM)
www.farmusa.org

International Fund for Animal Welfare
www.ifaw.org

Our Hen House
www.ourhenhouse.org

The Sea Shepherd Society
www.seashepherd.org

Where Oceans Hide
Their Dead

ROBERT

CHAPTER 1

THE KILLING BEGINS AT DAWN.

Men and barely men spill out of the backs of rusted
pickup trucks. Some are dressed for the job, wearing green
rubber boots and bloodstained white overalls; others are in
torn jeans, barefoot, shirtless. They carry axe handles or bats
or pieces of rebar.

They take their time, yawning themselves awake, slowly
cresting the craggy hill, pausing to take in the windblown
waves in the shallow distance, then divide themselves as they
approach their victims diagonally, picking up the pace, then
swinging with purpose.

The victims, seals no more than a year old, scatter,
clouds of sand and dirt rising. When one squirts through
the tightening gyre, a man gives chase, cutting it off before

it reaches the safety of water. He batters the creature into stillness, sticks a knife into its belly.

It takes a deep-seated desperation to do this sort of work, but in this part of Africa desperation is more abundant than jobs. That's what Noa had told him. She told him of the sands spotted black with blood, the mother seals, separated from their pups, helpless bystanders to the slaughter, heads swaying, sepulchral, their guttural voices calling out to lifeless bodies. And, as the men piled the bodies like sacks of soil onto the backs of pickups, the mothers made their sad retreat to the ocean, some with fatal injuries of their own.

The seals suffer this carnage every year, and still they return to these same sandy, rock-strewn shores. Robert suggested the seals were stupid, but Noa disagreed. They have run out of desolate beaches, she told him. This has been their home for thousands of years; they will not go down without a fight. *The seals*, she told him, *are the mirrors of our sins.*

Noa told him all of this more than five years ago, when they shared a ship's cabin and she was a hardened activist, he a seasick wannabe. They were passengers on a ship that placed itself with regularity between whales and whalers. Hull against hull, smoke bombs and stray bullets and shrapnel. Dangerous work by any standard.

But this was never good enough for Noa. She was impatient to do more, risk more. When the world awakened to their battle on the water and the cameras outnumbered the crew, she said she would move on to those animals the world still ignored. There were so many species without sponsors, without any hope of attention.

The Cape fur seals brought her to tears. She swore that she would come down here one day and place her body between the seals and those spiked wooden clubs.

Robert had sworn to join her. He swore it the last night they spent together, both of them squeezed into a one-man cot in their vessel in the far North Atlantic. He swore to follow her wherever she went, and he intended to make good on his promise.

But he was an FBI agent, working undercover, sworn to a higher power, so any promise he'd made—and he'd made many—had been, in the end, a lie.

CHAPTER 2

IN THE DARK OF EARLY MORNING, Robert pulls off the dirt road, behind a strand of dust-covered bushes. On the horizon he sees the moon reflected off the waves. This was supposed to be the road to Dunkel Beach, but without any signs he has been going on word of mouth.

A week before, he'd begun his Namibian odyssey 500 miles up north, at the Cape Cross Seal Reserve. There, Robert had comfortably played the part of tourist on holiday, with so many others around to blend in with. Slow-roaming herds of travelers discharged from tinted-windowed buses. Shoulder to shoulder with aimless, younger, round-the-world types with backpacks and beards.

He had been to Namibia years before, back when he was fresh out of the FBI academy and eager for passport stamps. He spent two weeks on the trail of arms traffickers on their way south from Angola. So he was already familiar with the country's slower pace, crooked cops, and crumbling infrastructure. The money, in U.S. denominations, was the only thing that kept this part of the world running—though judging by the number of Chinese tourists he'd seen crowding the viewing area, he suspected *yuan* might be equally effective these days.

Robert gazed over the dusty beach, undulating with the

motion of thousands of brown fur seals, crowded together like the humans who were watching them. It was the first hot day of spring, and many of the larger seals stood high on their black flippers, noses vertical, as if posing. Others lay prostrate, pups at their sides, nursing. And amid these motionless bodies, seals commuted to and from the water, pausing every so often to bark at a competitor or howl at nothing in particular— or at least nothing Robert could discern. Even with wind blowing hard out to sea, the chorus of yelps and grunts was loud enough to drown out the sounds of the tourists and their beeping cameras. Robert wondered if the tourists knew that this beach was often the scene of great violence.

His eyes swept the beach, then turned to study the faces of the crowd.

She was not there.

He got back in his rental car and headed south, meandering from one increasingly desolate port town to another, where the number of travelers dwindled along with his hopes of finding her. The locals weren't of much help. Any time he asked someone about seal culling, he got that familiar, off-putting look—as if he were one of them. An activist. One of those outsiders bent on telling Namibians how to live their lives.

Just last night, in the harbor town of Lüderitz, he asked the clerk at his motel, a heavyset woman transfixed by a *Real Housewives* rerun, where he could find seals. She shook her head and handed him the same faded brochure from the Cape Cross Seal Reserve he'd been given a dozen times before. In fading light, Robert walked two blocks from the motel to the rocks bordering the shallow and mostly vacant port. A few lonely sailboats kept rhythm off to one side. At the end of a pier were two rusted fishing trawlers, the remnants of a once-thriving industry.

Robert's mind began entertaining thoughts of getting in

his car, returning to Windhoek, completing the round-trip journey back to Washington. Gordon, his former boss, would surely take him back. Gordon had always said that it took a decade to create a reliable federal agent, and at thirty-five Robert was more than a decade into his tenure. Agents quit all the time in fits of madness or frustration, only to return a few days or weeks later. This little detour would qualify as madness. Searching for a woman he once believed dead, a woman who wanted nothing to do with him when she was still alive. A history he was now hoping to rewrite even though a part of him had grown comfortable with the current narrative. There was a comfort of sorts in assuming that, if alive, she would not take him back anyway. Perhaps he was not as scared of failure as he was of success—to find her and learn, finally, whether there could be a future on the other side of all those memories.

Robert stepped into a small bar named Kappy's and sat next to a man named George to watch a rugby match. George was chatty, and Robert's instincts told him that the man was worth listening to. George had been in town a week waiting for a road construction job to begin, drinking through the paycheck he hadn't yet earned. He talked about the jobs he had worked, meandering his way up the coast from South Africa. Fisherman. "I spent more time bent over the rail than catching anything," he said. Furniture mover. "Wrenched my *bladdy* back hoisting a fridge into the truck."

But there were worse jobs out there, he told Robert, pure *kak* jobs. "You ever seen them harvest seals?" George asked. Robert shook his head and bought him another round. "Check here, my friend. It ain't like plucking grapes." And that's when George told him about Dunkel Beach.

And now, with Dunkel Beach ahead of him somewhere in the darkness, Robert gets out of the car and turns his back to the biting wind. He should have packed a jacket. Even though the calendar reads late September and the days feel like Southern California, it is winter here, and the nights and mornings feel more like Northern Ontario. He continues down the road, and after about hundred yards hears the surf over the wind. Then the smell, foul and fishy. He stops and tilts his head and hears the yelps and grunts of a seal colony.

Noa had said that the sealers arrived before daybreak and were long gone before any tourists showed. The killing device of choice was not a gun. Guns were rare and bullets expensive. But wooden clubs were plentiful. The leaders usually carried the official killing tool—the hakapik, which looked like something mountain climbers use, a sharp ice pick at the end of a long handle with a flat hammerhead on the other side. The dull end was used for crushing the skull, the sharp end for dragging the body. From a distance, Noa said, the men could almost be mistaken for farmers sowing the land.

For so much of his adult life, the early hours of the day were the least enjoyable, not just because he was often hungover or sleeping in a third-world hotel room but because he always associated dawn with death. Years ago, while in training at the academy, the early hours were used to test them. In the pre-dawn hours they were shouted at for yawning, for not reciting the correct phrase at the correct moment, ever reminded that they may be called upon to protect a life or take a life before the rest of the world was awake. Robert was excited back then, in his early twenties and aimless and eager to be a part of this new workforce, one that operated outside of business hours.

Robert hears movement to his left, swivels to make eye contact with a large cat. A jaguar, he thinks, but smaller. A broad, curious face, eyes catching the moon, then turning and sliding into the bushes. A sighting so brief Robert begins to wonder if he saw it at all.

Robert gets back in his car and checks his watch. It's only 4:45. On the horizon he sees a tiny light, most likely a fishing trawler. Most likely illegal. He watches the light move slowly across the windshield and thinks back to that night in his hotel, high above LAX, watching the lights of planes approaching the runway, wondering if he would succeed in his first solo undercover assignment.

His name was Jake for that role, and he was in LA for the Rights for Animals Conference. Playing the part of animal rights activist, he dressed in old jeans, a faded black T-shirt, Converse sneakers, and a wristband with the word PEACE imprinted on it.

He spent the first day downstairs wandering the sessions, from *Activism Against Vivisection* to *In Defense of Predators*. As an FBI agent, he was there to meet Neil Patrick Cameron, known as Aeneas, the infamous founder of the anti-whaling organization Cetacean Defense Alliance. As Jake, he was there because he was committed to the cause, eager to join the next boat sailing out to do battle with whaling ships.

When he met Aeneas at the CDA booth, Jake told him of his desire to join the crew. Aeneas told him the boat was full and to try again next year.

But Jake wouldn't be around next year; Robert and the FBI didn't have the luxury of time. They were pursuing a domestic terrorist known as Darwin who had been torching mink farms in Idaho and releasing the animals. Darwin had caused millions of dollars in damage, which didn't include lost revenue for the farms. No one knew what Darwin looked like, and Robert suspected that it was Aeneas himself. What he did know was that Darwin was a member of the CDA and would be on that next boat out.

How could an outsider become an insider in less than a day? Robert was asking himself this as he exited a session and stepped straight into a woman in a long madras skirt and a white Kiss Me, I'm Vegan tank top. She grabbed his arms for balance, and he grabbed her waist. After an awkward moment, a moment that lasted a half second too long, a half second he would replay forever, she pulled back. Or he released his hands. When their eyes met, he smiled, and she wrinkled her brow. Then she began to walk away.

"Do you get many takers?" he asked.

She stopped and turned around.

"Your shirt," he said.

She eyed him suspiciously, studying him from head to toe. "You're vegan?"

"Of course," he said.

"Then how do you explain that?" She pointed at his wristband, the wristband that he suddenly realized was made of leather.

He smiled sheepishly. "I don't eat it; I just wear it."

"Perhaps you should visit the orientation session. Room 105. And take notes." She shook her head, and he watched her walk away. She had seen right through his disguise, though not far enough.

A car door slams, and Robert is jolted awake, eyes blinking into the dawn. He reaches up and grabs the steering wheel, pulls himself upright. The sun is still low, his car's shadow outstretched toward the water, and he notices a vehicle parked a hundred yards ahead of him.

It is an old commercial van made less so with bumper stickers wallpapered across its olive-green exterior. A roof rack carries large plastic bins of various sizes and colors. On another continent Robert would dismiss this heap as a bunch of surfers getting a head start on the waves. But not here, not now. These people are getting a head start, all right—but not on the surf.

Four people emerge, three men and one woman, a blonde with a ponytail. One of the men carries a video camera. The others carry signs. The woman is wearing sunglasses, and Robert can't tell if she's Noa, not from this far back. Noa's hair was dark when he was with her, twisted into dreadlocks. He curses himself for not packing binoculars.

He climbs out of the car and carefully approaches, keeping his distance. He watches them pause at the top of the hill before descending out of view.

What will Robert say if it is Noa? *Funny meeting you here? I just happened to be in the neighborhood? Took a wrong turn at Windhoek?*

And what if it's not her? What will he say then? The sightseeing line won't hold up, not at this hour, this far south. The truth is tempting but too risky. These people will be on guard as it is, and he'd only be perceived as another threat, particularly if he asked the whereabouts of one of their own.

But if he can't play the activist or the tourist, what role is left for him to play?

He notices his right hand behind his back, checking on a phantom gun. It is a strange feeling to be entering a situation, like so many others in which conflict appears inevitable, and not to carry a weapon. Though he had spent the previous twelve years silently resenting the weight of it, the perpetual pressure against his lower back, now that he is without it he feels unbalanced and vulnerable. His mind must adjust to a life of avoiding conflict rather than abetting it. From now on, evasion, not engagement, will be his life.

When he crests the hill he surveys the chaos unfolding on the shore below him. Spread across a sloping beach the size of a football field are hundreds of seals, yelping, heads waving, pups scattered about like schoolyard backpacks. Among them are a dozen men in two groups on opposite sides of the beach, swinging clubs at flapping, squirming pups.

Parked on the sand are two old pickup trucks, one towing an empty utility trailer. How did these trucks not wake him, he wonders, then notices the tracks extending along the sand for another half mile; they'd arrived by a different route.

Two of the activists stand far away, at the waterline, urging seals to escape, holding their pointless signs. The woman is screaming at one of the groups of men, bumping into them sideways to slow them down. This could be Noa—she'd always been the first to jump into the action—but this woman's body is leaner than Robert remembers.

Far off to the right is the activist with the video camera, a man in his twenties with shaggy brown hair and a beard to match, approaching another gang of sealers. His fellow activists, signs held high, form a backdrop. Two of the sealers are gesturing at the camera.

Robert picks up his pace until he is jogging down the hill, still unsure of what he is going to do or say. He needs to be closer to be sure, to see her eyes, but this is hardly the right time. He should wait, stay up on the hill. Yet something propels him toward the fight. Years of habit? Or maybe the simple fact that he wants the seals' crying to stop.

He gets closer, until he is standing behind one of the sealers, a kid maybe sixteen or seventeen years old, with no shoes and no shirt, oblivious to Robert's presence. As the kid raises high a rough-hewn wooden bat, Robert grabs it and pulls him around, and the kid's eyes widen with surprise.

The kid pulls back on the tool until Robert lets him have it. The end that Robert was holding is stained dark red, as are his hands.

"Beach closed," the kid says.

"So what are you doing here?"

The kid swings the bat at Robert, who ducks, then lunges into the kid's abdomen, knocking him to the ground. He grabs the bat again and turns to follow the woman's voice. Still standing, still screaming. He continues across the sand toward the cameraman.

The seals are kicking up clouds of sand and dust, and he now understands the meaning of the bandannas across mouths. The process, if there is one, entails men circling the seals, scaring them into one another and, eventually, one of the men landing a lethal blow. But so few of the blows are lethal. The seals keep changing direction, the objects of some primeval game of baseball.

A young man is stabbing a seal in the eyes with a Bowie knife. The throaty sounds of crying fill the air, and pups scurry about with milk leaking from their mouths. And now, drips and pools of red in brown-and-white gull guano on rock are mixed together, a grisly Pollock.

The cameraman is surrounded. The boy that Robert disarmed shouts at him, then slaps him hard enough for his camera to fall to the ground. A man in prison-orange pants comes forward and strikes the cameraman with a club, knocking him to the ground.

Robert comes up behind the man with the orange pants, grabs his long hair, and pulls him hard onto his knees. Then he pushes him onto his back and steps on his windpipe. He uses the bat to wave off the other men as they gather around.

"You all right?" Robert asks the cameraman, who is sitting up.

"Yeah, mate. Thanks."

A handful of sand hits Robert in the face. The kid stands a few feet away, improvising. More men have joined the semicircular fray, with Robert and the activist in the middle like renegade seals.

"You better get out of here," Robert says to the cameraman. "You and the rest."

"Can't leave you here."

"I'll be fine. Grab your camera, join the others. Now!"

The activist hesitates, looking for an opening between the bodies and bats.

"Leave him," Robert says, pointing with the club at the man under his foot. "Or your friend never gets up again."

Bodies part, and Robert watches the activist scramble up the hill toward the others. The woman at the top is taking pictures.

Seven of them now surround Robert. The shortest of the lot, a bearded man in a red T-shirt with a faded white soccerball print, takes a step forward.

"Man, you in trouble. Big trouble."

"Am I? That's funny. So's your friend. He's going to suffocate in thirty seconds if you and your friends don't back the hell off."

Robert increases pressure on the man's neck and watches his eyeballs bulge. The bearded man hesitates. Robert apparently picked the right captive.

"Make that twenty seconds."

The man takes a half-step back. "Let him go, and we won't kill you."

"That's very generous." Robert lifts his foot enough for the man to gasp for breath. "I don't want any trouble. I've got no dispute with any of you."

Then he steps off. The man lies there coughing.

"I'm leaving now," Robert says. "Peacefully."

"I don't think so." The bearded man smiles and displays a knife covered in blood, most likely the blood of seals. Human or animal, it all looks alike, and the thought enrages Robert. He wastes no time meeting the man halfway, leg to groin and both hands on his arm, twisting until the knife is on the ground, then spinning around with the man's head in a vise grip. Robert, on one knee, fumbles and then finds the knife.

"Back up. All of you!" He holds the knife under the man's jaw, tight enough so he won't dare open that mouth of his.

"Back up!"

Robert stands, pulling the bearded man along, and takes a step forward. He feels a wave of confidence he hasn't felt in a long time, realizing that he doesn't need a handgun. Any old knife will do. And he isn't afraid of them, isn't afraid of anyone, the adrenaline giving him the courage he thought had drained away.

The men shuffle out of his way, and he continues ahead, dragging the bearded man along by his sweaty neck. Robert feels almost disappointed. He wanted to fight them all right now, live or die, on this beach. That's what Noa would have done, and she would have loved him now, if she were watching.

Halfway up the hill, with a safe distance from the others, he turns and pushes the bearded man to the ground.

Robert walks quickly up the hill, then stops and glances back. The man is still watching him, while the others have gotten back to work, dragging seal carcasses, clubbing the ones still moving. Robert looks down at his knife, covered in the blood of the murdered seals, now also mixed with the blood of one of their murderers.

Stay tuned for the complete novel at:
www.ashlandcreekpress.com.

ABOUT THE AUTHOR

John Yunker writes plays, short stories, and novels about the conflicted and evolving relationships between humans and animals. He is a co-founder of Ashland Creek Press and editor of the anthologies *Among Animals, Among Animals 2,* and *Writing for Animals.* His plays have been produced and staged at such venues as Centre Stage New Play Festival, Oregon Contemporary Theatre, and the ATHE (Association for Theatre in Higher Education) conference. His teleplay *Sanctuary* was performed at the Compassion Arts Festival in New York, and his short stories have been published in *Phoebe, Qu, Flyway, Antennae,* and other journals. To learn more, visit <u>www.JohnYunker.com</u>.

Ashland Creek Press is a small, independent publisher of books for a better planet. Our mission is to publish a range of books that foster an appreciation for worlds outside our own, for nature and the animal kingdom, for the creative process, and for the ways in which we all connect. To keep up-to-date on new and forthcoming works, subscribe to our free newsletter by visiting www.AshlandCreekPress.com.

CPSIA information can be obtained
at www.ICGtesting.com
Printed in the USA
FSHW01n1427180818
51407FS